The Hot Scot

KATE EDEN

This is a work of fiction. Names, characters, places, and incidents are either the product of the author's imagination or are used fictitiously. Any resemblance to actual persons, places, or events is coincidental.

The Hot Scot

Copyright 2013 by Jaye Wells

All rights reserved. This book or any parts thereof may not be reproduced in any form without permission. The scanning, uploading, and distribution of this book via the Internet or any other means without the permission of the publisher is illegal and punishable by law. Please respect this author's hard work and purchase only authorized electronic or print editions.

BOOKS BY KATE EDEN

THE MURDOCH VAMPIRES SERIES
The Hot Scot
Rebel Child

ACKNOWLEDGMENTS

Thanks to Liliana Hart for encouraging me to take the plunge. Thank you to Lyndsey Lewellyn for the gorgeous cover. As always, thanks to Z for your unwavering support and for all the laughs..

PROLOGUE

Kira Murdoch seethed as she paced in front of the fireplace. "You may be 437 years old, but I am still your mother! That painting is the only thing left of your father, and I want it back."

"Mother, I want it back too, but I am in the middle of perfecting the Lifeblood formula. Why can't you send Callum to the museum?" Logan Murdoch lounged on the couch while he listened to his mother's lecture.

"We need to move on this immediately, and your brother is en route from New York as we speak. Besides, it would do you some good to get out of that sterile laboratory for a bit."

Kira sat next to Logan and took his hand. Her voice softened as she tried a new approach. "I know you don't like dealing with mortals, but I am asking you to do this for me."

Kira knew she'd won. Her son's superhuman strength, mind control abilities, and immortality were useless when it came to matching wits with his mother. Sure, being a 723-year-old vampire made her a formidable opponent for anyone. But when it came to her sons, she only needed the skills mothers everywhere, both mortal and immortal, had employed for centuries: manipulation and old-fashioned nagging.

Kira shook her head. "Logan, more than a century has

passed since we lost your father. You owe it to this family to get that painting back. You owe it to me."

Logan groaned inwardly as she twisted the knife a little further. If he didn't give in soon, the nagging would start.

"Mother, enough with the family-duty speech," he said with a wry smile. "Of course I'll get the painting back. They're mortals; how difficult can it be? If they give me a hard time, I'll just move things along with a mental push."

"I knew you would come through for me, darling" she said, her smile approving.

Logan stood and nodded resolutely. "Might as well get this out of the way. By the time I am done with them, they'll tie the painting up in a ribbon and thank me for taking it."

CHAPTER ONE

A sadistic man must have invented high heels, Sydney Worth thought to herself as she climbed the ladder. Three-inch heels were never her first choice of footwear, but two weeks earlier her boss had made a snide comment about her sensible flats. She loathed giving the man any more ammunition against her—thus the pointy-toed torture devices which currently clung to the tenth rung.

After she steadied herself, she used her glove-encased hands to straighten the frame of the Gainsborough landscape.

Most curators relied on maintenance staff to handle routine tasks like this, but not Sydney. The European gallery was her domain. She felt responsible for making sure it looked its best. Besides, she liked getting out of her small office and spending time with the art. It calmed her. And with a boss like Marvin Stiggler, she needed all the calm she could get.

"Is it straight, Jorge?" she called out to her assistant, who was supposed to be helping her.

Nothing.

She sighed impatiently.

"Damn it, is it straight or not?"

"It looks pretty good from here," a deep, very un-Jorge-like voice responded. Her female parts went on red alert.

Forgetting her precarious position, Syd swiveled her head to see the source of the compelling voice. But she only managed to make herself dizzy. She swayed, and her left heel slipped on the rung.

Balance gone, she fell fast.

"Ooooh shiiiiit!" she cried. A part of her brain registered the indignity of her words, likely her last.

Just when she thought she was a goner, she landed on something solid and warm.

"Oomph," it said.

She slowly opened her eyes to catch her first glimpse of the hereafter. An amazing pair of indigo-blue eyes gazed back at her.

"An angel," she breathed.

"Usually people call me something less complimentary," he replied with a devilish grin.

Syd closed her eyes again and groaned. "Great, my mother was right—girls who don't wait until they're married do go to hell."

"Did you hit your head on a rung?" he asked.

Something about the concern in his voice sounded decidedly undemonic to Syd, not that she'd ever met any demons, but still.

As it clicked she was not dead or in hell, she remembered the fall.

"Oh my God, don't drop me!" She quickly shimmied, wrapping her legs about her savior's waist and her arms around his head in a death grip. At once, his arms tightened around her.

"Mrph," a muffled voice said from the vicinity of her breasts. She instantly leaned back.

"Sorry, delayed reaction," she said, her cheeks flaming.

"Oh, it was my pleasure, I assure you," Blue Eyes said with a chuckle.

Syd really focused on the face in front of her for the first time. She took in the mouth made for sin, the square chin, the bold nose that complemented the face instead of overpowering it, and of course those amazing eyes. She knew this face.

"You're the Hot Scot," she said in a breathless voice.

The man studied her for a moment as if trying to decide if the fall knocked her senseless. Syd stared back. Could it be true? She shook her head. Of course he wasn't the Hot Scot. If he were, that would mean the man holding her was well over three hundred years old.

"Well, I am flattered, but how did you know I'm Scottish?"

"What? Oh . . . no," Sydney shook her head to clear out the cobwebs. "I mean you look exactly like the man in our new painting. Besides, the brogue kind of gave it away, even though it's subtle."

Sydney still couldn't believe the resemblance as she stared at him.

"Yes, well, my family came across the pond many years ago, so the accent has faded a bit," he said. "As for the painting, your reaction is somewhat understandable. You see, I'm him—I mean I'm his descendant."

After her muddled brain slowly absorbed that observation, Syd became aware of several things at once. First, she was not only straddling a complete stranger's hips, she damn near had him in a death grip with her thighs.

Second, he was an extremely well-endowed descendant if the pressure against her pelvis was any indicator.

Third, as she stared into his eyes, a jolt of connection zapped through her midsection. She told herself it was just his resemblance to the man in the painting, but that didn't explain the recognition she saw in his eyes, too.

She opened her mouth, hoping the right words would magically occur to her. Unfortunately, before inspiration could strike, a gasp sounded behind her.

"Miss Worth, what in the hell do you think you're doing?" Marvin Stiggler's outraged voice rang out in the cavernous gallery.

Syd closed her eyes and wished the floor would swallow her

whole. Of course her boss would walk in just in time to witness the most outrageously embarrassing moment of her life. Somehow, she would find a way to pin the blame for the entire episode on the troublemaking, yet very compelling, man she currently straddled.

She slowly dismounted from the tall, hard frame supporting her and tried to avoid the amused blue gaze of its owner. With all the dignity she could muster, Sydney lowered her skirt, smoothed back her curly auburn hair, and turned to face the outraged countenance of her boss.

"Well? Care to explain yourself?" he sneered.

"Mr. Stiggler, I . . . um . . ." she floundered.

Before she could find the words to defend herself, the man behind her stepped closer and placed a balancing hand on her lower back. The warmth of his touch made her aware of her other parts, which still tingled from the intimate contact they'd just shared. She pushed those thoughts ruthlessly aside and tried to focus on the tenuous situation at hand.

"Mr. Stiggler, is it? Before you jump to conclusions, I must take responsibility for this incident. I distracted the lady when she was on top of the ladder." He motioned to the ladder just to his left. "As a result, she lost her balance and fell. I was lucky to catch her before she seriously injured herself."

Sydney nodded vigorously to add credence to the explanation.

"That fails to explain why she was straddling you, sir," replied Stiggler, who looked both disgusted and pleased to have caught his least favorite employee in a compromising position.

"Nevertheless, she could have been seriously injured. An injury, I might add, which could have proved quite expensive for the museum. I am sure you are familiar with worker's compensation," the confusing man responded. As unsettling as he was, he seemed to be defending her.

Stiggler deflated a bit. But he wasn't done. "And who, may I ask, are you?"

"I apologize for not introducing myself sooner. Logan Murdoch," he said as he stepped forward to shake Stiggler's hand.

The director hesitated a moment and then reluctantly shook the man's hand, his own dwarfed by Logan's large square palm. Sydney started to like the stranger. Anyone who could intimidate Stiggler was a friend of hers.

"Murdoch? Are you related to the Murdochs?" Stiggler's voice rose with excitement.

"I wouldn't say the Murdochs, but as my family is well known here in Raleigh, then, yes, I am one of those Murdochs."

"Let me get this straight. My curator of European art was just saved from a near-fatal fall by a member of the family who owns Murdoch Biotechnology?"

"I am really not involved in the running of the company. I leave that to my brother, Callum."

Sydney held back a grimace as she watched Stiggler nearly swoon at this newest development. The man was a bloodhound when it came to money. And if what Mr. Murdoch said was correct, he belonged to one of the wealthiest families in North Carolina. She could almost see the calculations going on in Stiggler's head.

But she was more curious about what brought Mr. Murdoch to their museum. Her concerns about his ancestor comment earlier doubled at knowing he had the Murdoch name and bank account behind him.

She cleared her throat to get the men's attention. Stiggler began to gush all over the man who recently had his head in her cleavage. Really, the whole thing was just embarrassing. Had she actually thrust her breasts in his face? She started to blush again, but she needed some answers.

"Gentlemen, excuse me. But Mr. Murdoch has not explained his reason for visiting this morning," Sydney said.

"Please call me Logan, and I should call you . . . ?"

"Miss Worth would be fine," she said in her primmest tone.

After all, just because a woman wraps her thighs around a man with enough force to crush a casaba melon, he couldn't just presume to call her by her first name, could he? Absolutely not.

His lips twitched, but she ignored it and waited for an explanation.

"Miss Worth then." He executed a slight mocking bow in her direction. "As I mentioned earlier, the portrait you acquired is of an ancestor of mine, Royce Murdoch. I want to know how the painting came to be in your possession."

"As I am sure you heard from the press, the painting was donated to the museum by a benefactor who prefers to remain anonymous," Syd explained.

Stiggler jumped in, "But if you are a descendant, we would love to have you involved in the exhibition. How much would you like to contribute?" he asked without any apparent concern over his lack of tact.

"I'm not interested in donating to the museum," replied Logan.

"No? Why wouldn't you want to contribute and promote your good family name?" Stiggler asked.

"Let me cut to the chase. Someone stole that painting from my family two hundred years ago. We gave up any hope of finding it until we saw the news coverage. We want it back."

Sydney's mouth dropped open. A sheen of sweat appeared on Stiggler's pasty brow, and his eyes almost bugged out of his head as if a stroke was imminent. The gallery was silent as a tomb for a good minute before either gathered their wits enough to respond. Logan calmly met their stunned expressions, seeming content to wait out the silence.

"You want it back?" Sydney repeated, not quite believing her ears.

Stiggler regained his senses, but instead of addressing Murdoch, he turned on Syd.

"Miss Worth, this is just one more example of how your inexperience has hurt this museum," he hissed.

Syd rounded on him, "Excuse me? How is this is my fault?"

"If you had done your job, this never would have happened."

"We've only had the painting a week." She tried to keep her voice calm to cover the acid churning in her stomach. "You're the one who started a media blitz before anyone had a chance to authenticate the painting!"

A throat cleared, and Sydney suddenly remembered the man who started all of this. It brought her back to her senses enough to realize how unprofessional she must seem. But how dare Stiggler blame her for this? Really! She had put up with a lot since she accepted her position at the Raleigh Museum of Fine Art six months earlier. Because she was young by curator standards, only twenty-eight, it had been an uphill battle all the way to prove her talents.

"I told the museum board hiring an inexperienced woman for the role of curator would be a mistake. Fresh perspective, my foot," Stiggler railed.

Honestly, thought Syd, *the man thinks only stuffy middle-aged white men know anything about art.* Her two master's degrees, one in art history and another in European history, meant nothing to him. Nor did he care she was graduated from both programs with departmental distinction. Luckily, she'd proven herself to the museum board and landed her dream job. She had persevered through months of Stiggler's crap only to have this gorgeous man come in and muck everything up for her.

"Mr. Stiggler, I fail to see how this development is relevant to the origins of my employment here," she said. She would not let him bait her into losing her cool.

"You know the acquisition of this portrait comes at a time when the museum desperately needs attention. After all, attention means donors," Stiggler continued with a significant look at Murdoch.

Syd knew the importance of the painting in terms of public relations, especially with a bad economy making donors less generous, but she also saw it as her opportunity to put her name on the map as a curator. And she desperately wanted to prove herself, and not only to Stiggler.

"Mr. Stiggler, perhaps we should take a moment to refocus our attention to the matter at hand, hmm?" Murdoch interrupted Stiggler's rant.

Suddenly the anxiety she felt gave way to resolve. The man

couldn't just waltz in there and throw all of her hard work down the drain. And she knew if Stiggler could pin this on her, he would. She had to ensure that never happened. So she turned her attention away from her rodent boss and onto the man really responsible—Logan Murdoch.

"Mr. Murdoch, I apologize for our outburst, but your news has come to us as a bit of a shock. However, I assume you have some evidence to support your claim." Murdoch Biotechnology or no, this man was not going to intimidate her.

"Well . . . no." He seemed honestly baffled she would even suggest he needed proof. He stared at her intently for a second. She waited for him to say more, but he just continued to look into her eyes as if trying to read her mind.

Ok, that's weird, thought Syd.

"Are you telling me you waltzed in here expecting us to just hand the painting over to you without verifying your story? Really, Mr. Murdoch, did you expect us to gift wrap it, too?"

Ha, take that! She gave herself a mental high five.

"Miss Worth, apologize to Mr. Murdoch! That kind of sarcasm is not appropriate when speaking to such an esteemed member of our community," chastised Stiggler.

Syd rolled her eyes and then looked at Murdoch expectantly.

His eyebrows knitted together, and his jaw clenched as if he was trying to remain calm.

Well, tough, she thought. *He'd better get used to being challenged. No one pushes this girl around.*

He cleared his throat as if needing time to regroup. "I admit my family and I were in shock when we saw the news. In my rush to get here, I failed to consider the need for evidence. Perhaps we could come to an agreement."

Stiggler's eyes lit up. Syd could almost hear the cha-ching echoing in the man's head. She, on the other hand, was insulted.

"Are you suggesting we would be open to bribery?" she demanded.

"Hush!" said Stiggler as he slithered closer to his prey.

"Please ignore her. She has no decision-making authority here. Now about that arrangement . . ."

Murdoch looked at the man with distaste.

"No, I am not offering a bribe. If we could go see the painting, I will explain what I have in mind."

Looking a little baffled, Stiggler nodded his toupee-covered head and crossed his hands respectfully over his gut. Syd often thought, with the designer suits his outlandish salary afforded him, Stiggler appeared half-politician, half-used-car salesman. Lord knew why the museum board kept the man on. Most likely it was his ability to finagle credit for his employees' hard work while doing almost no real work himself. He really was a rat. Unfortunately for Syd, the rat also had the power to make or break her career.

"If you'll follow me, Logan," said the rat.

"You may call me Mr. Murdoch," said the man who confused her more by the minute. He sure seemed like the enemy, but she couldn't shake the odd feeling he was on her side.

"Of course, Mr. Murdoch," said Stiggler. "Miss Worth, please continue on with whatever it is you do all day. Besides throwing yourself off ladders that is."

Syd opened her mouth to protest being cut out of the discussions, but Murdoch beat her to it.

"Actually, I insist Miss Worth be included." Syd whirled to face him, her mouth hanging open with shock. Of course, she wanted to be included in negotiations, but she wondered why he insisted on her involvement. He calmly met her gaze. She took in his resolved expression but glimpsed a promise in his eyes. Syd tried not to focus on what the promise entailed because, given their interaction so far, she feared it would involve sticking her chest in his face again. Only this time it would not be an accident. She mentally fanned herself.

Get a grip, girl. This man is the enemy, she scolded herself and raised her chin, which only seemed to amuse him. She scowled at him. He grinned back. Stiggler was so beside himself he didn't notice the exchange.

"Absolutely not. This is a museum administration issue, and she is only a curator," the rat fink insisted, trying to assert some of his power. The grin immediately disappeared from Mr. Murdoch's face.

Syd almost felt pity for Stiggler. Almost.

"Miss Worth is involved, or I call the lawyers." From his tone, Syd suspected he was a man used to getting his way. Her suspicion became a conviction at the next words out of Stiggler's mouth.

"After you, Miss Worth."

CHAPTER TWO

Stiggler sucked up to their guest as they headed to the conservation studio, but Sydney didn't pay attention to the words. After all, how many ways were there to kiss someone's ass?

She had bigger things to focus on—such as how to deal with Mr. Logan Murdoch. He had no proof with him, but the Murdoch name carried a lot of weight in these parts. It didn't make sense for him to lay false claim on a high profile piece of artwork. Unless he wasn't really a Murdoch.

She considered the possibility. Maybe he was crazy or on drugs. She shook her head to discard those thoughts. The man was the picture of virile good health, not a dark circle or bloodshot eye in sight. Moreover, he didn't have any of the signs she thought a crazy man would exhibit, like wild eyes or a habit of talking back to voices in his head. Although, the strangely intense looks he'd given her earlier were odd.

On the other hand, she couldn't deny he was a dead ringer for the man in the portrait. She would have to do anything she could to discredit him. After all, if the museum lost this painting, Stiggler would find a way to blame her.

Sydney slowed and waited for Stiggler and Murdoch to join her at the elevator.

"Miss Worth, is there a problem?" Stiggler asked as he brushed past her to punch the button.

Sydney rolled her eyes before she could stop herself. She looked over and caught Murdoch studying her with a grin. Busted.

"After you," he said, gesturing for her to precede him into the elevator after Stiggler lumbered in.

"Thanks," she mumbled.

Don't be fooled. He isn't a gentleman. He just wants to get that painting, she lectured herself.

She tried to ignore him but failed miserably. His clean, masculine scent and powerful aura made the elevator shrink in size. She accidentally brushed his arm with her own. A tingle danced all the way down to her fingertips. While Stiggler rattled on about the museum, she glanced at Murdoch again and caught him watching her. She quickly looked away.

The trip down was mercifully short. As Stiggler forged ahead of them into the corridor, Murdoch put a hand on her arm.

"Miss Worth," Murdoch said, "I realize this development was unexpected."

"You can say that again. By the way, can I see some ID?"

He chuckled as he reached into his back pocket for his wallet and then flashed his driver's license. He wasn't lying about his identity.

And damn him, she thought, *even his driver's license picture is hot.* She frowned even more when she recalled her own, which resembled a mug shot.

"Sorry, can't be too careful," she said. He shrugged off her apology with a smile. She looked up to see Stiggler impatiently tapping his foot in front of the entrance to the conservation area.

"Miss Worth, did I just see you card our esteemed guest?" he demanded.

"It's no bother," Murdoch said. "After all, I imagine you don't let just any stranger off the street into this area of the museum."

"Of course, of course. I was going to ask to see your identification myself. Now shall we?" Stiggler said, motioning to the door next to him.

When Sydney entered the studio, the smell of turpentine acted like a balm on her frayed nerves. She always loved coming down here when she felt stressed. The conservation department resembled a small warehouse. Easels holding artwork in various stages of restoration or cleaning stood at odd intervals along the outer walls. Large worktables stood end to end along the middle of the room. The jars of paint thinner, paint brushes, magnifying glasses, and various other tools of the conservation trade were strewn along the tabletops. The room seemed devoid of life except for the sound of a radio drifting from a small office in the far corner.

"Lenny?" Syd called as she headed toward the head conservator's office. When no response came, she shook her head. When Lenny listened to the blues, he was in the zone.

Many of the museum staff found the conservation rats, as they were jokingly called, eccentric. But Sydney liked hanging out down here as they worked their magic. The conservation of priceless art was part science, part alchemy, and part luck.

Only certain people were talented enough to harness all three and restore artwork to its original glory. Dr. Leonard Kunst was one of the best in his field.

Reaching the door to the office, she watched for a moment as Lenny painstakingly cleaned the bust of a Roman senator. She knocked on the doorjamb, but he didn't hear her over the electric guitars whining from the radio on the bookshelf.

"Lenny?" she said as she touched his shoulder. The man jumped three feet in the air. Only his ingrained skills prevented him from knocking the bust over when his hands flew up.

"Jeez, Syd, give a man a heart attack, why don't you?" he exclaimed. He turned and lowered the volume on the song.

Syd smiled fondly at the man. His wild gray hair stood at irregular peaks, and his rumpled clothes added to his nutty-professor air.

"Sorry, Lenny, but we need to see the Scottish portrait," she explained.

"The Hot Scot," he said loudly and then chuckled. "This is the third time in two days. You got it bad for the man." Syd cleared her throat to indicate the presence of Stiggler and Murdoch just behind her.

"Oh jeez, sorry. Good morning, Mr. Stiggler." Lenny caught sight of Logan and his jaw dropped.

"Dr. Kunst," Stiggler said with a frown. "The painting?"

"Oh! Yes, sir." Lenny stuttered as he stared at Logan. "Sorry, he looks just like the man in the portrait."

"Mr. Murdoch is here because the painting was allegedly stolen from his family two centuries ago," explained Syd. To Murdoch she said, "This is Dr. Leonard Kunst, our head of conservation."

"I can't believe it!" Lenny said as he shook Murdoch's hand. "Have you ever seen the painting, Mr. Murdoch?"

"Of cour—, that is, no, I have not. However, I know from family records Royce and I share a resemblance," Logan explained.

"That is the understatement of the century," Lenny said. He shook his head and led the trio to a large easel set up in the corner of the room. He whisked the white cover off the painting with a flourish.

"This, Mr. Murdoch, is more than a resemblance," he said.

"Dr. Kunst, that will be all," Stiggler said, dismissing him. Lenny looked at Murdoch one more time before shaking his head and retreating to his office.

Sydney had viewed the painting several times, but she still got a flutter in her stomach. The image was one of the most powerful displays of rugged masculinity she had ever encountered. However, now, with Murdoch standing next to her, the impact was amplified. Lenny had it right. The similarity was amazing. If she didn't know better, she would believe Murdoch himself had donned a kilt and posed for the portrait.

In the image, the man with black, wind-blown hair and indigo eyes sat proudly atop a midnight stallion. He wore a white flowing shirt over a green and red kilt. Muscular thighs extended from beneath the kilt to grasp the horse's sides. Traditional green kilt hose extended to just below the man's knees. The image was compelling, but the expression on the man's face was somewhat out of place with the rest of the portrait. Although the composition was formal, the humorous tilt to his lips hinted he shared a private joke with the painter.

"I can't believe it is really here," Logan said beside her. She thought she detected a hint of emotion in his voice.

"I have to admit the resemblance is uncanny," Sydney mused.

"Yes, I suppose we do favor each other," Logan said, sounding uncomfortable.

"Alike? Hell, man, it looks like you posed for it yourself," Stiggler said.

Anyone with half a brain could figure out Logan Murdoch was a direct descendant of the man in the portrait. Sydney's hope this was all some kind of mistake vanished. Seeing the resemblance up close made it impossible to believe he was a con artist looking to scam the museum.

"I mentioned an agreement earlier," Logan began and then held a hand up when Stiggler started to speak. "No, I do not want to give you any money. Instead, I propose Miss Worth and I work together to find adequate evidence of my family's claim."

"Are you positive you wouldn't prefer to involve your attorneys?" Sydney asked. "After all, authenticating art and proving ownership can get quite sticky. Surely you are aware of the cases of art stolen during World War II by the Nazis. In some instances it took years for museums to legally identify the rightful owners."

"Yes, but in this case my family is approaching the museum directly about a specific painting. In addition, I will give you access to my family's archives. I am confident we can find the proof and handle everything with a minimum of fuss," replied Logan.

"What's in it for us?" asked Stiggler. "After all, if Miss

Worth finds the proof, you have your painting and we have nothing."

"You mean you have nothing other than good publicity for cooperating with us and knowing you did the right thing?" Logan retorted with disdain.

"Of course that has its own rewards, but you will need to use museum resources, and they don't come cheap," Stiggler shot back.

"Cut to the chase," Logan commanded. His face showed strain, as if he fought the urge to strangle the man before him.

"The museum will sorely miss this painting if your claim is valid, and we hope you will see it in your heart to compensate us for being so cooperative."

Sydney couldn't believe it. The man could not be tackier. The museum had the painting for less than a week, and he wanted money? Outrageous.

If Murdoch could provide legal proof of ownership, then it would nullify the contract the museum held with the deceased donor's estate, thus they would have no right to any money.

Logan gave Stiggler a hard look. But just when she thought he would rake the man over the coals for his impertinence, he surprised her by being civil.

"We'll discuss that when the time comes. Now, Miss Worth, when will you be able to begin?" he asked.

Syd looked back and forth between the men. Things were happening so fast she scrambled to quickly come up with a plan.

"First, I would need to check with Jorge to make sure he has time in his schedule to assist me," Syd said.

"No. Absolutely not. I forbid you to involve Jorge in this matter," Stiggler said.

"And why not? Jorge is an excellent researcher, and I would only need him to get the preliminaries out of the way. After the first day or so, I will need him here in the office to keep all our other projects on track," Syd argued.

"I doubt Mr. Murdoch would appreciate someone like that in his home," Stiggler sneered.

"You mean someone of Latin American descent? I am sure Mr. Murdoch is not as narrow-minded as some people," Syd said meaningfully.

"But that's not what I meant. I meant that assistant of yours is a homos—"

"Mr. Stiggler," Logan cut Stiggler off, "I assure you no matter what ethnic, cultural, or other categories Miss Worth's assistant falls under, he will be welcome in my home."

Syd let out a breath and sent a grateful smile to Murdoch, who nodded back.

"Then that's settled," she said. "I will need a day or two to clear my calendar and do some preliminary research. Today is Monday, so why don't Jorge and I start first thing on Wednesday?"

"That works for me. I must warn you, our archives are quite extensive. I might be able to help narrow down the search, though, if you can tell me the type of evidence you will be seeking," Logan said.

"Generally letters and journals are the most common sources. However, until I have a chance to dig into your family history, it is difficult to guess where proof will be found."

"Dig into the family history?" Logan repeated, sounding troubled.

"Yes, you said this painting was stolen two hundred years ago. I will need to know more about the circumstances surrounding its commission as well as the events coinciding with its theft. Usually, in cases where we have no records for a piece, our first step is to determine its provenance, or a record of ownership."

She was impressed as Murdoch nodded and listened attentively to her explanation. Most people tuned her out when she switched over to her art geek persona. Case in point: Stiggler, who stifled a yawn. She ignored him and continued.

"In most cases, we start with the most recent owner and work our way back. However, for Royce's painting that information is not available since the owner is not only dead, but also stipulated anonymity in his or her will. So we start in the past and work forward."

"This process is much more involved than I thought," Logan said. He ran his hand through his hair.

"Mr. Murdoch, you can rest assured I will make every effort to expedite this process for you," said Stiggler.

Murdoch ignored the statement and turned to address Syd.

"I suppose I should let you get to work. Heaven knows I will be taking up enough of your time in the coming days. If you require any special equipment or supplies, call me, and I will make sure you have them by Wednesday."

As he handed her his business card, their hands brushed. Again, that jolt of awareness zipped over her skin. He held her gaze a moment longer than necessary. Syd forced herself to look away before she did something stupid, like drool on him.

"It was nice to meet you Mr. Murdoch. I look forward to working with you," she lied. The man unsettled her, and the prospect of spending more time with him had her feeling a little panicky. But she was a professional, and she would put aside her hormonal reactions to get the job done.

"I assure you, Miss Worth, the pleasure was mine," he said. His smile was polite, but the glint in his eye left Syd convinced he was alluding to the unfortunate ladder incident from earlier.

He turned to Stiggler. "I don't need to remind you this matter should be kept quiet."

"Mr. Murdoch, I assure you, I am the soul of discretion," Stiggler said with a trustworthy smile and a firm handshake.

Murdoch said his good-byes and was gone.

Stiggler slowly turned toward Syd, his expression turning from amicable to menacing.

"I have one thing to say to you," he growled. "If you mess this up, you will be out on your ass so fast you won't know a van Gogh from a velvet Elvis."

#

"Her boss is an ass," Logan said to his mother an hour later. He hadn't needed to use his psychic powers to figure that one out, but the thoughts he picked up from the man put Logan in a bad mood. Normally reading people's minds was a handy skill to have, but at times likes these he wished he could be as blissfully unaware as a mortal.

"I understand your concern, but you must remember the reason you are doing this. We will finally have a piece of your father back," replied Kira.

She sat across from Logan in the blue parlor of her elegant townhouse. The light blue silk-upholstered Queen Anne chair complemented her ivory pantsuit. But her curly hair, as black as a raven's wing, stood in stark contrast to the pastel colors surrounding her. Knowing his mother, she had chosen the colors specifically because they made her dark beauty stand out. She looked damn good for a woman her age. After all, most 723-year-olds were dust in the wind while his mother looked no older than a college coed.

"I have already talked to the lawyers. Since possession is nine-tenths of the law, it is up to us to prove our case to the museum."

"Well, darling, that should be no problem. I will simply have the boxes moved to your house."

Logan groaned. "Why bother moving them at all? Miss Worth can do the research here."

"Logan, you are already overseeing this matter quite capably. Besides, I am sure this curator will be much more comfortable with you since you have already met. And don't give me the line about your experiments. Alaric can assist you both at the lab and with the curator," she said, waving off his concerns.

"I still have a bad taste in my mouth about including Miss Worth. Having her dig through our files could be risky, but I got a clear message that Stiggler is trying to get rid of her. I couldn't in good conscience leave her without any way to save her job."

"Why don't you offer a donation to the museum with the stipulation she keep her job?" his mother asked.

"I find resorting to bribery with that man extremely distasteful."

"Well, I think what you did is honorable—chivalrous even," she said with a smile.

Logan nodded absently as the front door opened. A few seconds later his brother Callum strode into the room. He gave his mother a kiss on the cheek and then dropped next to Logan on the couch.

"So, big brother, I hear you found your painting."

Logan nodded.

"Why don't you look happier?" Callum asked.

"It seems Logan didn't anticipate some road bumps in the painting retrieval process," Kira supplied.

"Like what?" asked Callum.

"Proof," Logan responded sullenly.

Callum laughed. "Poor Logan's not used to dealing with pesky mortal bureaucracy."

"Instead of laughing, why don't you help me figure out how to prevent a very clever woman from discovering our family's little secret while she digs through all our old papers," Logan retorted.

"I am sure it will be fine," said Kira. "We are always very careful when wording our correspondence. Besides, we can weed out anything incriminating. And you're forgetting we were alive when the painting was completed and when those hooligans stole it. It's simply a matter of putting the right papers in front of Miss Worth."

"So what is this curator like?" asked Callum.

"She's . . . competent," said Logan, trying to avoid the subject of Sydney Worth with his brother.

"Tell him about the ladder incident, Logan," his mother said with a grin.

He scowled at her. He hadn't revealed the more interesting details about the interlude to his mother, but she got the gist of it.

Callum immediately noted his brother's discomfort and pounced. "Do tell," he said with a wicked grin.

Logan reluctantly told his brother everything from saving Sydney to Stiggler's ridiculous claim about discretion. By the end of the story, Callum was doubled over laughing. Logan wanted to punch his brother but knew his mother wouldn't tolerate their immature antics in her favorite parlor. But he'd get his revenge. Perhaps he'd mix skunk's blood in with his brother's next meal. That would teach him.

"Let me get this straight. She was straddling you with her . . . assets in your face? Then she carded you? Priceless!" Callum snorted again with laughter.

"You know, I have been meaning to ask you why you didn't just use a mental nudge with the girl." asked Kira.

Logan shifted in his seat. "I just thought we should do this the correct way."

Kira's eyes narrowed suspiciously. "When you left this morning, you were determined to get this done quickly. What aren't you telling me?"

"Wait a minute," Callum interjected with suspicion clear on his face. "Logan, you could read her mind, couldn't you?"

Logan grimaced.

"Royce Logan Murdoch! You couldn't read her mind!" his mother declared, ready to launch out of her seat in excitement.

Callum slapped his knee. "Hot damn! Big brother's found his soul mate!"

Logan's glare would have stopped a mortal's heart, but his brother carried on unaffected. "Logan's in lo—" he began before Logan's elbow to his ribs cut him off. "Ooof. Hey!"

"That's enough," Kira barked. "Callum, you know I don't consider soul mates an issue to take lightly."

She turned on her eldest. "Logan, I can't believe you tried to hide this from me. You really couldn't read her mind?"

"Mother, it's no big deal. She could just as easily be a psychic or witch. It doesn't automatically mean she's my soul mate."

"Did you pick up the scent of magic on her?" Callum asked.

Logan shook his head reluctantly. Then he narrowed his eyes at his mother.

"I am telling you right now to leave this alone. Even if I believed in the soul mate myth, which I don't, it wouldn't matter. I do not get involved with mortals. Period. Do not, I repeat, do not pursue this. I have humored you with this painting debacle, but if I get the slightest hint of matchmaking from you, I will wash my hands of the whole mess."

Kira just stared back at him for a moment. He refused to feel guilty about his words. This was his life—his very long life—and he'd be damned if his mommy was going to play *yenta* between him and some mortal woman. His mother knew the scars he carried around on his heart from his last encounter with a mortal woman. So, no, Sydney was off limits.

Even if she represents a prime example of her species. Even if her impertinence makes me want to kiss the sass right off her mouth. Even if . . . He shook his head. He couldn't risk it.

"Logan," Kira began softly. "Darling, I know why you are hesitant to get involved with another mortal. We both do," she said looking over at Callum, who nodded sympathetically. Logan couldn't stand the pity he saw in their eyes. "But give it a chance. All mortal women are not like Brenn—"

He slashed his hand through the air, cutting his mother off. "This isn't about the past. The simple matter is you are reading things into the situation that don't exist. Sydney Worth is not my soul mate. I want you to promise you will not interfere."

Kira took a deep breath. Again, he felt a twinge of guilt, but he knew if he gave her an inch, she'd take a mile. He couldn't chance it. His reaction to Sydney today had been too strong to risk involvement with her beyond the minimum required to get the painting back.

He still couldn't believe he'd flirted with her like some mortal lothario. How long had it been since he had flirted with a female? He couldn't read her mind, but her interest was as clear as the breasts she'd shoved in his face.

However, she had reservations too. Her actions at the museum showed her dedication to her career came first. He could relate. He had too much riding on his own research to complicate it with a dose of estrogen.

"I promise from now on I will not try to convince you Sydney is your soul mate," his mother conceded. He knew her carefully worded response left her plenty of room to interfere. Nevertheless, he'd said his piece and knew she would be careful to respect his wishes, at least to his face.

"However, I want both of you to listen," she said. "I have lived for almost three-quarters of a millennium. I do not want to see my 750th year without a daughter-in-law to adopt and a grandchild to spoil. You both owe it to me as your mother and to the Brethren to produce a new generation. So I am warning you: The time is coming when I won't accept the 'no mortals' or the 'I'm too busy' excuses any more. Am I understood?"

Logan and Callum exchanged uneasy glances and then nodded in unison. They each had won battles with their mother over the years, but her feminine wiles and maternal instincts gave her the edge to ensure she would win this war in the end. If she wanted them to settle down with a nice woman and produce heirs, they'd soon be picking out bassinettes. Fortunately, being immortal meant the definition of "soon" was subjective.

"I am glad that's settled. Callum, tell us about your trip," said Kira.

"The Brethren Council was quite excited about the direction of our research. They are anxious to know when Logan's synthetic blood will be ready for distribution," said Callum.

"I am close. I am awaiting a shipment of blood for comparison against the synthetic product. Once the testing is done in the lab, I will try it on volunteers," Logan explained.

"I can't tell you how excited everyone is. Imagine a day when we don't have to rely on human sources for nourishment. Utilizing bagged blood made everything easier, but this will mean true freedom for all of us," Callum said.

"Any other news from the meeting?" Logan asked.

"Word is Raven is stirring up more trouble. Seems she found out what Logan is up to and has vowed to fight it. I guess it makes sense. Once Logan's product hits the streets, the Brethren Council will raise the penalties for feeding from humans," Callum explained.

"Raven," Kira said with distaste. "One of these days the council is going to lose patience with that young one, and she will have hell to pay."

"Did you hear what she said to the council when they insisted she try the sun shield therapy? 'No vampire worth his blood would be caught dead in the sun!'" Callum chuckled. "I know she's a nuisance, but you have to admire her spunk."

"Spunk? Callum, she is a threat to everything we work toward with our research: To one day be able to safely live among mortals. Her kind perpetuates the fears most mortals still harbor about our kind," Logan chastised. "She is a menace that needs to be reined in. Imagine any vampire in this day and age refusing to go in the sunlight. And don't get me started on the velvet capes and the coffin she sleeps in. It's ludicrous."

"Either way, we need to keep our eyes open. You know Raven never goes in for a direct attack. She'll most likely just make a nuisance of herself," said Callum.

"I'll warn Alaric," said Logan. "But I honestly doubt she could do much to hinder our efforts."

"Plus you have other things to worry about," Callum said with a smirk. "When does your girlfriend start work?"

Logan sent a menacing look to his brother. "Miss Worth will begin on Wednesday. Would you like to volunteer to help her go through the archives?"

"But, Logan, if I worked with her, she would probably just become smitten with me. And we can't have that since she's your soul mate."

Logan groaned. Where was a sharp stake when he needed it?

CHAPTER THREE

Jorge Smith's black Ferragamo loafers were propped on Sydney's desk when she found him. He didn't look up from his phone conversation when she entered.

"Get off my phone," she said.

Jorge held up one manicured finger and continued talking.

"Now!" Sydney shoved his feet off her desk, grabbed the phone, and hung it up.

"Geez, boss lady, what's got your panties in a twist? It's not that time of the month is it?"

Sydney took what she hoped would be a calming breath. Nope, not working. She counted to ten. Twenty. Another breath. Okay, maybe she could refrain from murder for a few more minutes.

"How many times have I told you not to use my office for personal calls?"

"You weren't using it. I don't see what the big deal is. You know I do it all the time."

Sydney plopped down on the chair across from Jorge, who was still enthroned in her desk chair.

"You're right; it's not about the calls. Where the hell did you disappear to this morning? You were supposed to help me straighten the Gainsborough landscape."

"I had to pee. And I hadn't had any coffee, so I decided to go grab some. Then on my way to the kitchen, I ran into that hot new security guard. You know, Bruce? Lordy, girl, I tell you that man is so hot he's smokin'!"

"Let me get this straight. You left me perched on a ladder without backup to go ogle the new security guard?" She fought to remain calm. Yelling at Jorge was futile.

"Syd, Syd, Syd. You were doing fine. Plus, I didn't leave with the intention of checking out Mr. Hot Pants, I just got sidetracked. You make it sound sordid."

Sydney just looked at him. Jorge was at best a barely competent assistant; at worst, he was a flighty drama queen. Although he was only quarter Cuban, Jorge played up his Latino roots when it pleased him. In fact, Sydney knew his real first name was "George" pronounced the English way, not "whore-hey" as her assistant preferred. She never questioned him about it though; the Spanish version seemed to fit him better.

Today, Jorge's outfit included a bubble-gum pink button-down shirt accented with a pink and lavender polka dot necktie. The black trousers were the only conservative element of the outfit, except they were tight enough to highlight his world-class buns, now unseen as he continued to laze in her desk chair. Mischief danced in his heavily lashed emerald eyes. The expertly mussed dark brown hair completed the look, which he spent a fortune on styling products to attain.

At times like this Syd didn't honestly know why she kept him around. His typing was abysmal. He spent more time filing his nails than paper and had a bad habit of disappearing when heavy lifting was necessary. On the other hand, he had great aesthetic sensibility, knew the art world like the back of his hand, and his catty comments never failed to make her laugh. Maybe she was being unfair in taking her bad mood out on the guy.

"I'm sorry. It's just been a day from hell, and it's barely lunchtime."

"Why don't we go to Herrera's for fajitas and margaritas, and we can talk about it?"

"You know we aren't supposed to drink during work hours."

"Technically we're off the clock during lunch, so it doesn't count," he rationalized.

"I'd love to, but we have a serious problem," she said with a sigh.

"Oh no, you have that look on your face like the time I spilled the copier toner all over the forms you spent hours filling out for The Enforcer."

"This is much worse."

"Worse than the time I accidentally wrote the new program for the deaf was 'good pubic relations,' but we didn't catch it until it had been distributed to every media outlet on the Eastern Seaboard?"

"Worse."

"Well damn, girl. Did your vibrator break?"

"Jorge!"

"Well, you've been cranky. I'm just sayin'."

"This is serious, okay? We may lose the Hot Scot."

"The Hot Scot? My dishy dream lover in a kilt?"

"Exactly. Logan Murdoch, of the infamous Murdoch family, is the Hot Scot's identical twin. Apparently the painting was stolen a couple of hundred years ago from his family, and they want it back."

"You're kidding! I hit on Bruce when I could have seen the Hot Scot in the flesh? Damn!"

"Can you focus for a moment, please? If they can prove their claim, Stiggler will use it as an excuse to get rid of me."

"That little weasel," he said while slamming his fist on the table. "Wait, if you lose your job, then I lose my job! I feel faint."

"Settle down. We can't do anything about Stiggler right now. On Wednesday we are both going over to look through the Murdoch archives," she told him. "But before then we have to find out everything we can about the painting and the family.

Hopefully we can find a way to keep our jobs."

"We'll figure something out. Maybe if we can convince them to donate some money, Stiggler will be pacified," Jorge said.

"Agh, this is all giving me a headache," Syd complained.

"Tell you what. Why don't I call the deli and have them deliver some sandwiches for lunch? You can get started on the research."

"Not so fast, mister. You're in this with me. If you have a hot date tonight, cancel it. We're going to be here late," Syd warned.

"You want some Midol with that sandwich, dragon lady?"

She just stared at him. He took the hint and whisked out of the office on a cloud of Issey Miyake cologne, his signature scent.

Syd reclaimed her chair and then banged her head down on her desk a few times. Maybe if she knocked herself out she could forget this day and start over. Yes, a nice case of amnesia would do nicely. The buzz of the intercom interrupted her.

"Syd, The Enforcer is on line two," said Jorge.

"Why didn't you tell her I was in a meeting or something?"

"What do you think I am? You don't pay me enough to lie for you, lady."

"Fine, just fine. This is exactly what I need right now."

Syd took a deep breath before picking up the phone.

"Good morning, Geraldine. How can I help you?"

"Sydney, I am calling about the expense reports you filed yesterday. How many times must I remind you both the forms and the receipts must be copied in triplicate and stapled before you submit them to me for approval? Paperclips are not acceptable."

Syd winced. Geraldine Stern, a.k.a. The Enforcer, served as gatekeeper for Stiggler's office as well as taskmaster to the curatorial staff. The woman was so anal retentive it was creepy. Make an error in filing paperwork or show up thirty seconds late for a meeting with Stiggler, and The Enforcer would bear down on you like the wrath of God.

Luckily, Syd had learned the woman's weakness early on and

used it to her advantage at times like these.

"I apologize. I appreciate you letting me know. Next time I will remember to staple them," Syd responded, trying to sound sincere.

"Look, this is the fourth time—"

"By the way, I saw you in the galleries this morning. That suit you're wearing is fabulous," Syd cut in, trying to head off the tirade.

Geraldine's tone went from disapproving to giddy in a heartbeat. "Oh! It's new. Don't you just love Ann Taylor?"

"Who doesn't?" Syd said. Of course, she couldn't remember the last time she'd had the money even to set foot in the store. "And the olive color really brings out the highlights in your hair."

"My stylist, Pierre, is wonderful. I can give you his number," the woman enthused. Syd grimaced. Was she implying Sydney needed help with her hair? She self-consciously lifted a hand to smooth it back from her face.

"Uh, thanks. So, you'll take care of the expense report?"

"Well, I really shouldn't ... But, I'll let it go this time. Just try to remember next time."

"Thanks, Geraldine. I really appreciate that."

"Let's do lunch later this week. We can go to Saks and try out Laura Mercier's new eye cream. It's never too early to hydrate, Sydney."

"Uh, let me get back to you, okay? I might be out of the office for a while working on a special project," she said and quickly ended the phone call.

Geraldine was an attractive fifty-ish woman whose looks had begun to loose their luster. Syd had seen Geraldine one day in the restroom reapplying her makeup. The woman carried a mind-boggling array of beauty products in a purse larger than a small elephant.

A lot of museum employees couldn't stand the woman for her nitpicking about every minor infraction. But Syd supposed Geraldine's anal tendencies came from a need to control her environment since she had no control over the march of time.

Syd might have laughed at how easily Geraldine was manipulated by a few well-placed compliments, but in reality, she pitied the woman.

#

Less than five minutes after her conversation with Sydney, the intercom on Geraldine's desk buzzed. She finished applying her new lip-plumping serum before pushing the button on her phone.

"I need to see you in my office, Miss Stern," Stiggler commanded.

She checked her reflection once more in the mirror she kept in her desk drawer. She sighed when she saw the serum hadn't reduced the fine lines around her lips. She closed the drawer with a thud and went to see what the bane of her existence needed now.

Stiggler sat behind a massive mahogany desk with his hands steepled beneath his chin.

"Yes, sir?" she said, trying to sound respectful.

"Sit down. We have a problem," he said without preamble. "I had a visit today from a man who claims his family has rights to the portrait of the Scot."

"But that's impossible. The law firm that handled the donation verified everything was legal."

"I talked to the lawyers. If what Murdoch says is true, and the painting was stolen from his family, it would nullify our legal right to it," Stiggler explained.

"Murdoch?" Geraldine asked. Excitement raced through her limbs.

"Yes, Logan Murdoch. His family owns Murdoch Biotech."

"I've heard of him," she said thoughtfully. "So what's going to happen?"

"We have reached an agreement to assist him. Miss Worth will be doing the research herself. "Normally I would not let her near this, but Murdoch insisted she be involved. Besides, it could work to my benefit. After all, when the proof is found—and I believe it will be—we will find some way to pin it on Miss Worth and finally be rid of her," Stiggler said. "Plus, I am counting on Murdoch to show his appreciation for our help with a generous donation."

The glee in his expression would have been distasteful to Geraldine if the development didn't serve her own purposes as well. In fact she felt a bit giddy herself. After all, Stiggler didn't know it, but he had just handed her information that would be very valuable to a certain party. A party Geraldine wanted very much to impress.

"What can I do to help?" she asked, playing up her role of indispensable assistant. In reality, Stiggler was such an incompetent fool the museum would run itself into the ground without her there to keep things running smoothly. But if she had her way, she would soon leave it all behind to fulfill her destiny.

"Just keep an eye on Miss Worth and that assistant of hers. Any additional evidence we can gather to make her look bad to the board the better," Stiggler said.

"Yes, sir." She ruthlessly tamped down the guilt that niggled at her over the idea of spying on Sydney, but sometimes a girl just had to squeeze a few limes to make a good margarita.

"Miss Stern, what would I do without you?" Stiggler asked with a smirk.

You'll soon find out, you pompous ass.

#

Geraldine waited until Stiggler left for the day to make the call. At four in the afternoon, it was still too early for Raven to be awake, but she needed to get a message to her mistress.

She grimaced. Sleeping during the day would be the biggest drawback once she was immortal. Honestly, a person couldn't be very productive at night. But she supposed the benefits outweighed the drawbacks.

She smiled. She was so close. For months she had worked her way up in the minion ranks of the Sanguinarian sect. As a neophyte her duties consisted of mundane chores like doing laundry. But as she proved herself loyal and resourceful, she was given more important duties. In fact, instead of the normal year it took most minions to attain acolyte status, it had taken

Geraldine only six months. The quick rise through the ranks was especially important given her age. Most of her fellow minions were teenagers, while she was already fifty.

The Murdoch information would guarantee her advancement to the next stage of minionhood—the Turning. And not a moment too soon. Just the other day she had noticed a few extra crow's feet around her hazel eyes. She was eager to kiss the wrinkles and grey hairs of midlife good-bye and finally feel young again.

Yes, Raven would be very pleased with the information. Just last week the mistress began planning to sabotage Murdoch's latest breakthrough. While Geraldine thought synthetic blood sounded like an efficient solution to one of the less desirable aspects of vampire life, the mistress lectured about the importance of keeping to the old ways.

She shrugged. If passing on the tip guaranteed an end to sagging breasts, she would put up with feeding off the hoof, so to speak.

She picked up the phone and dialed.

"This is minion Stern. I need you to pass an urgent message on to Mistress Raven."

#

Sydney closed the cover of her laptop with a thud. She had hoped to be able to find enough information on her own about the painting without having to use the Murdoch archives. She knew when she started it was a long shot, but she had to try. Unfortunately, none of her usual web-based resources provided any clues about the origins of the portrait.

She couldn't believe no one seemed to know either the artist or the original owners of the painting. Usually she could gather enough clues from the art itself to know where to find the right information. But since the portrait arrived with none of the usual provenance paperwork, she had little to go on.

She had dated the portrait from some time in the late eighteenth century using clues like the kilt and the style of painting. However, portraiture was so common in England and Scotland during that period that trying to track down the painter would be impossible without more clues.

Mr. Murdoch said the name of his ancestor was Royce Murdoch. A search on the name had resulted in twenty-two thousand hits. When she narrowed it down to results from the correct time period in Scotland, she hit a dead end. In addition, Jorge returned from the museum library an hour ago empty-handed after four hours of research. As much as she hated to admit it, it seemed working with Logan Murdoch was the only way to solve this mystery.

She tried to tell herself it was the threat to her job that had her so anxious. But her disloyal conscience pointed out part of her worry resulted from her physical reaction Logan and the fact she would have to see him every day until this was all over. She still had trouble wrapping her mind around her attraction to him. She had heard about sexual chemistry in romance novels and in chick flicks, but had never experienced it first hand.

Until now.

Sure, she had been attracted to men before, including her ex-fiancé. But Cole had never made her feel a primal urge to mate. Looking back, she knew his personality defects were to blame for her lukewarm interest in sex with him. But she barely knew Logan Murdoch, and she'd wanted to rip his pants off with her teeth the moment she looked at him.

Luckily, the professional concerns surrounding their interaction precluded any further lustful thoughts from her corner. She had given up too much to pursue her dream of being a curator to let another man mess it up for her. After all, a man, Cole, was to blame for her almost not pursuing the dream to begin with. While she regretted the pain it had caused everyone involved, she knew she had made the right decision. If Cole had really loved her, he never would have insisted that once they were married she forget her art history studies and focus instead on playing hostess for his law firm partners.

A stab of regret hit Sydney as the memories of that time resurfaced. She would never get over her parent's callous disregard for her feelings. Sure, she shouldn't have waited for the wedding day to reveal her misgivings. But Cole and her parents railroaded her from the beginning. Her mother and father were so determined that Syd make the perfect society match that they never considered her wishes.

Granted, back then she was so caught up in trying to live up to the Worth family expectations she almost didn't understand what was happening until it was too late. Her parents would never forgive her for publicly humiliating them. Their rejection still ached three years later and probably always would. But if they couldn't understand her need to be happy, then she didn't need them. She was proud of her achievements. If she felt a little lonely sometimes, it was a small price to pay for living life on her own terms.

Syd shook the gloomy thoughts away. She needed to focus on the present. Having abandoned research for the day, she decided to focus on clearing her schedule for the next week. She wouldn't let herself think any more about men, especially the one who made her hormones stand up and cheer. And she didn't mean Jorge.

CHAPTER FOUR

"Hey watch out! You almost made me spill my venti, nonfat, no-whip caramel macchiato!" Jorge said after Syd belatedly slammed the brakes at a red light. "What's your deal today anyway?" he demanded with narrowed eyes. "You're driving like a lunatic, and you're looking way hot. Something's up."

Syd glanced down at herself. The lightweight black V-neck sweater had already been in her closet but had coordinated perfectly with her new knee-length tan suede skirt and midcalf black boots. The outfit shouted confidence. Too bad she didn't feel that way.

"I just felt like trying something new. And I am not driving like a lunatic—that yellow light was way too short," she insisted.

"Nuh-uh, not buying it. You're actually wearing red lipstick and kick-ass boots. And in the last ten minutes you have bumped two curbs, and that old woman flipped you the bird when you cut her off," he said and then raised an eyebrow. "Nervous about seeing someone?"

"If I am nervous, it is because my job is on the line. Mr. Murdoch has nothing to do with it."

"Liar. Sydney has a crush," he said in a singsong voice.

"Jorge, I am not sixteen years old. Now drop it," she demanded, knowing she sounded bitchy but not caring. "I need you to promise me you'll be on your best behavior today. No flirting and no dirty jokes."

"Who me?" he asked innocently. "If anyone is going to be flirting, it's you."

"I will not!"

"Will too."

She let out an exasperated sigh. The last thing she needed this morning was to get in a childish argument with Jorge. She had bigger fish to fry. In less than two minutes, she would be at Murdoch's house. She knew he intended to be there all day because of their phone conversation yesterday.

Just thinking about that call made her nervous all over again. Their talk had been professional and brief, but she'd still found herself rattled afterward. It was bad enough he looked like a sin waiting to happen, but to sound like one too? The combination of the deep timbre and the slight Scottish accent sent shivers down her spine. He should be illegal.

What was she doing getting all weak in the knees over that man? Sydney Ellen Worth was a professional. She would not let the embodiment of masculine perfection sway her from her duties. Hopefully, Murdoch would stay out of her way today and let her get the job done without taunting her with his gorgeous self. She was suddenly glad Jorge would be there to run interference.

"Jorge, can we just agree our behavior needs to be courteous and professional?" she asked as she turned into the driveway of Murdoch's house. The heavily wooded lot and long drive prevented Syd from getting a view of the house.

"Lady, I don't know what you're implying. My middle name is 'Professional,'" he countered.

"Yeah, but your last name is 'Flirt,'" she joked.

"Very funny, but also true," he said with a chuckle. "Don't worry; I know how much is riding on this. Don't forget, if Stiggler gives you the boot, I will be right behind you in the unemployment line."

"I'm sorry. I know I am being difficult this morning. Maybe you're right. I am a little nervous," she admitted.

"Honey buns, don't you worry. It's gonna be easy peasy. You'll see," he promised.

She rolled to a stop in the circular drive in front of the house. Built in the conservative Georgian Revival style, the house towered three stories above them with ornate dormers crowning the roof. Black shutters and white cornices neatly accented the red brick. The morning sun sparkled against the numerous windows lining the façade.

Jorge let out a low whistle. "Nice digs."

She studied the place. The residence looked perfect for a well-to-do family who preferred the privacy afforded by living farther from the city, not for the home of a bachelor. She'd pegged Murdoch as one of the types who preferred the low maintenance, trendy condo developments that were so popular among the upwardly mobile single set of Raleigh. The man just continued to confound her.

"Guess we better go in," she said without enthusiasm.

They got out of the car and climbed the wide steps to the front door. She lifted the heavy brass lion's head doorknocker.

"This guy must be loaded. Do you think he'd consider being my sugar daddy?" asked Jorge.

Syd didn't have time to reiterate her "no hitting on the client" lecture before the door swung open to reveal Logan Murdoch.

#

Logan stood in the open doorway, but before he could greet his visitors, a man in tight khaki pants and a lavender polo shirt rushed forward and shook his hand vigorously.

"Mr. Murdoch, I am so excited to finally meet you in person. Wow, your house is gorgeous. Almost as gorgeous as its owner," the man said. Logan focused on his face. Was that lip gloss? He looked at Sydney for help.

"Jorge, you can stop shaking his hand now. Mr. Murdoch, this is Jorge Smith, my assistant. Forgive his enthusiasm. We don't let him out of the museum very often," she joked.

"No, that's quite all right. It's nice to meet you, Mr. Smith," Logan said.

"Honey, you can call me Jorge," he said with a leer.

Logan didn't need his vampire mind skills to know for which team Jorge batted. But the flirting didn't faze him. A person didn't live for four centuries without developing an open mind about things.

"Jorge it is then," he said amicably. "Miss Worth, it is good to see you again. Please come in. I am sure you are both eager to get to work."

They entered the large foyer. Logan tried not to stare at Sydney. He had appreciated her beauty when they first met, but today she took his breath away. Lipstick the color of ripe berries made her lips fuller and inviting, and the subtle smokiness of her eye shadow made her hazel gaze more seductive. Her outfit accentuated her curves, especially the V-neck of her sweater. He quickly averted his gaze lest she catch him admiring her assets.

"So do we get a tour?" Jorge asked, dashing Logan's hopes he could just deposit them in the library and get back to the lab.

He was eager to finish Lifeblood now that he was so close. Plus he really didn't want to be more involved with Sydney than necessary. His mother's predictions about Sydney being his soul mate left him nervous to spend too much time with her. Not that he believed in that nonsense. As a scientist he knew there had to be a more rational explanation for his inability to read her mind. He just hadn't thought of it yet. In the meantime, he couldn't let anything distract him from his work.

"Jorge, I am sure Mr. Murdoch has other things to do than play tour guide. Besides, we really do need to get to work," Sydney said. She met his look almost shyly. He wondered suddenly if she felt the tension between them too.

"As you wish. The library is down this hall," Logan said, leading the way.

"You should have plenty of space to work in here," he explained as they walked in.

"I should say so," Sydney said, looking around. When Logan said library, she thought it would be a cozy little space with a desk, not a room almost as big as one of the galleries at the museum.

"Did you read all of these?" Jorge asked, motioning to the two long walls covered floor to ceiling with books.

"I don't think anyone could read all these books in a single lifetime," he responded.

Although, given several lifetimes one could, he thought with an inward chuckle.

"This will work nicely, Mr. Murdoch. That table is large enough for both of us to spread out on," Sydney said, motioning to the rectangular table in the center of the room.

Jorge choked out a startled laugh. Then Sydney's face turned red as the double meaning of her comment sank in.

Logan stifled a chuckle of his own.

"I meant, that is…" Syd struggled to recover.

"It's quite all right. I know what you meant," Logan said and received a grateful look from her.

"Now, let me explain what you'll be looking through," he said. "We tried to gather only those boxes pertaining to the late eighteenth century. My family is enthusiastic about preserving our history, so I am afraid there is a lot for you to go through—letters, bills of sale, contracts, etc."

Syd looked at the boxes as Jorge wandered around the room admiring the knickknacks.

"Don't worry, Mr. Murdoch. We're used to plowing through archives larger than this," she said.

"Good. And please call me Logan. After all, you are going to be digging through my family's past. We might as well be on a first-name basis," he said with a smile.

She hesitated a second. "Alright, Logan. Call me Sydney."

"Okay, Sydney. I will get out of your way so you can get started. There is an intercom by the door. Just buzz if you need something," he said as he made his way to the doorway.

"Logan, could you spare some coffee? I'm parched," Jorge said. Logan could swear the man batted his eyelashes.

"Of course. I apologize for not offering sooner. I'll have Alaric bring in a tray for you," he said. Then he nodded to

Sydney before leaving them to their work.

#

"I guess we'd better dig in and see how everything is organized," Syd said, eyeing the boxes dubiously.

"Can't we wait for the coffee?" Jorge whined.

"Logan's butler will bring it soon enough. Sit down and help me," she said.

"Fine, slave driver," he said and dropped into a chair at the large dining-room-sized table.

Syd looked meaningfully from him to the mountain of boxes next to the table. He stared back and then slouched even further into the chair. She sighed and hefted one up onto the surface herself.

"Okay," she said after she opened the lid to the first box. "Luckily everything is grouped by year. This box is labeled 1794-95. Unfortunately, none of the file folders inside are labeled."

"Wait," Jorge said, sitting up straighter. "Don't we just have to focus on the years the piece was painted and stolen?"

"Good question," she replied. She thought for a moment. "Honestly with all the craziness of the last few days, it never occurred to me to ask Logan if they knew the exact years. I'll have to check with him about that. But for now, let's just concentrate on getting a feel for how things are organized. I doubt we'll find anything concrete today."

Jorge groaned. "This is going to ruin my manicure."

"Quit your bellyaching and pick up a box," she said and sat in a chair to start on her own box.

They worked in silence for about fifteen minutes before a brief knock sounded on the door. At Syd's acknowledgement, the door swung open.

Syd felt her eyes widen at the man who strode into the room carrying the tray with their coffee. Wearing khaki cargo shorts and a bright red Hawaiian shirt which accentuated his broad shoulders, he was the embodiment of the classic surfer dude. His flip-flops made a thwapping sound as he walked toward them.

"Hey, I'm Alaric. Logan said you wanted some coffee?" the blond god said.

Syd glanced at Jorge, whose mouth had fallen open. He was practically drooling on the table.

"You're Logan's butler?" Syd asked.

Alaric smiled. "Actually I am his lab assistant and friend. I am just helping out by bringing you coffee."

Embarrassed both by her assumption and by Jorge's continued open-mouthed adoration of the man, Syd jumped up to grab the tray from Alaric.

"I'm Sydney, and this is Jorge. Jorge?"

She waved a hand in front of his face, and he seemed to snap out of it. He rose slowly from his seat and sauntered over to Alaric, who was eyeing him dubiously.

"Well, hellooo," Jorge cooed.

"Um, hi," Alaric responded, backing away a couple of steps.

Syd had to intervene before Jorge got them both kicked out for sexual harassment.

"Jorge, your coffee's here," she tried.

"How sweet of you to bring us coffee. Please, you have to stay and have a cup with us," Jorge said eagerly.

"Actually, I have to get back to the lab. And I am sure you have a lot of work to do too," Alaric said. He looked at Sydney for help.

"You're right. Thank you for the coffee," she said.

"No problem," he replied as he quickly made for the exit. "See you later."

"Oh, you can count on it," Jorge said with a smile. Alaric all but ran out the door.

"Dammit, Jorge. Didn't we talk about not flirting this morning?"

"I am only a man. I have no control over my baser instincts. It was bad enough when it was just that adorable Logan but to add the hunky surfer into the mix?" He shook his head. "It's like taking someone on the Atkins diet to a donut shop."

"I am only going to say this once. Are you listening?" She waited to make sure she had his full attention. "If I see you harassing either of those men again, I will send you back to the museum and ask The Enforcer to give you a tutorial on proper organizational skills."

At his shudder, she nodded. "I see you understand how serious I am."

"Syd, I promise I'll try to control it. But when you got mojo like I do, it's hard not to expose it to the world."

"Yeah, well, keep your mojo to yourself," she said, trying to hide her grin. "Now can we please get back to work?"

"Okay, but would you mind if I had some coffee first? I am feeling spent from the morning full of eye candy," he said.

"Tell me about it." She sighed. "Pour me a cup while you're at it. And make it a double."

#

"No way," Alaric said.

"Come on, I'm busy," Logan replied.

"Look, I know you're busy, but I am not going back in there to be ogled again," Alaric said.

"Sydney ogled you?" Logan exclaimed. He tried to ignore the stab of jealousy that hit his midsection.

"No, that assistant of hers," Alaric said with a shudder.

"Who, Jorge? He's harmless."

"Logan, I am a vampire. Every mortal is harmless to me."

"So what's the problem?"

"He made me feel like a sex object," Alaric said, his expression sheepish.

"Oh, please." Logan laughed.

"Okay, the real problem is you can't hide out in the lab all day. Those are your guests. You can't keep using me to avoid them," Alaric said.

Logan frowned. Was it that apparent? He knew he was avoiding having to deal with them, but he didn't want it getting back to his mother he wasn't trying his best to get the painting back.

"I am not avoiding them. You know how important my work is. If I had my way, they would be at my mother's right now."

"But they're not. Sooner or later, you're going to have to go talk to them. Although, I don't really think it's them you're avoiding so much as her," his friend said with a knowing smile.

"I am going to kill Callum."

"Honestly, I thought he was crazy when he told me about the whole soul mate thing. But now that I've seen Sydney, I think you should go for it."

"That's ridiculous. First, she's mortal. I don't have to explain that one to you. Second, she's here trying to do her job. The last thing she needs is a bunch of matchmaking vampires bothering her."

"Chicken," Alaric said, followed by some annoying clucking noises.

"I am not scared. I am just not interested," Logan said and turned to adjust the gauges on a nearby centrifuge. Alaric was just trying to get a rise out of him. And it was working. All he wanted was to be left alone to work on his formula. He wanted to ignore his attraction to Sydney. Being around her would make that almost impossible to do.

"Fine, but just remember denial ain't just a river in Egypt."

"Oh, that's original. You'd think after one hundred and twelve years on this earth you would be a little more creative."

"Forget the whole mutual attraction issue. You still need to talk to her," Alaric said seriously.

"*Mutual* attraction?" Logan said, trying to sound nonchalant.

"Just because you can't read her doesn't mean the rest of us can't."

"She's attracted to me?"

"You said you're not interested, so I won't bore you with the details." Alaric turned away but not before Logan saw the sly grin on his face. "Now get down there and play the good host. Why don't you invite her to stay for dinner?"

"Like a date?"

"No, genius, like a business dinner. You know, so you can discuss her findings, and she can ask you any questions she has."

"Hmm. Maybe I'll do that. After all we both have to eat,

right?"

"Whatever works for you, dude."

\#

Syd glanced up as Logan came into the library. She sat alone at the table. Jorge had cleared out an hour earlier after calling a cab to come get him. She stayed later than she originally intended, hoping to catch Logan and pick his brain.

She looked at her watch. Seven o'clock. He had avoided her for ten hours.

"So how goes it?" Logan asked with a friendly smile.

"We went through a lot today, but I am afraid we're going to need more information if we want to speed up the process."

"Actually, I was just going to fix a quick dinner. If you join me, I would be happy to try to answer your questions."

Syd stared at him, taken aback by the offer. The last thing she'd expected from him was an invitation for dinner. Was it like a date?

Logan must have read the concern in her expression because he quickly added, "We both have to eat. And since we need to talk anyway, why not kill two birds with one stone?"

Okay, not a date. She should be relieved, right? But she still felt nervous about being alone with him.

"Will Alaric be joining us?" She asked, trying to keep the hope out of her voice.

"No, he left a few minutes ago. Why?" He frowned.

"Just wondering," she said nonchalantly.

"So how about it?"

"Okay, but I insist on helping you cook."

"Deal. Although, I should ask: You're not a vegetarian are you?"

"Nope," she smiled. "Carnivorous all the way."

Logan returned the smile, and she felt the butterflies in her stomach start dancing again.

"A woman after my own heart. Steak it is."

\#

Logan stood in front of the large gas grill on the back terrace of his house. The aroma of sizzling steaks swirled around him.

Sydney stood a few feet away, leaning against the low wall that bordered the patio. He took a moment to admire her silhouette. A light breeze caressed her auburn hair as she lifted her face to the soft moonlight.

He mentally shook himself and focused on making sure he didn't overcook the meat. They had begun the meal preparation in the kitchen, as she prepared a salad while he rubbed the steaks with spices. Their conversation had been polite as they worked. But now out on the patio, with it's soft light and beautiful view, things had gotten quiet.

Keep it professional, he reminded himself.

"What made you want to become a curator?"

She took a sip of her red wine before answering.

"I have always had a passion for history, and I love using art as a tool to interpret the thoughts and events of different time periods. And working with priceless works of art every day is amazing."

"Did you always want to work in a museum?"

Syd laughed. The throaty sound echoed off the walls of the house. "For the most part. There was a period where I was ready to throw it all away for a more practical life, but luckily I came to my senses."

Logan sensed more to the story but didn't want to pry.

"So tell me about your work," she inquired.

"I help develop new therapies for our company. Callum has a full research staff, but I do independent experiments."

"Funny, you don't really fit the scientist stereotype."

"How is that?" he asked, curious about how she viewed him.

"You're not geeky."

Logan chuckled.

"Oh, I think you'd be surprised," he responded. "My mother swears she's going to padlock my lab one of these days because I spend more time with beakers and Bunsen burners than people."

"You certainly don't look like a geek. No pocket protector, no pants pulled up to your armpits, and definitely not a geek's body."

A flush spread over her cheeks. Logan guessed she hadn't meant to mention that last part.

"What kind of body do I have?" he asked, wanting to tease her.

"You know, uh, not geeky," she said, looking everywhere but at him.

"How is it not geeky?" he pressed.

"You're just, um, toned, I guess."

"You're blushing."

"No, I'm not. I am just flushed. It's hot out here."

He decided not to remind her it was October. To ease her embarrassment, he asked, "How do you like your steak?"

"Medium, please," she responded.

"Overcooked, you mean. Rare is the only way to go," he said.

"Yeah, if you like it bloody," she joked back.

He laughed uncomfortably as he took his steak off the grill. Her comment had hit a little too close to home considering he had chugged a bag of blood in the lab earlier.

"Yours should only be a couple more minutes," he said.

"Great. I think I'll use the restroom before we eat."

#

"You're an idiot," she said to her reflection in the bathroom mirror. She finished washing her hands and sighed as she dried them.

What was she doing here? She should not be flirting with this man. She should be at home reading scholarly texts and planning her strategy about the painting. But no, she had to tell him he had a hot body. Might as well have said, *Take me now, big guy*.

She took one more look at herself. "Be professional. This is a business dinner," she said aloud. Then she turned and marched back to the terrace.

Logan was setting the platter of steaks on the table when she returned. She took her seat, and they spent a few minutes filling their plates.

She took her first bite and groaned. He could cook, too.

Granted, men learned to grill practically in the womb, but this was the best steak she had ever had.

"I take it you like it?" Logan asked, amusement clear in his voice.

"Mmmm hmm," she murmured because her mouth was still full.

"I'm glad you like it. Steak is my second favorite meal."

"What's your first?" she asked.

He glanced up at her for a moment. "Uh, prime rib," he said. His hesitation seemed odd to Syd. Why did she get the impression he wasn't telling the truth?

"But that's practically the same thing," she said.

He shrugged. "What can I say? I like red meat."

His grin made her forget to chew for a second. Snapping her mouth shut, she tried to refocus her thoughts.

"So, I suppose we should talk about the research. I realized today we never discussed exactly what you know about the origins of the painting or its theft."

He took a sip of wine, and she got the impression he was stalling.

"Actually my mother knows more about that than I do. She is the one who elected me to approach you about getting it back," he said.

"I guess I'll need to talk to her then. But isn't there anything you can tell me? With what little we know, it's like searching for a needle in a haystack."

"I . . . uh . . . don't know exact years, but I can tell you it was painted in the 1780s. I believe it was stolen around the 1850s."

"Do you know anything about Royce Murdoch? Maybe some insight into him would help me."

"He was the eldest son of a powerful family. I have heard he was into science and learning more than commerce or fighting," he said.

"Sounds a little like you," Sydney joked.

He cleared his throat. "Yeah, I guess he does. Anyway, I doubt you'll find anything about him in the history books."

"Thanks, that gives me a little to go on. Do you think you

could arrange a meeting with your mother soon?"

"Actually, she left today to go visit our place in Asheville. She should be back in a few of days," he said.

Syd sighed. She knew it wasn't Logan's fault, but nothing about this task seemed easy.

"Honestly, I hope to find the evidence before then, so it may be a moot point."

"Sydney, I'm sorry this is taking you away from the museum. I got the impression things there are tough for you. I'm sure being here doesn't help that situation since you have to be away from your work," he said.

"You're right. I am frustrated. It's not really your fault. After all, if proof exists, then your family has every right to want it back. But let's not talk about that anymore. I'll just use what you told me tonight and hopefully things will work out soon."

They continued their meal in silence for a few moments, each lost in their own thoughts. Then a question occurred to Sydney.

"Were you born in Scotland?"

"Yes, I was born near Edinburgh, but we have been in America so long that none of us really has much of an accent anymore."

"You mentioned you mother and brother. What about your father?" she asked.

A shadow passed across his face. She instantly regretted indulging her curiosity.

"You don't have to—" she started.

"No, it's fine. My father's death was the main reason we moved to America. He was killed during a...robbery. My mother thought it best we move to get a fresh start."

"How horrible for all of you. Your poor mother had to leave everything behind and raise two young sons on her own. She must be a strong woman."

"You have no idea," he said. She detected both respect and exasperation in his tone.

"I assume you're a close family."

"Yes, although sometimes they drive me crazy," he said with

a grin.

"It wouldn't be family if they didn't," she joked back.

"Is your family close too?"

Syd paused. She didn't really want to reveal too much about her family. The pain she felt over their rejection was still fresh.

"I don't really speak with my parents."

"I'm sorry," he said with sincerity. "Do you have siblings?"

"No, just me."

"I can't imagine that. You must get lonely," he said.

"Sometimes," she shrugged. "But you get used to it."

"I'll admit the prospect holds some appeal. When I just want to be alone to work, it seems like some family member is always knocking on the door or calling."

"Actually that sounds kind of nice. Always having someone to care about what you're doing."

Logan must have sensed her sadness at the topic, so he changed subjects. "So I have to ask, who is your favorite artist?"

"Hmm. That's a tough one. There are so many," she said. Syd took a sip of wine while she pondered the question. "I guess if I had to chose just one, though, it would be Klimt."

After that they continued to discuss art for some time, debating the merits of one artist over the other. Sydney found herself amazed by his knowledge of art history. She figured a scientist wouldn't have a lot of time to study the arts. Logan continued to surprise her.

The topic gradually moved on to books and movies. Then Logan shared some amusing stories about his exploits with Callum and Alaric, whom he considered a brother.

Syd looked over at him as her laughter finally subsided after a particularly funny story. She didn't know if it was the wine, the beautiful night, or the laughter, but she hadn't felt this good in months.

Logan looked back at her with a smile. She was struck again by the contrasts he presented. She originally found him somewhat intimidating, but seeing him now, she felt comfortable. He leaned back in his chair, swirling the wine in his glass.

"This was fun," he observed.

"Yes, I never thought I'd find someone who could keep up with me in an obscure Monty Python quoting contest."

"I meant the whole dinner," he said, suddenly sounding more serious.

"Uh, yes, it was very nice," she said. Suddenly she felt shy again.

An uncomfortable silence descended.

"So, do you have a boyfriend?" Logan blurted.

"Uh, no," she said hesitantly, wondering where he was going with that.

"Good," he said with a nod.

"Good?"

"I mean it's good this project isn't keeping you away from someone special," he amended.

"I guess," she said with a shrug. She took a nervous sip of wine to cover her unease with the tension that hung between them suddenly.

Logan put down his own glass and leaned forward. "Look, I lied. The real reason I asked is that I know we're working together, but I keep having . . . unprofessional thoughts where you're concerned."

Her breath caught. *Holy crap!* Talk about cutting to the chase. The last thing she expected when she agreed to dinner was for this gorgeous man to tell her he was warm for her form.

He put his hand over hers on the table and met her gaze.

"I'm sorry. I didn't mean to make you uncomfortable."

"Uh, no, I just didn't expect you to say that."

"So . . . what do you think about . . . what I said?"

"Uh, I admit there is some sort of . . . something there."

He chuckled. "That's specific."

"Well, I don't really know what to say. Um, thanks?"

"So you don't feel anything?" he asked with furrowed brows.

"I didn't say that," she said quickly.

He chuckled and leaned in farther. "What are we going to do about that?"

She felt herself leaning toward him, the seductive sound of his voice entrancing her.

"I don't know," she breathed.

"I'm sure if we put our heads together we can think of something," he responded a breath away from her lips.

Oh. My. God. He's going to kiss me! Syd's mind shouted as Logan cradled her face in his hands and began his descent. *Shut up and enjoy it*, her body countered. Before she could think of anything to say to him, his mouth caressed hers tentatively.

She breathed in the heady scent of red wine and warm male and gave into the inevitable. She stroked his lips with her own, emboldened by the electricity arcing from her mouth to her pelvis.

Everything changed as her nervousness faded and her craving for him took over. Their tongues intertwined as he deepened the kiss. Suddenly he lifted her from her chair, and then the strong muscles of his thighs cradled her. She felt her libido spin out of control. Yet at the same time, the warm shield of his body her made her feel oddly safe.

She twined her arms around his neck and tilted her head for a better angle. His arms wrapped around her back, caresses quickly giving way to urgent kneading.

Her groan echoed into the silence of the night surrounding them. His hand moved around to stroke her breast. She scooted back to give him better access and barely noticed when her elbow bumped something.

The sound of shattering glass broke the spell surrounding them. Syd jerked up when she felt something wet hit her leg. She slid toward the ground, but Logan steadied her—his reflexes so fast she barely knew what happened. She stood quickly and surveyed the scene.

Shards of wine glass crackled under her feet, and a small pool of red stained the flagstone patio. Her heart pounded in her chest, whether from the interruption or the kiss itself, she couldn't decide.

"Logan, I am so sorry. I guess I bumped it when I . . ." she trailed off.

He smiled back. "It's just a wine glass. No harm done, except to your skirt. I'm afraid you're going to have to get rid of it." He touched the stain on her thigh. The contact brought Syd back to her senses.

She glanced at Logan, who seemed intent on a second round of tongue jousting—minus her skirt, apparently. She abruptly stumbled back from him.

"Oh no, what the hell are we doing? No more kissing!" She held her hands up to slow his advance. He stopped and looked at her.

"Syd, it's just a skirt. I'll buy you a new one," he said calmly and then continued his advance.

"It's not about the skirt. Logan, we shouldn't be kissing, period," she said.

"Why?" He raised a challenging brow.

Her thoughts still a bit scrambled from his taste and touch, she struggled to formulate a compelling reason for them to stop. "Because?"

He chuckled. "Surely you don't expect me to believe that was one-sided."

"No, it was both of us," she admitted, "but we have to forget it happened." Now that the sensual fog had cleared, her mind had kicked into flight mode. The realization she had been just shy of ripping his clothes off caused her to panic. How could she forget she was there because of her job? She hadn't read the museum manual lately, but she was pretty sure sleeping with patrons was a no-no.

Logan took a deep breath. "I don't think I'll forget it. But I agree it would complicate things to pursue this . . . whatever it is between us."

Syd sent him a grateful look. "I appreciate you being so understanding."

"Believe me, I am kicking myself mentally as we speak," he said with a wry grin.

"That's my cue to leave, then. Good night." She reached out to shake his hand. He hesitated and smiled at her formality. Then, he took her hand and lifted it to his mouth. The brief caress of his lips on her skin sent a tingle up her arm. She withdrew her hand and turned to go before her resolve was tested any further.

"Thank you for the dinner. Bye," she said over her shoulder as she rushed to get out of there.

As she flew through the patio doors, she heard him say, "It was my pleasure."

CHAPTER FIVE

The shrill ring of the phone startled Logan awake. He glanced at the clock and groaned. Five a.m. After Sydney had left, he tried to concentrate on his work to take his mind off of her. But he finally gave up and headed to bed around two.

"Yes," he snapped into the phone, ready to tear into whoever had the audacity to call this early.

"It's me," said Alaric. "We have a problem."

Logan sat up. Alaric wouldn't call unless it was something serious.

"The delivery of blood disappeared. The driver from the shipment company never checked in with his boss. His manager got nervous and sent someone out to check the route. Logan, they found the driver unconscious and the truck empty."

"Raven," Logan said with a snarl.

"That's what I think, too. No one else would have a reason to raid a shipment of blood."

"Damn! This is going to set us back," Logan said and hit his fist into a pillow. Several feathers flew into the air after the pillow ripped from the impact.

"I've already been in touch with Francesca at Brethren

headquarters. She is going to start collecting fresh samples from the elders as soon as possible. Then she'll bring the blood to us herself in a day or two. After all, we're so close we don't need much."

"I suppose I could convince mother to donate a couple of pints in the meantime. Her blood is old enough to do some preliminary tests against the samples of the Lifeblood," he said, referring to the synthetic blood they were testing.

"Isn't she out of town?" Alaric reminded Logan.

"Damn, I forgot," he said. "Okay, maybe we can do some tests on blood samples in the labs at Murdoch Biotech. Meet me there in an hour."

They said their good-byes, and Logan hung up. He shook his head and got up to dress. Some days it just didn't pay to be immortal. The last week alone brought a rogue vampire trying to thwart his research, a vixen curator tempting his flesh, and a nagging mother insisting he pursue stolen artwork. He shuddered to think what the next week would bring.

#

Syd looked at the clock on her dashboard as she drove toward Logan's the next morning. Ten o'clock, much later than she normally got to work. Her eyes felt like sandpaper. For the last few nights, stress-induced dreams had her waking constantly. Her favorite one involved falling off a cliff and waking an instant before impact.

One moment she felt good about the agreement she and Logan had made, and then the next she felt her stomach drop at the prospect of seeing him again. Currently anger won out as she railed against herself for her lack of willpower.

"What kind of idiot kisses a man just because he knows some stupid movie quotes?" she asked herself aloud. "The same kind who falls off ladders and thrusts her breasts in men's faces, that's who.

"Today you will be a rock, unaffected by him in every way. Do not stare at his rear end, do not look at his lips, and for God's sake, woman, do not spend any time alone with him."

Luckily, Jorge was not there to witness her ravings. She

needed him at the museum today to lead a tour group from the Raleigh Ladies' Auxiliary. Jorge made the perfect tour guide for a group of older women. He flirted outrageously with them and complimented their shoes and handbags, and they in turn shared the best gossip from Raleigh society.

Syd stopped the car in front of Logan's house. Despite her tough talk, she was nervous again. What if it was awkward? What if he thought less of her? What if she threw herself at him in a weak moment? *Not gonna happen, sister*, her mind demanded.

She took a calming breath and headed for the door. Before she could knock, she noticed a piece of paper stuck in the jamb.

Sydney—
Had urgent business. The door is unlocked. Make yourself at home. Should be back this afternoon.
L.

She wondered why anyone in this day and age would leave his door unlocked. She looked around the front of his house and recognized the answer. Logan lived about fifteen minutes outside of Raleigh on a tract of land set back from the road and covered with pine trees. Not much chance of a stranger wandering into his unlocked door. Still, she felt uncomfortable as she let herself in.

"Logan?" she called from the foyer. She didn't want to chance that he had returned from his business early and forgotten to take the note off the door. She called his name once more, but the only sound was the echo of her voice in the large marbled entryway.

She heaved a sigh of relief and went to the library. At least she could put off having to see him so soon after their embarrassing interlude. She set her briefcase on the table and got to work.

#

Six hours later, she rubbed her eyes. Reading old documents was hell on the vision. But she couldn't complain about the progress she had made today.

She still didn't have conclusive proof, but she found a few references to family portraits done by a man named Cornelius Murdoch. The name surprised her because it meant a member of the family might have painted Royce's picture. If so, the man obviously had great talent, but she had never heard of him. She made a note to search for the name in one of the art databases she frequently used for research.

She also found a letter from a friend of the family commiserating with them after vandals broke into the home and stole many valuable items. It didn't take a genius to figure out that Logan's story meshed with what she was seeing here. But she still needed a specific reference to a painting of Royce Murdoch as well as a description fitting the painting at the museum.

She decided to call it a day. She needed to go by the museum before heading home to catch up on her sleep. But deep down she knew she wanted to get out of there before Logan returned.

She grabbed a piece of paper to leave him a note. Chewing on the end of her pen, she struggled over what to say. Finally she wrote: *Logan, hope you had a great day! I know I did. See you tomorrow!*

Nope, she sounded like a cheerleader on speed. She crumpled up the note and tried again.

Logan. Thank you for the use of your library. I accomplished much today. I shall return tomorrow. Sydney.

Jesus, now she sounded like a Victorian barrister. That note joined the other one.

Logan. See you tomorrow. Sydney.

She nodded and decided the short-and-sweet approach was the way to go.

She gathered the discarded notes and her briefcase and headed to the foyer. She left the final note on the console table. As she turned to go, she heard the sound of a garage door opening from the rear of the house.

He was home. Panic set in, and she ran to the front door and was in her car in no time.

Whew, that was close! Her body thrummed with adrenaline.

She looked in the rearview mirror as she pulled away and saw Logan standing on his front porch watching her escape.

So much for professionalism.

#

Logan watched the dust curl behind Sydney's car as she rounded the bend and disappeared behind the trees lining his driveway. He figured she must be late for an appointment given the speed with which she drove.

He went back into the house and saw two pieces of crumpled paper lying near the doorway. Had Sydney dropped these as she left? He bent to pick them up. He opened the first one, and his eyebrows furrowed. It was a note from Sydney sounding like an anal retentive lawyer. He opened the second one and chuckled.

He looked up and saw the third note on his console table, finally clueing in that these were practice notes. Logan found it endearing that she practiced what to say. He retrieved the note she had decided to leave. His laughter echoed through the house. The woman continued to amuse him. He considered leaving them for her on the table in the library. He could just imagine her face when she found them in the morning.

Chuckling some more, he climbed the stairs to his bedroom. Deciding they would be good to read when he needed some comic relief, he placed the notes in the drawer of his nightstand. Then he plopped on his bed with a sigh.

He and Alaric had worked nonstop since six a.m. They finally decided to call it a day when it was obvious they couldn't do much more until the Brethren liaison arrived in the morning.

He still could not believe Raven's audacity. She had a reputation for rebellion among the Brethren. However, messing with his family indicated a level of boldness that surpassed her previous exploits. The Murdoch family was well respected in the vampire community. His mother had her hands in many of the council's initiatives, and even he and Callum had some influence due to their contributions to the betterment of vampire life.

The Brethren Council was created one hundred and fifty

years ago to aid their kind in a rapidly changing world. A group of visionary elder vampires created laws to protect vampires from discovery by humans. Their philosophy that vampires could peacefully coexist with mortals influenced their laws. Thus feeding from and turning humans was forbidden, except in rare cases. Any vampires who broke that law were banished to areas where they could no longer harm mortals.

Logan's work provided an array of products that allowed them to live like mortals. Vitamin therapies helped counteract the sun allergies that plagued all vampires, and iron supplements counteracted the extreme anemia which was to blame for many of their weaknesses. In fact, one of the reasons vampires needed blood so much was for the iron it provided. Of course, the blood also provided nutrients needed to maintain their strength and to constantly repair the damages of daily living. Bagged blood was a decent solution since they couldn't feed off humans directly, but Logan knew Lifeblood would be the key to finally ending their dependence on human sources of nutrition.

He rubbed his eyes. He wanted to take a nap, but Callum was coming over to strategize about the Raven problem. His mother was on her way back from Asheville and would probably be there in a few hours as well. He hoped his mother had found some evidence there that would help Sydney finish her research.

He smiled again as he remembered Sydney's notes. Could they explain her speedy retreat this afternoon? Did she hear him coming in the back door and decide to leave quickly instead of talking to him? He frowned. He hated it that she might be nervous. If things hadn't been so crazy, he would have been able to talk to her today and apologize for last night.

He had been out of line kissing her, especially after the protesting he had done with his family. Disgusted with himself for his lack of control, he decided maybe it was best he was so busy. Obviously he couldn't be trusted around the woman.

Sydney was amazing, but she deserved better than a vampire who could offer her nothing more than a few nights of pleasure. And that was all he was willing to give. He would not risk getting his heart involved with a mortal woman again. They tended to react badly when they found out their boyfriends drank blood.

He shook off the memories of Brenna and stood. He needed to go grab some blood before everyone showed up. He'd need the strength to make it through the next several hours.

He stretched and headed downstairs. Time to get back to work.

#

Sydney arrived early the next morning. She was excited to get started again after yesterday's discoveries. Jorge worked from the office today, scouring the museum library and the Internet for any information he could dig up.

She got out of her car, and the front door opened. Logan and a stunning blond stepped onto the porch. Blondie laughed at something Logan said. Syd's blood began a slow simmer when the woman leaned in to hug Logan. He met Syd's eyes over the tramp's shoulder.

She'd seen enough. Syd slammed her door with more force than necessary.

"Sydney," he said, pulling away from the woman. As he came down the steps to greet her, he smiled and said, "Good morning."

She pasted a false smile on her face.

"Good morning," she said and turned toward the woman. "Hello."

"Forgive me," Logan said. "Sydney this is Francesca Duchamp, a . . . business associate. Francesca, this is Sydney Worth, the curator I was telling you about."

Business associate, my foot.

"Nice to meet you," she said to Miss Perfect.

"Logan has said wonderful things about your work," Francesca replied with a friendly smile.

If Syd hadn't already despised the woman for her familiarity with Logan, she would have hated her now for being both beautiful and nice. Standing about three inches taller than

Sydney, the leggy blond looked like a she had stepped off the pages of *Gorgeous Supermodels You Love to Hate* magazine. She wore a tailored grey suit with a pink shell that made her peaches-and-cream complexion glow.

Syd merely nodded at the woman. She was too busy trying to tamp down the jealousy Francesca aroused. She tried to talk herself out of the reaction by remembering the reasons she was not interested in Logan, but her baser instincts prevailed. She might not want Logan, but she'd be damned if this Charlize Theron look-alike was going to get him.

"Well, I must be off. Sydney, it was a pleasure meeting you. I hope to see you again," Francesa said with a smile. "Logan, may I speak with you for a moment?"

If they kiss, I am going to rip her lips off.

Logan nodded and walked Francesca to the silver Mercedes sitting on the opposite side of the drive from Syd's red Ford Focus.

"Thank you for coming at such short notice," Syd overheard Logan say.

Francesca murmured a response too low for Syd to hear. Syd wasn't actively trying to eavesdrop, but found herself inching towards a shrub at the edge of the driveway to admire its foliage.

Unfortunately, she could only pick up a few confusing words.

"Your brother . . . ," Francesca said.

". . . pain in the . . . ," Logan responded.

Francesca laughed, ". . . mate . . . chance . . . love."

Syd frowned. That didn't sound like a business discussion.

Francesca whispered, ". . . thinks I spent the night . . . explain."

"Damn . . . never work . . . mortal . . ."

Syd glanced at them from the corner of her eye. Francesca shook her head at Logan with a smile. Logan frowned at the woman.

Good. If he's frowning at her, then there will be no kissing, she thought.

Francesca gave Logan another hug. "It will all work out," she said, her voice no longer quiet. "Sydney," Francesca said. Syd jumped and then turned toward the pair, trying to look nonchalant. "I wish you luck. You're going to need it."

With a chuckle, Francesca said good-bye to Logan. Logan frowned fiercely at the car as it drove away. Syd didn't know what had just happened but wanted to run inside before Logan noticed her again.

As if suddenly remembering her presence, he turned toward her. His frown melted, but he ran a frustrated hand though his hair as he walked toward her.

"Sorry about that. She came over very early to bring by some important materials Alaric and I need to complete our current project."

"You don't have to explain it to me," Syd said, sounding defensive even to her own ears.

Logan smiled. "So you didn't assume she had spent the night when you saw us standing on the front porch together?"

Syd stared at him for a moment, shocked that her thoughts were so easily read. "Even if she had, it's none of my business."

"Well good, I wouldn't want you to be jealous," he said with a baiting smile.

"*Jealous*? You're delusional. We're just friends, remember?"

"Sydney, we agreed to be friends after a very passionate kiss. It would be normal for you to be bothered if you thought I slept with another woman just twenty-four hours after that."

"I think we need to stop talking right now," she said, and to prove her point she marched up the front steps.

Logan's laughter followed her into the house. She stalked toward the library. She set her things on the table and put her chin to her chest. Her day already sucked, and it wasn't even nine a.m. yet.

"Sydney, I want to apologize for the other night."

She nearly jumped out of her skin. She swung around to see Logan walk into the room and close the door behind him.

"Jesus! You scared the crap out of me!"

He frowned. "Sorry, I thought you knew I was behind you."

"You must be the quietest walker on earth. Lions aren't that quiet hunting prey," she said.

Logan just waited for her to finish her rant. When she calmed down, he spoke again.

"Like I said, I just wanted to apologize for the other night. I know this whole mess is hard enough without me making passes at you. I hope you aren't nervous to be here. I'd like to try being friends."

Syd saw the sincerity in his gaze and felt like a heel. Here the guy was trying to make her feel more comfortable and she just raved at him about sneaking up on her.

"I'm sorry too, for snapping at you. I'd like to try the friends thing," she said.

He walked over and took her hand. Looking into her eyes, he said, "I want you to know if things were different, I wouldn't settle with just being friends."

Syd swallowed loudly.

"Sometimes responsibility sucks, huh?" she said and then instantly wanted to kick her own ass. *Nice going, smooth talker.*

Logan chuckled, "I couldn't have said it better myself."

He released her hand and walked over to the boxes on the table. Syd was relieved he ended the moment. His genuine regret over their situation ate at her resolve to keep things light.

"Sorry I couldn't be here yesterday. Did you find anything interesting?"

"I did. Does the name Cornelius Murdoch ring any bells?"

Logan abruptly turned to look at her. She stared in confusion as a parade of emotions passed over his features.

"Are you alright?" Syd asked.

"Yes, fine. Sorry, I didn't get much sleep last night, so I'm a little punchy. Cornelius, you said?"

"Yes, I found several references indicating he painted portraits of the family. I assumed he was a relative."

"Yes, he was the head of the family. Royce's father, in fact."

She felt her eyes widen. "That's interesting. I am amazed the leader of a powerful family would have any spare time to paint. Not to mention the talent."

"He was a true Renaissance man," Logan said with a sad smile.

#

Logan escaped a few minutes later after telling Syd he had to get back to work. It wasn't a lie; he needed to begin the final experiment now that Francesca had brought the new samples. But more than that, he needed to end the discussion about his father.

Sydney's use of his father's name so unexpectedly had shaken him. After all this time his father's loss was a devastating blow, especially given the circumstances of his death.

Logan admired his father, not just for the respect he commanded within the vampire community, but also for his dedication to his family. Logan inherited his love of science from him, and had spent many hours assisting his father in his lab. Of course, back then science was a fledgling subject, so their experiments were elementary compared to the work Logan did today. But without his father's influence, Logan never would have accomplished as much as he had.

His father also pursued other interests besides science, such as art, literature, and politics. Unfortunately, a clan of rogue vampires took exception when his father tried to implement some radical reforms.

Reforms that cost him his life. While vampires were immortal, they were vulnerable to certain forms of attack. No amount of blood could cure a stake through the heart or a severed head. The rogues had done both to his father. Logan would never forget his mother's face when she heard what they had done to her beloved husband.

Logan shook away the depressing memories and tried to focus on the good ones. He remembered the jokes and long talks they'd shared over the hours it took for his father to paint Logan's portrait. Logan was elated to be so close to having the painting back. His mother was right; it would be like regaining a piece of his father.

Logan entered the lab. Alaric looked up from the test tubes he was labeling.

"What's wrong?"

Logan smiled. "Nothing. Life is just interesting."

"You're telling me," Alaric laughed. "I take it Sydney arrived."

Logan nodded. He walked over to the set of samples Francesca had delivered.

"We're close, my friend," he said.

"Amazing isn't it? Although I can't help but wonder what Raven will try next," Alaric responded.

"I'm not worried. After all, all of our samples of Lifeblood are here, and she wouldn't dare enter my home."

"True, but I am sure she has something up her sleeve."

"Probably, but I can't think of anything she could do that would get to me."

Logan rubbed his hands together and walked over to the refrigerator that contained the test samples of Lifeblood.

"Now enough talk about Raven. Let's make history."

#

Syd's head jerked up. She must have dozed off for a second. After her initial enthusiasm this morning, she'd spent the rest of the day slogging through box after box of documents without finding anymore leads. She glanced at her watch. No wonder she had fallen asleep, it was already midnight. She rubbed at the crick in her neck.

Where was Logan? She had seen him that afternoon when he and Alaric invited her to eat lunch with them. But since the quick meal, she had neither seen nor heard from either of the men. They must still be working in the lab.

She stood up and then immediately dropped back into the seat. She was exhausted. The stress and poor sleep of the last few days must have caught up with her. She decided to rest her head on the desk a few more minutes. Then she'd find Logan to say good-bye and go home.

CHAPTER SIX

Logan walked into the library shortly after midnight and found Sydney facedown on the table.

He smiled when he heard a soft snore come from her. He felt a twinge of guilt that she had exhausted herself to this point. After all, she was doing all of this to help him.

He put a hand on her shoulder and gently shook. When she didn't respond, he whispered her name.

One of her hands came up to scratch her ear where his breath tickled it. He smiled again. She slept like a child, totally unconscious. He tried to rouse her once more before giving up. But he decided even if he had been able to wake her, it would be unsafe for her to drive in her exhausted state.

He bent and picked her up with his arms under her shoulders and knees. She sighed contentedly and snuggled into him with her head on his shoulder. He clinched his jaw against the feel of her and the protective instincts she inspired in him. She presented an irresistible blend of seduction and innocence that intrigued him.

He quickly strode through the foyer and up the winding staircase. Not once did Sydney stir. He entered the first guest room, which happened to be across from his own room. Not bothering to turn on a light, he gently lowered her to the bed. He tried to lean back, but she held tight to his shoulders.

"Logan," she breathed as she nuzzled her face in his neck. The throaty sound of his name on her lips made his member stand at attention. He had to get out of there.

But Syd had other plans. Her hand caressed its way down his chest. He reached up to still its progress before she reached any place interesting.

"Sydney, it's time for bed," he said. He hoped he could wake her enough to get her to lie down all the way and go back to sleep.

"Yes, come to bed," she murmured and pulled him down with her. He extracted her hands from his waistband and pulled back.

"Syd!" he hissed.

She opened her eyes to half-mast and yawned.

"Logan?" His name sounded groggy this time. A definite improvement from the sex-kitten tone she'd used a moment before.

"What?" she asked, but she was still half-asleep.

"Shhh, it's okay. You're going to sleep in my guest bedroom. You're too tired to drive." He quickly removed her shoes and backed away from the bed.

"Mmmm, sleepy," came her slurred response.

He finally reached the door and looked back. She turned away from him and nestled into the pillows. Relieved she was finally out again, he turned to leave.

"Mmmmm . . . Logan, yummy."

He stopped in his tracks. He turned to look again, but she hadn't moved. Syd was dreaming about him? More importantly, the dream involved him being yummy?

He sprinted out the door before he woke her up and showed her just how yummy he could be.

#

Syd woke up feeling deliciously refreshed. Birds chirped in the tree outside her window, and sunlight warmed the room.

She rolled over and stretched.

Wait a second.

She didn't have a tree outside her bedroom. Hell, she didn't even have a window in her bedroom. She cocked one eye open. She first noticed the silk-covered canopy above her. Definitely not her bed. She quickly looked to her left. She let out a relieved sigh. Thank God, she was alone.

She took stock of the room while her mind scrambled to make sense of her situation. The soft green of the walls glowed in the morning light. The ivory furnishings and soothing Japanese watercolors which adorned the walls added to the room's tranquil feeling. She thought about her own cramped apartment with its stark white walls and shabby furniture. She suddenly wanted to cocoon herself in the luxurious down comforter and go back to sleep. But something niggled her.

Rubbing the sleep from her eyes, she tried to remember the night before. Her last lucid memory was her decision to rest her eyes in the library. Following that were flashes of Logan putting her to bed.

She bolted upright. Logan had carried her to bed, tucked her in, and she had called him yummy!

Scrambling out of bed, she decided she had to get out of there before he woke and she had to apologize for sleep flirting.

She ran into the bathroom and splashed cold water on her face. She looked in the mirror, and a wild-eyed Medusa stared back at her. Scratch that. She needed to get out of there before Logan saw her looking like that.

She crept to the bedroom door and listened. The silence that greeted her sounded like music to her ears. She slowly opened the door, pausing when it creaked loudly. She glanced around and then continued down the hall when Logan didn't come out of one of the doors nearby.

She quickly made her way to the library to grab her briefcase. Then she tiptoed back through the foyer and out the front door. Unfortunately her escape was hampered by the woman who stood on the porch, her arm raised to knock on the door.

"Hello. You must be Sydney," the woman said with a friendly smile and a twinkle in her eyes.

"Uh, yeah. And you are . . . ?"

"I'm Logan's mother, Kira. It is a pleasure to meet you on such a glorious early morning." Syd caught the implication immediately.

"Mrs. Murdoch, it's not what it looks like. I fell asleep last night while I was working, and Logan let me sleep in his guest room," she explained, sounding guilty to her own ears.

"Please, call me Kira. And no need to explain why you're here so early. I know how hard you have been working. I am just sorry it has taken so long for us to meet."

Syd took the opportunity to inspect her companion for the first time.

"Are you sure you're Logan's mother?"

Kira laughed. "Last time I checked. That boy took fifteen hours of pushing to deliver."

"It's just you're so . . . young," Syd said.

"I did have him relatively early in life, and I was blessed with good genes," Kira replied with a shrug. Syd wasn't sure how to respond. After all, the woman almost looked younger than her.

She barely resisted the urge to reach up and restore order to her bed head. In addition to her youthful appearance, Kira was gorgeous. Syd suddenly felt like the ugly stepsister. Then it dawned on her—Kira Murdoch had the resources to hire an entire team of plastic surgeons to keep her looking young.

"I assume the research is going well?" Kira asked, changing the subject.

Syd realized her eyes were narrowed as she looked for telltale signs of a cosmetic surgery on Kira's face. She halted her inspection to respond.

"Your family has an interesting past, but I am afraid I have yet to find the proof we need. I was hoping you and I could sit down soon and discuss what you know about the history of the painting."

"That sounds fine. In the meantime, I will go through some additional files at my home to see if I can help. I am sure something will turn up soon.

"On another note, how are you and Logan getting on?" she asked.

Syd opened her mouth but was unsure how to respond. Syd didn't know Kira enough to know if she was asking in a matchmaking capacity or was just making polite conversation.

"Logan has been very helpful," Syd responded evasively.

"Oh, come now, you can be honest." Kira leaned forward conspiratorially. "He's handsome isn't he?"

"I don't really think—"

"Don't be shy. Mothers know these things. I think you two would make a splendid couple."

"But you don't even know me," Syd protested. Were they really having this conversation?

"Call it intuition if you like, but I think you would be very good for my son. He spends too much time with test tubes and not enough time living."

"He seems pretty lively to me," Syd said before she could stop herself.

Kira smiled knowingly. "Don't worry, my dear. I know you probably didn't mean to say that out loud. It will stay between us. But please know if you ever need to talk, I am a good listener. Now I suppose you probably have other things to do than talk with an old woman."

Syd shook her head. First, the old woman comment was so ironic she had to bite back a laugh. Second, she knew she should be shocked by the woman's candor, but she felt strangely comfortable with Kira.

"Actually I do need to get to the museum to catch up on some work. It was nice to meet you. I hope we can talk again soon."

"Oh, I think we'll be seeing a lot of each other," Kira said mysteriously and then waved before going through Logan's door.

#

Logan chuckled to himself in his room. Sydney would never make a career out of being a cat burglar. At least if her targets were vampire households. Perhaps a mortal man wouldn't have heard her moving around, but Logan's enhanced hearing had picked up her movements from the moment she woke.

He stretched and got out of bed. Thankfully, it was the weekend, so he would have two days without Sydney around to distract him from his work. Not that she was all that bad as far as distractions went. But he was so close to finalizing the formula for Lifeblood, and it was crucial nothing divert his attention right now.

He whistled a tune as he retrieved a bag of blood from the small refrigerator in his closet. Back in his room, he heard voices below and craned his neck to see where they came from. He almost spewed blood all over the glass when he saw Sydney and his mother talking like old friends in front of his house.

This couldn't be good. His mother had that calculating look on her face. He could only imagine her joy at finding Sydney sneaking out of his house this early. Great, now he'd have to have another talk with her about her matchmaking.

He watched as the two women parted ways. He counted the seconds until he heard his mother's knock on this bedroom door. He opened it, and she immediately held up her hand to forestall his lecture.

"Don't say anything. I know nothing happened. I can read her mind, remember? But darling, I have to say this: If you can't see that woman is your soul mate, then you're crazy."

"Stop it."

"But, Logan, she's intelligent, beautiful, and is totally hot for you."

"Mother that's enou—she's hot for me? Wait, no, I am not having this conversation with my mother."

"Darling, you're such a prude. You think I don't know about sex after all this time? How do you think you and your brother got here?"

"Enough, you're going to make me gag on my blood."

Kira laughed. "I am just saying that I think it's time you got over Brenna and started living your life."

"I don't want to talk about this. What is or is not between

Syd and me is our business."

"You're right, darling. I just want you to be happy."

Logan nodded to acknowledge her concern.

"Did you find anything in Asheville?" he asked, wanting to change the subject.

She smiled. "Sorry, darling. Looks like you're going to have to work with Sydney for a while longer."

#

Once in her car, Syd breathed sigh of relief. She would have expired on site if Logan had discovered her sneaking around. Not to mention the mortification she would have felt if he had overheard her conversation with his mother. Luckily, she had two days to compose herself before seeing him again.

She glanced down as her cell phone chirped from inside her briefcase. Immediately she worried it might be Logan calling. She breathed a sigh of relief when she finally wrestled the phone out and saw the museum number on the caller ID.

"Miss Worth, where the hell are you? I have been calling all morning!" Stiggler demanded after she answered.

"Sorry, Mr. Stiggler. I left my cell phone in the other room when I went to bed," she said, proud of herself for telling the truth.

"You need to get over to the museum right now. I have called an emergency meeting."

"But sir, I—"she began.

"I don't want to hear excuses," he interrupted. "Just get here. Now."

He hung up on her. Syd looked at her phone for a moment. That was abrupt even for Stiggler.

Syd turned her car in the direction of the museum. She had hoped to be able to go home and change before going to catch up on work. What could be so urgent that Stiggler called an emergency meeting?

She looked in the rearview mirror. Great, now she had to face Stiggler with Medusa hair, morning breath, and a sheet crease on her cheek. Today was going to suck.

#

THE HOT SCOT

When she arrived twenty minutes later, police tape and somber-looking uniformed policemen greeted her. Only after flashing her museum identification was she allowed access to the building. Unfortunately, no one would answer her questions about their presence.

She hurried through the galleries on her way to the conference room near Stiggler's office. She burst into the room to find Jorge, The Enforcer, Lenny, and other members of the curatorial staff looking worried as they gathered around the massive oval table. At the other end of the room, Stiggler paced as he railed.

"Incompetent . . . inconceivable . . . thieves . . . " were the only words she could make out.

She stepped further into the room, gaining the director's attention.

"Ah, Miss Worth, so glad you could join us! Hope we didn't interrupt your beauty sleep," Stiggler said and sneered. She tried to look poised as he took in her appearance.

"What's going on?" she asked, ignoring his sarcasm as she took a seat next to Jorge.

"We've been robbed!" Stiggler said as he slammed his hand on the table. "And I want an explanation!"

Syd looked around the room only to realize everyone was looking at her.

"Um, why do you want an explanation from me? I didn't even know about this until thirty seconds ago. What was stolen?"

Stiggler just continued to stare at her intently. Finally Jorge leaned over and whispered, "The Hot Scot."

Sydney jumped out of her seat in shock. "What? You're kidding! When was it taken?"

"Last night," said Lenny. "I was working late and must have fallen asleep. When I woke up, it was gone."

"You slept through the theft?" Syd asked in disbelief.

Lenny raised his hands in a helpless gesture. "I must have. One minute I was working and heard a noise. The next thing I knew it was a couple of hours later. That's when I noticed the painting was gone," Lenny replied. He sounded as confused as Sydney felt. How could he have slept through something like that? She felt a twinge of guilt when she saw how distraught he seemed.

"Dr. Kunst, we can discuss your ill-timed nap later. First we must figure out who took it," said Stiggler as he sat in his chair at the head of the table. "Obviously our main suspect is Mr. Murdoch."

"*What?*" Sydney said. The shocks just kept coming.

"He obviously has the motive. Perhaps he became impatient with the snail's pace you call research."

"First of all, I resent your implication I am dragging my feet on this project. I assumed you wanted it handled correctly, and that means I have countless boxes of archives to sift through by myself," Syd said, automatically going on the defensive. "Second, Logan would never stoop so low as to steal from this museum."

"Logan, huh? Getting friendly with the man, Miss Worth?"

"Mr. Stiggler, please don't be crass. I am working in his home, and he has been a gracious host. I think he deserves better than to be accused of something this nefarious."

Maybe she was being a little too vehement in her defense of Logan, but she *knew* he was innocent of the theft. She just had to get Stiggler to forget this line of thought without revealing where she had spent the night.

"Regardless, the man does have the motive. And then there is the message," Stiggler said enigmatically.

"Message?" Syd asked, looking around the table.

Jorge gave her a shrug and an apologetic smile. "Syd, there was a message left by the thief."

"And?" she said as she circled her hand, indicating he should continue.

"It said, *rinunci la ricerca,*" explained Lenny.

"Huh?" Syd said, more confused than ever.

Lenny looked at her and translated the Italian. "Stop the research."

Syd's eyes widened. That did sound bad for Logan, but why

the Italian? Wait!

"No, no, no. Logan is a scientist. He is currently working on some major research for his family's company. Perhaps whoever stole the painting is connected to that. Maybe they're Italian . . . or something," she said.

"That's a stretch," said Stiggler. Obviously he had tried and convicted Logan already.

"Since the police are involved, I suggest we leave the evidence gathering to them," Syd said. She decided debating Logan's guilt would get them nowhere. "In the meantime, I need to call Logan."

"Why?" demanded Stiggler. "The painting hasn't been proven to belong to him. Or has it?"

"While I have not found conclusive evidence the painting belongs to his family, I have every reason to believe that is the case. He deserves to know about this."

"I suppose he should be informed. After all, I am sure the detective in charge will have some questions for him."

Syd decided to wait to panic about the veiled threat until she could get a better handle on the situation. She grabbed her cell phone and dialed.

#

Half an hour later, Sydney met Logan at the entrance to the museum.

"I'm sorry to interrupt your research, but I thought you'd want to know about this," she explained.

She looked so distraught that Logan felt an urge to take her in his arms and comfort her. Instead, he waved off her apology.

"You were right to call me. Where is the detective?"

A short time later, Logan had handled the detective's questions with ease. Even though he was innocent, he couldn't reveal Sydney was his alibi since it would mean admitting she had slept at his home. So he had been forced to give the detective a slight mental nudge. That done, he went to find Syd.

He found her pacing nervously in front of the museum gift shop.

"How'd it go?" she asked in a low tone.

"Fine. No problems."

"You didn't . . . uh . . . tell him that I slept—"

He raised a hand to interrupt. "Syd, it's fine. There was no need to even bring it up to him."

She took a deep breath. "Thank God. Oh, I mean I appreciate you helping me last night, but I was afraid someone might misinterpret things."

He put a hand on her shoulder, hoping to relieve her anxiety. "Understood. But really, no one has to know."

"Your mother does," she blurted.

Logan laughed. "Yes, she mentioned she ran into you when you were leaving this morning."

"Yes, she was very nice. I can't believe she's old enough to be your mother though."

"I hear that all the time. But I assure you she is definitely older than she appears."

"Look, thanks for letting me crash last night. I can't believe I fell asleep. It's so unprofessional."

"Please don't worry about it. It was bound to catch up with you sooner or later. Besides, we're friends, remember? No need to be professional all the time," he joked.

He was relieved when a slight smile lit up her face. He hated that she felt so uncomfortable around him.

"The detective agreed to let me examine the crime scene. Care to join me?"

"I can't believe in all the confusion I haven't seen it yet," she said.

They headed down to conservation. Police taped cordoned off the scene, and uniformed officers stood guard outside the doors. They waved the pair through.

The room seemed undisturbed except for the easel where the painting had been. They walked carefully to the spot.

A fresh canvas with Italian words written in angry strokes stood on the easel that once held his portrait. One sniff and Logan knew the neat lettering was not paint as the museum staff assumed, but blood.

Raven.

This time she had gone too far. Taking the shipment of blood was bad enough, but stealing the painting was personal. Now she had the only link remaining to his father. He had yet to tell his mother what had happened, but knew she would be enraged by the younger vampire's gall. This had to stop. Now.

"It says, 'Stop the research.' It's Italian," Sydney explained. He smiled at her to show his appreciation even though the translation wasn't needed. He spoke five languages fluently.

"I think I know who did this," he said softly to Sydney.

"Really?" she whispered back. "Why are we whispering? No one else is in here. Besides, shouldn't you tell the detective?"

"The group who did this has caused trouble for us before, but they are very good at leaving no evidence so the police could not help. I think my best bet is to track it down on my own."

"Isn't that dangerous?" she asked.

"They are more of a nuisance than anything. They should be more worried about my mother's wrath when she finds out the painting was stolen again."

"I want to help," Syd said, placing her hand on his arm. Her light touch sent pure sensation up his arm and straight to his groin.

"Absolutely not," he said, his tone harsher than intended. The last thing he needed was to get Sydney involved in the middle of this mess. It would be difficult enough to track down Raven without a mortal asking questions he wasn't prepared to answer.

Syd straightened to her full height, which barely reached his chin, and looked him in the eye. "Look, mister, that painting still technically belongs to the museum. You either let me help you find it, or I will go to Stiggler and let the police know you are withholding information."

Logan resisted the urge to ruffle her hair. She was adorable when she talked tough. Unfortunately, she also held some cards that could complicate things even further. If she went to her boss, the police would be all over the place, and it would be harder for him and his family to track down Raven.

So he'd let her help, but he would have to give her tasks that kept her out of his way. He could not let her find out the truth of the situation, and he absolutely would not put her in harm's way.

"Okay."

Syd blinked at him. "Okay? That's it?"

"Sure, you have every right to help with the search."

She looked suspicious but pleased. He knew he'd have to play the next couple of days very carefully to keep this savvy woman from discovering the truth.

"I am going to go call my mother and Callum. I am sure you have things you need to take care of here. Why don't we all meet at my house tonight to formulate our plan?"

Syd nodded. "That sounds good."

"I'll see you later then," he said. Then he walked away before he kissed the spunky woman who was becoming more important to him every day.

"Oh, Logan," she said from behind him. "About last night. I didn't . . . um . . . say anything in my sleep, did I?"

He watched the blush spread quickly on her beautiful face before letting her off the hook.

"Don't worry. You didn't say anything to be embarrassed about." He watched her shoulders droop with relief before going in for the kill. As he turned again to leave, he said over his shoulder, "After all, I think you're pretty yummy too."

CHAPTER SEVEN

Logan smiled as he remembered the look on Sydney's face after his parting shot at the museum. As much as he tried to behave himself around that woman, he just couldn't help teasing her.

Of course, his comment wasn't entirely teasing in nature. He did find her sexy as hell. While her smart mouth and intelligence challenged him, he found the glimpses of vulnerability irresistible. His instincts wanted to gather her close and let her know she didn't have to be strong all the time—to ask her to let him be strong for her. He shook his head. Now he sounded like a bad romance novel.

"Logan, what are you thinking about?" his mother asked. She stood near the bar across the living room from where he sat.

"Just thinking about work," he evaded. Then he silently lectured himself for spending so much time having thoughts about Sydney when he should indeed be thinking about work. The council wanted results yesterday, and he still had a lot of testing to do. But for some reason, he found the luscious curator much more interesting than beakers and test tubes.

"Sure, brother, my work often makes me grin lecherously, too," Callum said from his chair near the fireplace. Logan shot his brother a glare. His meddling sibling seemed to be having a lot of fun at his expense lately. Logan couldn't wait until their mother set her matchmaking sights on Callum.

"Don't you have some deals to make tonight or something?" Logan asked.

"Nah, I have some time, so I figured I'd pitch in with the Raven search. Plus I can't wait to meet the enchanting Miss Worth I have heard so much about."

"Where have you heard so much about her?" Logan asked, suddenly suspicious. He turned to look at Alaric, who ducked his head and pretended to examine his flip-flops.

"Alaric?" Logan said..

The traitor looked up with feigned confusion "Yes?"

"Do you need more work to do in the lab?"

"Why do you ask?"

"I just figured if you have so much free time to spend gossiping with my brother that you need more to do," Logan said.

Alaric didn't even try to hide his grin.

"Hey, we're guys. We can't help talking about an attractive female. Besides, I didn't tell him everything," Alaric said.

"What do you mean 'everything'? There's nothing to tell," Logan said, glad that no one in the room could read his mind and recognize his statement for the lie it was.

Alaric shot Logan an amused look. "My friend, do I need to remind you that you are the only one in this room incapable of reading Sydney's mind?"

Logan paused for a moment as Alaric's words sunk in. Fantastic. Even if Alaric hadn't told everyone already, they all would have known about the kiss the moment Syd walked into the room. The mortification he felt at being the subject of family gossip paled in comparison to the protective instincts it brought up.

He addressed the trio troublemakers. "I want to make this perfectly clear, so listen up. If you have questions about Sydney and me, you talk to me. Sydney deserves more respect than to have her private thoughts mined for juicy gossip. I already feel bad enough having to deceive her without you invading her privacy on top of it."

Callum and Alaric both shuffled their feet at the end of the speech. Apparently, neither had considered mind reading invasive. Come to think of it, Logan never had either. But then again he had not had much interaction with mortals in a couple of centuries. Besides, he wasn't all that noble. He really wanted to ask what other tidbits Alaric had gathered. But he would never stoop to that level. He meant what he'd said; he respected her too much to use such underhanded tactics to get information. Sure, the frustration definitely got to him when she was around, but on the other hand, it was refreshing as well.

As far as deceiving Sydney went, well, that was a necessary evil. After all, they couldn't very well sit her down and explain that they were all vampires and a rogue vampire stole the painting. Thus, they had concocted a story about an extremist group. Since he didn't plan on letting Syd anywhere near the real action of finding Raven and the painting, he didn't feel too bad about the lie. Besides, in vampire circles, Raven was an extremist.

"Good for you, son," Kira said. "Perhaps it is a good lesson for us all to use more discretion when using our powers. As far as Sydney is concerned, she especially deserves our respect. The poor dear has done so much for us." Logan nodded, relieved his mother had not joined the teasing.

"I agree," Alaric said. "After all, she is Logan's soul mate."

Logan leapt from his seat, ready to teach his impertinent friend a well-deserved lesson. However, before he could get to Alaric, the doorbell rang. Logan stopped in his tracks.

Sydney.

He shot a warning glare at Callum and Alaric before turning toward the foyer. On his way, he stopped by his mother's chair and turned to address all three of his companions.

"Everyone better be on their best behavior tonight. No mind reading, no innuendos, no embarrassing stories. Sydney is here to help us."

"But Logan, we would never try to make her uncomfortable," Callum said with a chuckle.

Logan ignored the second chime. He had to make it clear to everyone that he would not stand for any antics.

"Watch it, brother. If you don't behave, I'll tell mother about the time—"

"All right, all right. I'll behave," Callum said, holding up his hands in surrender.

Logan nodded. He chuckled when he saw the suspicious glance his mother sent his brother. He slid a look at Alaric, warning his unusually quiet friend to keep it that way. Then, he hurried to the foyer as the doorbell rang again.

Out of the frying pan and into the fire. He felt his pulse race knowing she was just beyond that door. He couldn't remember the last time he'd been this anxious to see anyone—mortal or immortal. He reached for the door just as he realized he'd never gotten this excited about seeing Brenna.

#

Syd watched the door swing open to reveal a frowning Logan. She hesitated. After his teasing comment as he left the museum earlier, the last thing she expected was to see him looking so serious tonight.

"Logan? Is everything okay?"

He shook his head and smiled. "Sorry. I was thinking about a confusing problem."

She laughed. "I am glad it's not my arrival that put you in a bad mood."

"Never. Please come in." He held the door open wider to allow her access. As she passed him, she caught the scent of him—subtle aftershave with an undertone of virile male. She tried not to inhale too deeply lest she throw herself at him.

He led her through the foyer and into the living room. Kira met her at the entrance and gave her a friendly hug.

"Sydney, this is my brother, Callum," Logan said as they walked farther into the room.

She looked up to see a gorgeous man walking toward her.

THE HOT SCOT

He looked as if he'd stepped straight off the pages of GQ with his charcoal suit and wingtips. A hot corporate raider, but with eyes that twinkled with mischief and a smile hinted at flirtation.

"A pleasure," Callum said. "I am honored to finally meet you, Sydney." He bowed over her hand and kissed it.

"All right, little brother, that's enough," Logan said. She wondered at his tone. Could he be jealous of a little harmless flirting?

"And you have already met Alaric," Logan continued. Alaric stepped forward and shook Sydney's hand. He wore what Sydney thought of as his uniform. Tonight's Hawaiian shirt sported images of tiki gods on a blue background.

"Nice to see you again. Your assistant isn't joining us tonight?"

"No, I try not to let him loose on the public too often," Syd joked. Alaric and Logan chuckled while the other two looked curious about the comment.

Logan tried to explain. "Jorge is . . . uh . . ."

"He's a flirt," Syd cut in. "I am afraid he took quite a liking to Alaric when they met."

Alaric looked uncomfortable at the reminder but laughed good-naturedly.

"So, should we get started?" Logan said, motioning to a chair for Sydney.

"Sydney, why don't you sit here next to me," Callum suggested with a boyish grin.

She started toward the couch where he sat. But Logan stopped her with a hand on her arm.

"Actually, you would probably be more comfortable in one of the chairs. The couch is very lumpy." He started to guide her toward the chair next to his. Callum smiled at her again and shrugged. Sydney looked up at Logan in time to catch him shooting a glare at his brother. She obviously missed something here. She didn't for a minute believe Callum was actually hitting on her. It almost seemed like Callum was trying to make Logan jealous. And Logan took the bait. She stifled a smile.

Kira offered Sydney a drink, which she accepted. She took a

sip of the red concoction and choked.

"Oh, I'm sorry. Did I make it too spicy?" Kira asked, concern clear on her face.

"Uh, no. I just wasn't expecting a Bloody Mary. It's actually quite good," she said, taking another sip. She thought the choice of drink odd for an evening meeting, but noticed everyone else held glasses filled with red liquid.

"Yes, I personally love a good Bloody Mary at the end of a long day. So many vitamins," Kira said. She took a long gulp of her own drink. When she glanced at Sydney after she lowered the glass, Sydney could have sworn the woman's eyes lit up. Guess someone likes a lot of vodka in her drink, Syd thought.

She heard a chuckle from Callum, and Kira looked embarrassed all of a sudden. Alaric tried to disguise a snicker by taking a sip of his own drink.

"So, has there been any more news at the museum about the painting?" Callum asked.

She shook her head. "I am afraid not. The police have zero leads at this point. I'm sorry. I wish I had more to give you."

"Don't worry yourself, dear. It's not your fault. After all, no one can predict the actions of extremists."

"Extremists?" asked Syd. Logan said something earlier about a group causing problems, but she began to suspect something more serious was going on here.

"Yes, we have had some problems with a radical group that opposes the research we do. They have caused a few inconveniences in protest," explained Callum.

"In fact, the urgent business which kept me away the other day was due to them," Logan explained. "We believe they stole a shipment of supplies I needed for an important project. But stealing the painting is the most serious offense thus far—a personal attack on our family. I don't know how she found out about the painting, but I plan to personally prove to her you don't mess with the Murdoch family," Logan said fiercely.

"Her?" Syd asked.

"What?"

"You said 'her.'"

"I did?"

"Yes, Logan, you did," his mother said.

Syd thought she saw a flicker of a smile on Kira's lips but couldn't imagine the cause.

"Oh. Uh, the leader of this group is a woman. She is vehemently against scientific advancements."

"You're telling me she hates science?" Syd asked dubiously.

"Well, let's just say she has a certain affinity for old ways," Callum said with a smile.

"That's odd," said Syd. Who was against all science? She knew extremist groups could be a little bizarre—they were called extremists for a reason, after all—but she had never heard of a group like this.

"But how do you plan to handle it? Are they dangerous?" Syd asked.

"Don't worry, my dear. The boys and their contacts should be able to track down the people responsible in no time," explained Kira. Syd thought it odd for a mother to be so nonchalant about sending her sons on a dangerous mission. And who were these "contacts"? Were Logan and Callum involved in something more illicit than simple scientific research?

"Mother, that makes us sound like Mafioso," said Callum. "We will simply call some of our contacts who are familiar this group."

Callum spoke as if he had read her thoughts. She shrugged it off when she realized her expression must have given her away.

"So where do I fit in all of this?" she asked.

"Sydney, I totally understand if you just want to stay clear of this whole matter. After all, while we don't plan on it being dangerous, there is always that possibility," said Logan.

She thought about it for a moment. On one hand, he had a point. She didn't feel excited about tangling with an extremist group. On the other hand, if she helped Logan and his family, it could give her some leverage with Stiggler. Another part of her balked at the idea of using their misfortune for her own gain. But if she was honest with herself, she really wanted to help them. She cared about Logan, and she wanted to do anything she could to help him get back the item that meant so much to him and his family.

Her four companions waited silently while she thought over her options. She looked up to see three smiling faces—Kira, Callum, and Alaric. But Logan's frown gave her pause. Had his suggestion been his way of trying to get rid of her?

"Before you make your decision, I want to say I would love for you to help us," said Kira. Before Sydney could question that statement, Kira added, "After all, you might have some connections in the art world that could assist us."

"But Syd, you must understand that while I can assure you we would do everything in our power to keep you out of harm's way, there are no guarantees," Logan hastily added.

She was more confused than ever. Kira seemed to want her there, but Logan didn't. She wanted to help, but if Logan wanted her gone then she might as well leave now.

"Logan," Kira said with a pointed stare at her son. "Don't scare the girl. She'll think you're trying to get rid of her."

"Huh?" he said, sounding confused. She saw Alaric and Callum were both shooting looks at him. Suddenly, his eyes widened as if he finally caught on.

"Syd, no. I just don't want you to feel obligated here. You already have done so much for us."

Relieved, she smiled at him. "You know what? The fact I did so much work only to have those cretins steal the painting pisses me off. I would love to help you get the panting back."

"That's the spirit!" said Kira, who then slapped her hand down on the chair arm. "Now that that's settled, what's the plan?"

#

"Alaric and I will try to track down the group's hideout. Callum, you'll call your Brether—I mean law enforcement contacts. Mother will work the . . . um . . . information gathering angle from the police detective. I think that covers it," Logan said.

He rubbed his temple. Trying to choose his wording

carefully in front of Syd proved more difficult than he'd imagined. After all, he couldn't let Syd know that, in reality, he and Alaric were going to scour vampire bars for information on Raven's hideout; Callum was going to the Brethren Council for assistance; and his mother had the job of reading the detective's mind for any clues he might have found.

"What about me?" Syd chimed in as Logan stood up.

Damn. He had hoped she wouldn't notice he hadn't given her a task.

He sat back down and struggled to think of busywork to give her. He had to keep her out of the way and ignorant of the truth of the situation.

"I know. How about you get online and research the group? See if there is any gossip in chat rooms and the like about their plans," he said, mentally high-fiving himself for his genius. "Great, I guess we're done here." He started to rise.

"Wait," she said and grabbed his arm to make him sit again. "Logan, you haven't told me the name of the group yet."

"I haven't?" he stalled.

"No," Syd said in a no-nonsense tone that let him know she didn't find his evasions amusing. "You haven't, and frankly, I am beginning to wonder if you are trying to brush me off so I'll stay out of the way."

Logan heard a quick chuckle disguised as a cough coming from the vicinity of his brother. He glanced at Alaric, only to find his friend grinning. He didn't risk a look at his mother, knowing he'd see her enjoying herself at his expense.

Looking back at Syd, whose stare defied him to give her busywork, he said, "Nonsense. It simply slipped my mind with all the confusion. Their name is . . . the Society for . . . Undermining Contemporary Science."

The faces around him just stared for a moment.

"Are you telling me an extremist group goes by the acronym SUCS?" Syd asked dubiously.

Logan heard another smothered laugh from the other side of the coffee table.

He shrugged. "Who can understand these wacko groups?"

Syd still looked dubious, but nodded. "Oookay. I guess I can see what I can find. What is the name of their leader? I should run a search on her, too."

"Her name is Raven Coracino," his mother said.

Luckily, Syd had turned to look at the traitor who gave birth to him, so she missed the glare he sent Kira's way. The damned woman merely shrugged in return.

"Okay, seems easy enough," Syd said as she turned to face Logan again. He quickly replaced his frown with a smile.

"Great, well I better get started contacting people," Callum said as he stood.

"Good idea," said Kira. "The sooner we get started, the sooner this will be done. But I want to say something. We must remember we are only going to get the painting back. It is up to the proper authorities to deal with Raven,"

Logan sorely wanted to teach Raven a lesson for all the trouble she had caused, but he understood his mother's reasoning. The council would surely see these latest transgressions as reason enough to take serious action against Raven. In the past, they had merely given her slaps on the wrist, but now they would be forced to ensure she changed her ways. While the council forbade any type of physical punishment, they were very creative when it came to administering justice.

"Agreed," he said. "Let's all meet back here tomorrow afternoon. Syd, does that give you enough time to do your web search?"

"If there is anything to be found, I'll have it by morning," she said. Her tone let him know she had suspicions about the information he gave her. Luckily, he just needed her out of the way tonight. If things went as planned, he would find Raven by the time they met again tomorrow.

She stood and reached to grab her drink. Logan noticed at the last moment she had accidentally grabbed his glass instead. He leapt toward her and grabbed the cup from her hand. She sent him a startled look as some of his blood and vodka cocktail sloshed onto the floor between them.

"Sorry, uh, I have been fighting a cold and wouldn't want

you to catch it," he explained lamely. He feigned a weak cough to add legitimacy to his claim. He ignored the renewed round of snickers from his family.

She nodded slowly and looked down at the priceless rug under their feet.

"I'm sorry your rug is stained. If I am correct, that's Aubusson. I don't think tomato juice comes out."

"Don't worry, dear, we drink a lot of Bloody Marys. We're pretty experienced at getting red stains out of things," Kira said. Sydney wondered how much vodka they all had in their drinks when Kira's comment made everyone else in the room chuckle.

"Sydney, can I walk you to your car?" Callum asked.

"I'll do it," Logan said. Syd looked back and forth between the brothers as if watching a tennis match.

"Logan, since Callum's leaving anyway, there's no need for you to bother. Besides, if you're coming down with something, you should probably stay inside," she said.

"Don't worry about Logan," Callum said with a grin as he took her arm. "He probably just needs to sleep like the dead, and he'll wake up tomorrow feeling immortal."

Logan jabbed his elbow into Callum's ribs. His brother didn't even flinch at the impact. He simply turned Syd toward the door and led her out. Sydney looked over her shoulder as she walked away and sent a lame wave at Logan. He felt like a thunder cloud ready to burst.

CHAPTER EIGHT

Logan tamped down the jealousy that reared when he saw Syd laugh at some joke his brother made as they walked out together. Did she always walk with that seductive sway to her hips?

He didn't like the idea Syd might find his brother's legendary charm appealing. As a scientist, he didn't quite buy the soul mate theory his mother used to explain his inability to read Syd's mind. But he couldn't deny the attraction he had felt for her from the moment they met.

He shook his head and turned to Alaric and his mother. They both watched him with knowing expressions.

"What?"

"I may not be able to read your mind, my friend, but the look on your face just told the whole story," said Alaric.

"Yes, dear, if you want us to believe you have no feelings for the girl, you must try a little harder at pretending you're unaffected," said his meddling mother.

"I don't know what you mean. I was simply thinking about a particularly troublesome equation."

Alaric laughed. "Yeah, Logan plus Sydney equals what?"

"Shut up," he said.

"Logan, don't take your sexual frustration out on your friend," his mother chastised.

"Please, can we change the subject?" he pleaded.

"All right, when do you want to head out to the bar?" Alaric said, taking mercy on him.

Logan looked at his watch. "It's only eight o'clock—still early yet. The places we're going don't get rolling until near midnight. Let's try to get some more work done before we head out."

"Actually, Alaric, why don't you go on? I need to speak with Logan for a moment," Kira said.

Alaric shot Logan a sympathetic look before nodding and heading toward the lab.

Logan groaned inwardly. The last thing he needed was another lecture right now.

"Wipe that martyred expression off your face and sit down."

Logan dutifully sat down in his chair and waited. He knew the less he said the better.

"Son, you're being an idiot. Anyone with half a brain could see the sparks between you and that girl. I know Brenna hurt you, but it's time to move on and give yourself a chance at happiness."

"This isn't about Brenna," he said.

"I wasn't born yesterday, young man. In fact, seven hundred years of living teaches one a thing or two. I know what a man looks like when he's falling in love. And I know how he acts when he's fighting it tooth and nail. That girl is perfect for you. And from what I have seen, she is also intelligent and open-minded."

"Open minded? I'm a vampire. No mortal is that open-minded."

"I was."

Logan paused. He had forgotten his mother was once a mortal too. While he and his brother were born vampires, his father made his mother into a vampire after they fell in love.

"So you see, not all mortals react like Brenna. Darling, I

know you cared for her, but it's time you realize she was not your soul mate."

Logan thought about her words. He'd never let himself think about Brenna over the years. But he had to admit his mother was right. He recalled his last conversation with Brenna.

They'd met secretly in the cloister of the convent she attended for schooling. He had been in love and foolishly decided to tell her the truth. He figured if she loved him, too, they could find a way to make everything work out. He would never forget the fear and disgust he saw in her eyes. She said she could never love a monster and ran.

The next night Logan, upset but not beaten, went to the convent to try and reason with her. The novice nun who opened the gate told him Brenna had fled back to London before dawn. At that moment, he vowed he would never trust his heart with a mortal again.

"You're right," he said slowly to his mother. "She never really loved me, or if she did she couldn't see past her own superstitions. But the point is I loved her, and she rejected me. I can't risk that happening again. Better to find some nice vampiress who understands me."

"If the evidence wasn't already there that you and Sydney should be together, then I'd agree with you. But Logan, when was the last time you came out of that lab and lived a little? Even when you drag yourself away from your test tubes to attend a Brethren event, you keep to yourself. I see the women at those functions throw themselves at you."

"Maybe I just want to be left alone," he countered.

"Perhaps you just need to admit being vampire isn't the real issue here. You're afraid of getting hurt, period."

"I have a responsibility," he said.

"Your responsibility is to yourself. Son, I know you work so hard because you want to live up to your father's legacy, but he wanted you to be happy on top of everything else. You just need to learn to strike a balance between work and fun," she said.

Logan sat quietly for a few moments, letting her words sink

in. Was she right? Did he hide behind his father's legacy because he feared getting hurt again?

"Maybe you're right about the work thing, but we can't just sweep the whole I-drink-blood-for-food issue under the rug," he said.

"Yes, that is an issue. But I think if you have a little faith, things can work out."

"I am a scientist. I don't deal in faith. I deal in hard evidence. I don't believe Sydney is my soul mate just because I can't read her mind. And even if I did believe it, asking a mortal to accept the reality of our lives is difficult. How did you deal with it when father told you?"

Kira laughed. "Honestly, I didn't deal with it too well at first. I mean we're talking the late 1200s here. But your father anticipated that and was patient with all of my questions. Of course it helped I was already madly in love with him when he told me."

"That's encouraging," Logan said sarcastically. "But Sydney and I aren't in love."

Kira gave him a knowing smile. "Darling, how could either of you know if it's love or not when you both spend all of your time fighting the attraction?"

Logan didn't want to admit she had a point. In fact, he didn't want to talk about Sydney anymore.

"I know you only want me to be happy, but you have to understand Sydney and I both have reasons for not pursuing a relationship. Perhaps after everything settles down we could get to know each other better, but to even consider something right now is madness."

"One of these days, son, you are going to have to learn that you can't logic your way through life. Love happens when it happens. You can't plan for it or talk your way out of feeling it. But now I have said my piece, and I promise to stay out of it."

He smiled at her. He couldn't fault her for her concerns. In fact, Sydney had been right the other night. It was nice to have someone who worried about him.

"Thanks," he said sincerely. They both stood and hugged.

"And, Logan, one more thing. Sydney didn't seem too thrilled about the assignment you gave her. She's also suspicious about our cover story."

"What do you think she'll do?" he asked, frustrated that the one mind he wanted to read was closed to him.

"I'm not a fortune teller, darling. Just be warned. She is a clever girl, and I don't think she'll accept being kept in the dark about this."

"I agree she is clever, but I can't imagine what she'd do that I wouldn't figure out," he said.

"Never underestimate a determined woman—mortal or vampire—my dear," his mother responded with a laugh. She kissed his cheek and then left.

Lord, save me from meddling mothers and strong-minded mortal women.

#

"Of all the condescending, pig-headed, macho stunts . . ." Sydney fumed as she paced her apartment later than night.

The minute Logan told her the name of the group supposedly responsible for the theft, she knew something was fishy. In fact, the entire discussion at his house had her mind waving red flags. They were all hiding something; she was sure of it. The problem was she had no idea what or why they would hide things from her when they made it clear they wanted her help—everyone but Logan, that was.

Her suspicions were confirmed once she entered the information he gave her in all the major search engines. No Society for the Undermining of Contemporary Science existed on the web. One could argue that maybe they weren't organized or large enough to have a web site, but the way Logan talked there was bound to be some mention of them somewhere on the Internet. Her conclusion had to be that Logan made up the name.

She also entered the name "Raven Coracino" into the engines. A few matches came up with that one, but they were also dead ends. The main page Syd read seemed like one of those role-playing game sites where the people thought they were vampires. She even searched for groups who protested science and technology. But it hit her that a group against science would not want any involvement with the Internet. Her aggravation at Logan calmed a bit at that point. Maybe he hadn't made it all up. But the fact remained her task was a big waste of time.

She plopped down on her shabby couch. Why did she even bother? It seemed more and more as if she was banging her head against a wall. Stiggler definitely had plans to fire her. He continued to issue veiled threats every time she called him with a progress report. She knew now that finding the painting wouldn't save her job. Maybe she should just call Logan and tell him she couldn't find anything about SUCS or Raven and wish him luck. Then she could concentrate on finding a new job.

But then she remembered Kira's enthusiasm about her helping out and the passion in her voice when she spoke of the painting and the family's ancestors. And as frustrating as Logan Murdoch could be, Syd couldn't force herself to cut all ties and never see him again. She was becoming emotionally invested in the man, but something kept her from running away.

So where did that leave her? Obviously, Logan wouldn't give her any real tasks to help in the painting search. She knew from their planning session earlier that Alaric and Logan were going to split up and canvas some local bars for any information that might lead them to the group. They were eager to get the matter taken care of and planned to go out tonight.

If she could follow Logan, she could kill two birds with one stone. First, she could do something tangible to help gather information. Second, and most intriguing, perhaps she could observe him undetected to find out why he was being so secretive about the theft.

That decided, she stood up and headed to her bedroom. From her closet she pulled a pair of jeans, a turtleneck, and her trusty cowboy boots. She glanced at herself in the mirror after she changed clothes. Perhaps wearing all black was overkill. But hey, maybe this cloak-and-dagger thing would be fun. After all, how often did a woman get to spy on a gorgeous man with a secret? Besides, she figured she'd blend in when she followed Logan into the bars. She smiled. *Eat your heart out, James Bond—Worth, Sydney Worth, is on the case.*

#

"You about ready to head out?" Alaric asked Logan.

After his mother left, Logan threw himself into his work in the lab to escape the lingering doubts raised by their discussion. He glanced at his watch. His concentration had been so complete he hadn't realized the lateness of the hour.

"Yeah, you go ahead. I'll clean up here. You want to take the Chalice Club?" Logan asked.

"That leaves The Church. You up for that?"

Logan understood his friend's concern. While the Raleigh-Durham Chapel Hill area only encompassed a population of about a million mortals, the region had a relatively high vampire population. Four vampire clubs existed. Brethren Sect owned two, and visitors had to prove membership in the sect to enter. The other two—the ones they'd be staking out (pardon the pun) tonight—were frequented by rogue vampires.

Occasionally some college kids interested in the gothic scene would venture into the Chalice Club, which was located near North Carolina State University. They usually made it back home with their lives.

Any unsuspecting mortal who accidentally wandered into The Church rarely made it past the threshold with their lives. Raven might be a rebel, but the vamps who frequented The Church made her look like Mary Poppins. They would not take kindly to a Brethren Sect member entering their turf.

Rogue was a term the Brethren Council used to refer to those vampires who did not adhere to Brethren law. Most of the rogues were actually young, recently turned vampires who thought drinking blood made them gods. Their bloodlust gave them no respect for mortal life.

"Nah, I'll be fine. I just hope none of the rogues decide to pick a fight tonight. I don't have time to teach any strutting baby vamps a lesson," he said.

"As a New Blood myself," Alaric said, referring to the fact

he was a turned vampire and not a born True Blood like Logan, "I take exception to your attitude. Remember when you and Callum found me?"

"Yes, I do. And as I recall I had to put your baby vamp ass in its place as well."

Alaric laughed. "True. I was lucky though. If you two hadn't taken pity on me, I would have ended up just like those misfits who frequent The Church."

"You would have figured everything out eventually. But for the record, I'm glad we found you too. After all, good lab assistants are hard to come by."

"Bite me," Alaric said.

"You're not my type." Logan laughed. Alaric responded by flipping him the bird.

"You're definitely not my type for that," Logan said dryly. "Now get out of here. Check in later, and let me know what you find."

Logan began cleaning after Alaric left. Unfortunately, the mundane task left time for his mind to wander. Watching Sydney leave with Callum had raised the green beast within him.

He shook his head. Something about that woman gave him the primal urge to grab her and yell, "Mine!"

Because of the protective instincts she raised in him, he couldn't feel guilty about the joke of an assignment he gave her. He decided it was best to keep her in the dark and out of harm's way. Besides, he hoped to find the information he needed tonight. Then he could deal with Raven, and things could return to normal. Maybe once this whole fiasco was out of the way, he and Sydney could spend some time together to see if there was a chance. In the meantime, he had work to do.

#

Syd sat in her dark car and waited. From her vantage point she could see the entrance to Logan's driveway. Luckily, some well-placed trees provided cover. Earlier she had seen Alaric's red Jeep drive past. She hoped Logan's car would soon follow. She supposed she could have snuck up through the woods on his property to verify he was still at home, but honestly, she wasn't that comfortable with her spy role yet. Besides, her boots weren't made for hiking.

A few more minutes passed before the reflection of headlights hit the trees by his driveway. She put her car in gear and waited. When the black Porsche Carrera zoomed out of the driveway and turned onto the main road, she scrambled to follow him, cursing her sensible midsize sedan. At the speed he was going, she'd never catch up. Luckily, the road was straight, so she'd see if he turned off, and she needed to keep her distance anyway—another good spy maneuver.

As they neared the city, Logan slowed, and the added traffic of the more populated area helped camouflage her car. Syd let out a relieved breath. Her knuckles gripped the steering wheel so hard they ached.

His car turned onto Glenwood Avenue, one of the main routes into downtown. Since she knew he was headed to a bar, she didn't question his direction. Raleigh's nightlife, such as it was, could be found there. But when he passed the block where most of the bars where located, she started to get nervous. *Where is he going?* She looked around at the industrial warehouses that lined the road.

She prayed Logan had not been lying earlier about going to a bar. His car made a quick turn and pulled to a stop in front of a seedy-looking warehouse. She backed up and pulled into an alley behind the building. Fighting her dread at being alone in this part of town at night, she got out and started toward the front of the building on foot.

When she got to the corner of the warehouse, she peeked around. Logan was out of his car and headed toward the front door. A very scary-looking man waited there. Shorter than Logan but twice as wide, the hulk stood in front of the door with his arms crossed over his massive chest. The muted beat of music pulsed through the building. Maybe this was a club after all, but its location indicated it wasn't her kind of place.

Logan stood talking to the bouncer, who seemed to be giving him a hard time about entering. Syd was so intent on what was happening in front of the building that she didn't hear the footsteps behind her until it was too late. She turned to see who was coming up behind her, and a rough hand reached out and grabbed her arm.

"Hey—" she started but then got a good look at her attacker. Long, greasy black hair fell limply around razor blade cheekbones. A black Guns N' Roses T-shirt hung on his bony frame. She struggled, but for someone so gaunt, he had a surprisingly strong grip.

"Well, well, look what we have here. Are you lost little girl?" Syd flinched away from him as his putrid breath fanned over her face.

"Let me go!" she hissed.

"My buddies and me are always looking for someone new to play with. You're coming with me." He started to drag her down the street toward the alley.

Syd panicked. Part of her wanted to call for help, but she didn't want to blow her cover and have Logan discover she'd followed him. She dug her heels into the concrete, which only seemed to amuse the thug.

"What? You wanna play? I can arrange that," he growled. Syd looked up and gasped at his glowing red eyes.

Screw the cover, she thought.

"Logan!" she screamed as the freak with the red eyes dragged her to the alley.

#

Logan stopped arguing with the bouncer when he heard it. For a moment he thought he imagined Sydney's scream. Then he heard more sounds of distress coming from the side of the building.

He sprinted around the corner to see a greasy vamp dragging Sydney down the sidewalk. He didn't think as his primal instincts took over. His canines extended as he raced toward the fiend. The punk heard him coming and pushed Sydney toward the wall. Logan moved with preternatural speed. He grabbed his opponent and pushed him into the alley, hoping to get out of Sydney's line of vision.

"Come on, gramps, let's see what you—"

Logan's fist connected with the younger vamp's nose before he could finish his taunt. Logan knew he should probably just grab Sydney and go, but he couldn't tamp down the rage he'd felt at seeing the asshole's hands on Sydney.

"You need to learn to show the lady some respect." Logan grabbed the snarling miscreant by the neck of his T-shirt, which ripped, and threw him across the alley, where he bounced off the wall and landed in a heap. The thrill of battle danced through Logan's limbs. He grabbed the rogue off the ground and punched him again. *Ah, that felt good*, Logan thought.

Now that he had worked out some of his anger, he remembered Sydney was nearby. He couldn't risk her seeing him in battle mode with his fangs extended. It was time to end this and go check on her. He lifted the lid on a nearby dumpster and threw the other vamp in.

He took a deep breath and willed his fangs to recede. Thankfully the drugs he took prevented his eyes from glowing like the other vamp's. Then he turned and rushed toward Syd, who stood at the mouth of the alley with her mouth hanging open.

"Syd? Are you all right," he asked quietly as he approached. When he reached her, he cautiously ran his hands over her face and arms to check for injuries.

She stared at him with wide eyes. "You . . .he . . . what?"

"Are you okay?" he repeated as he stared into her eyes, looking for signs of concussion.

"Yeah, I'm fine. Banged my head a bit when he pushed me, but . . . um, Logan?"

"Yes," he said.

"Did you just lift that guy and throw him in a dumpster?"

"I guess I did," he said with a shrug.

"But . . . but . . ."

"I don't know what came over me," he said. "I got scared when I saw him dragging you down the street. I guess it was adrenaline or something."

Syd stared at him for another moment. He tried not to squirm under her scrutiny. She looked to the dumpster and then back at him again. Her gaze roamed down his body, and he felt it like a caress. He really wished he knew what she was thinking. He hoped she wasn't afraid of him. But she surprised him.

"That was awesome! That guy must have been on drugs or something. Did you see his freaky eyes? I was so afraid when he grabbed me, but luckily you were there." She grabbed him and gave him a hug. He held onto her tightly for a moment. His eyes closed as he breathed in her scent, relieved he had been there to save her. *Wait a minute.*

He pulled back and held her arms with his hands. She smiled up at him.

"Sydney, what in the hell are you doing down here? Following me?" he demanded. His blood pressure ratcheted up with each word. But before he could get his answer, the dumpster start to rattle. He grabbed her hand and pulled her down the street toward his car.

"I can't believe it! Of all the idiotic things to do," he railed as he dragged her behind him.

"Logan, slow down. I can't keep up," Syd said and tugged on his hand.

He spared a glance over his shoulder at her and tugged her arm. Behind him, the rogue's running footsteps and snarled curses echoed in the night.

"Keep up. He's moving fast," Logan chided. She turned to look and yelped when she saw the bedraggled hooligan gaining on them. She instantly increased her pace.

When they finally reached the Porsche, he threw Syd into the passenger seat. He stalked around the front of the car, and then they were speeding down the road in no time. In the rearview mirror Logan saw the rogue give chase for a few seconds before giving up.

"Wow," she panted, trying to catch her breath. "You're crazy fast. Did you run track in college or something?" Syd asked.

Logan mentally kicked himself. He had been so angry and in a hurry to get out of there he'd forgotten about his supernatural speed. Luckily, he hadn't gone as fast as he could have. That really would have amazed her.

"Yeah, something like that," he said. He looked at her with an arched brow. "Did you take Spy 101 at school?"

She grimaced.

"Logan, about that . . . I um . . ."

"I don't care why you followed me," he cut her off. "Wait, strike that. I do care, but we'll discuss that in a minute. What I really want to know right now is why you continued to follow me when you saw this neighborhood. This is no place for a woman alone at night."

"I know I was careless, but I had to know what was going on. You blew me off with that ridiculous web search! I wanted to know why you were all being so secretive. I am starting to think something illegal is going on."

"So you decided to follow me to a dangerous neighborhood in the middle of the night and almost get yourself killed?"

"Oh please, Logan, you wouldn't have told me the truth."

He gripped the steering wheel as he shot through the empty street toward his house. She had a point, but it didn't excuse her reckless disregard for her own safety.

She turned in her seat and stared him down. "Logan, please tell me what's going on."

He took his eyes of the road for a moment to glance at her. He wanted to throttle and kiss her at the same time.

"I can't tell you, Syd," he started. She threw her hands in the air and started to say something. "But, please know we aren't doing anything illegal."

She turned toward the window and didn't say anything.

"Syd?"

Silence.

"Hello?"

Nothing.

"Oh great, that's just fine. I don't want to talk to you either. But just know this discussion isn't finished."

With that, he reached down and turned on the radio. Pat Benatar's "Love is a Battlefield" exploded from the speakers. He winced and switched it back off.

Damned '80s station, he growled in his head. He glanced over at Sydney. Her back was still to him.

Damned woman.

CHAPTER NINE

The rest of the silent ride pulsated with tension. When Logan finally pulled to a stop in front of his house, Sydney's indignation had reached a dangerous level. She supposed she should be a quivering mass of nerves after the attack and Logan's superhuman show of strength that followed. But for the moment, she preferred focusing all that energy on working up a really good lather toward the hardheaded man next to her.

She threw open the car door and stomped toward the house. She heard Logan get out too, and before she could take more than a few steps, his hand grasped her arm and swung her around.

"We're not done talking," he said.

She tried to yank her arm out of his hand, but he held on tightly enough to let her know he meant business.

"I have nothing to say to you. I am going to go call a cab since you forced me to leave my car behind," she said. His eyes narrowed, and she raised her chin.

"I didn't make you leave your car; we were running away from the asshole who attacked you. I'll take you to get it tomorrow. You will sleep here tonight."

"Like hell I will," she said, her voice rising an octave. "Unless you want to tell me what is really going on, I want nothing to do with you and your secrets."

Logan's jaw worked for a moment.

"Don't turn this around on me or my family. You just don't want to admit you were wrong to follow me and put yourself in danger," he said. She grimaced at the reminder.

"I didn't know it would be dangerous. Besides, it worked out okay."

"If you call being attacked by a psycho okay, then I'd hate to see what you consider dangerous, lady. If I hadn't been there to bail your ass out, what would have happened?"

Sydney knew he was right, but she would never admit it. She didn't know what had gotten into her tonight. First she acted completely out of character by following Logan. Then she got totally turned on watching him handle the thug who attacked her. She only knew she couldn't back down now, even if he had a case. "If you think I am going to apologize for following you, don't hold your breath."

"I can hold my breath longer than you think. But if I ever catch you doing something so harebrained again, I am going to lock you up for your own good," he declared.

"Harebrained?" she yelled. "You . . . you . . . ass! Who do you think you are, ordering me around?"

"Apparently, I am the only person here with a logical bone in his body. Sydney, did you happen to notice that bar was in the worst part of town? Did you not hear me tell you tonight that the group we're dealing with is dangerous? But no, you completely ignored common sense and took off without any thought to your safety. Lord, what I wouldn't give to be able to read that mind of yours!"

Sydney narrowed her eyes as she stepped closer to him. "I have news for you, buddy. I do whatever I want, whenever I want. You can't allow me or not allow me to do anything," she said.

He grabbed her finger, which she had used to poke his chest while she spoke.

"I don't think you want to test me," he said in a low voice.

"Oh yeah, or what?" Sydney taunted, practically panting from the combination of anger and lust boiling inside her.

He leaned down until they were nose to nose. "Or I'll spank you."

The words hung in the air as they glared at each other. Their labored breaths mingled in the chilly October air. Sydney felt her nipples pucker as his eyes roamed to her mouth.

"You wouldn't," she finally whispered. His gaze left her lips and he met her eyes again. The lust she saw there took her breath away. Obviously, she wasn't the only one aroused by their exchange.

"You're right. Maybe I'd have to tie you up instead," he said, grasping her wrists as his low tone caressed her. She closed her eyes to fight the assault he waged on her senses. But closing them did no good—she could still feel him, smell him, hear him.

"Sydney, look at me."

She opened her eyes slowly. He was closer to her this time, his lips a fraction away from her own. His hands came up to frame her face.

"Don't ever scare me like that again," he whispered fiercely. She licked her lips where his breath caressed them.

Before she could respond, his lips crashed into hers. All of the pent up emotions from the night crested as she plastered herself to his body. The feel of his hard frame and the deep thrusting of his tongue made her go liquid with heat. After either a few hours or moments, she didn't know which, Logan lifted her into his arms and headed for the house.

He broke from the kiss to fumble with the door. Once inside, he stopped in the foyer and kissed her more slowly.

"I need you, Sydney," he said. She didn't allow herself to analyze the repercussions of her decision; she merely nodded and took his lips again. While he ran up the stairs, she busied herself with his neck, learning every sinew. Once in his room, he set her gently on her feet next to the bed.

He sprinkled kisses along her cheeks and down to her neck.

She gasped when he found the sweet spot just below her ear and sucked the tender flesh there. A jolt of electricity raced straight to her groin, which clamored for attention. He gently grazed her throat with his teeth, but then abruptly pulled back.

She opened her eyes to see what caused the reaction, but he stalled her question by taking her mouth again. Desperate to touch his flesh, she ran her hands up and down his hard torso. She ripped the shirt out of his waistband and caressed the rock hard muscles of his stomach beneath the fabric. But soon that wasn't enough. She needed to press herself against him—to put her face to his skin and inhale his scent. She pulled her hands back and started working on the buttons of his shirt. Frustrated by her slow process, Logan grasped the placard and tore it open for her. Buttons flew and ricocheted off the floor.

Sydney rained kisses all over the wide expanse of his chest while inhaling his scent. A sprinkling of crisp, dark hair tickled her nose. She found a nipple and ran her tongue over it before taking it between her teeth. She smiled at his sharply drawn breath. The ability to make this gorgeous man react to her touch caused a rush of pride and satisfaction to surge through her. She quickly lapped at the nipple again and then sucked. His responding groan enhanced her excitement even more.

He drew her back up to his mouth for a quick kiss before pulling her own shirt off. Leaning down, he sucked through the fabric of her lacy bra. The sensation of his wet mouth and the rasp of the scratchy lace against her already sensitive nipple had her gasping. Before she knew what happened, her bra flew across the room. He worshipped each nipple with his mouth for a few moments before straightening up and pulling her to his chest.

"Ahhh," she breathed as their skin met.

He looked down as they held each other for a moment. The passion in his eyes almost made her look away. She felt more exposed by looking into his eyes than she had when he'd had his mouth on her breasts. But then he smiled. She couldn't help but smile back.

Slowly he lowered his head and kissed her again. This time

he maneuvered her to lie back on the massive bed. He kissed his way down her body and ran his tongue along the waistband of her jeans. She squirmed.

"Are you ticklish?" he asked, looking up to meet her eyes.

"A little," she admitted. "But I like it."

He chuckled before kissing her there again. Soon she was gasping and laughing at the same time.

"Logan!" she pleaded.

"Sorry but you're fun to watch when you're wiggling around like that."

Her cheeks heated, but then he started working on the zipper of her jeans. Every inch or so he'd kiss her until she was squirming again, only this time it didn't tickle. She reached down to help him push the pants off, but he stopped her hand.

"Slow down. We have all night," he said. The sensual promise in his voice only served to make her more impatient.

"I am going to die if you don't touch me," she pleaded.

"I know the feeling, love."

Finally, he pulled off her pants and underwear in one sweep. She closed her eyes in anticipation of his touch. A few seconds crept by with nothing but silence. She cracked open one lid to see him gazing at her.

"What are you doing?" she asked, embarrassed by his intense perusal of her exposed flesh. But when he met her eyes, she forgot her self-conscious reaction. The raw admiration she saw there made her feel like an enchantress.

"Sydney, you're beautiful," he said with awe. Without a word, she held her arms out to him. He came in for another kiss as his hands memorized every curve of her body by touch.

She held her breath as his hand caressed her hip bone and stroked its way to between her legs. Rubbing the sensitive flesh of her inner thighs, he teased her for a moment. She struggled not to arch her hips and beg him to touch her more intimately.

Finally, he ran one fingertip softly along her cleft. Giving in to her body's demands, she arched her hips. His long fingers swirled around the slick area—the center of all her concentration. Sweat broke out on her brow as he continued to torture her.

Unable to stand the torment anymore, she grabbed his head and thrust her tongue in his mouth. Taking her cue, he dipped one finger into her. She rode his hand until she felt the first wave of an impending orgasm hit her. Gasping, her mind went blank as she went rigid with pleasure.

As the aftershocks melted away, she felt a soft kiss on her lips and then his weight lifted from the bed. Easing open one lid, she saw him quickly removing the remainder of his clothing. She unabashedly took in every inch of tantalizing skin he uncovered for her viewing pleasure. Saliva pooled in her mouth when he stood before her finally naked—a prime example of masculine beauty. She kneeled on the bed and reached for him to gain access to the buffet of delights he presented.

Logan clenched his jaw as Sydney's hands explored his body. While he wanted to her to feel comfortable with his body, he had already been about to explode from her orgasm. But looking down to see her small hand wrapped around his straining member, he almost came again. Without thinking, he tossed her back on the bed and pressed his full length between the folds of her sex. She gasped as he rubbed back and forth along the moist warmth there. He knew he was torturing himself, but he couldn't get enough of her. He needed to explore every inch of her—with his tongue.

He kissed her hard before beginning his descent. He didn't bother with teasing this time. He dove in and feasted on her until she writhed and moaned. Her passion made him drunk as she neared her climax. The scent of her caused his canines to lengthen, and he struggled to control of his primal urges. But he knew it was no use. The scent and sound of Sydney's passion overrode his control.

As she began to peak he thrust one finger into her. Screaming his name, she lifted her hips clear off the bed. He couldn't help but smile at the gorgeous sight she presented—all flushed cheeks and opened-mouthed ecstasy.

He was glad for the cover of darkness, which hid his canines as he rose up to stroke her face. He needn't have worried though. She seemed so lost in her pleasure she wouldn't have noticed if he bit her right then. He shook his head to clear those thoughts. It had been so long since he had fed off a human that his body yearned to feed from this gorgeous creature who aroused so many passions within him. The need to mark her, to claim her as his with his bite was nearly overwhelming. But her eyes flickered open then, and he saw the trust, the bliss there and knew he could never betray that trust.

He dotted soft kisses on her lips and cheeks. This woman was meant to be cherished. And for tonight he would do just that. Beyond tonight he had no idea. He pushed the worries about tomorrow aside and kissed her lips again. She rewarded him with a sleepy smile.

"Hey," he whispered.

"Hey yourself," she said.

"Don't fall asleep yet. I'm not done with you."

She chuckled softly. "You mean there's more?"

"We're just getting started," he said and took her lips again. As they kissed, her movements became increasingly frantic. Obviously, she had recovered and was ready for more, which suited him just fine.

He shifting so he was on top of her, and he reached down to position himself for entrance.

"Wait!" she whispered urgently.

His head snapped up. "God, Syd please don't tell me you changed your mind."

She laughed. "No. We just forgot the condom."

Logan rested his forehead on hers. "I don't have any. I'm sorry. I was totally unprepared for this."

His heart dropped as he realized he had been so careless. Disease wasn't an issue since he was immune to catching or passing on mortal illnesses, but pregnancy was still a concern. Being a vampire made him more potent than most mortals. If Syd was at the right part of her cycle, she'd be pregnant before she knew it. Definitely not an option. He took a deep breath, ready to suggest they call it a night, as much as it pained him.

"I do," she said quietly.

He looked up, his smile radiant. "That's great. Where is it?"

"Wait, you don't think it's weird I carry condoms around?"

"Sweetheart, considering the alternative if you didn't carry them, I am ready to worship at your feet."

"I hadn't thought of it that way," she said, her smile lighting up the dark room. "I just don't want you to think I am the type of woman who does this all the time. I, uh, just bought them recently. You know, in case."

"In case?"

His keen eyes saw the blush before she spoke again. "In case you and I . . ." she trailed off. Getting the picture, he planted a quick kiss on her lips.

"I'm glad. Be right back. Don't go anywhere."

He got out of bed and padded over to her purse. In no time he was back in bed ready to resume his position.

"Ready?" he asked, praying the interruption hadn't killed the mood. He may have been immortal, but there was only so much sexual frustration a vampire could take.

She nodded and grabbed him for a fierce kiss. Relieved she seemed as eager as he, Logan reached between them to position himself. Then, finally, he was there, sliding into her tight, hot passage. She sighed as he filled her. Slowly he started to move within her. When she wrapped her legs around him and met each thrust enthusiastically, he groaned and picked up speed.

"Oh God, Sydney. You feel so damned good," he said into her ear. She moaned in response and kissed him deeply. He pulled back from the kiss and buried his face in her neck. He found the sweet spot again and sucked her tender flesh. He fought the urge to bite again as she raked her nails down his back and thrust her hips in time with his.

"Look at me," he commanded. He needed to watch her eyes glaze over with passion as she reached for fulfillment. When her eyes met his, they burned with an intensity that made him feel as if his soul was exposed. But he couldn't look away. Never had he felt so completely connected with a woman than he did at this moment.

He knew she was close as her movements became more

frenzied and her eyes widened. Struggling not to explode, he picked up the pace. Suddenly she stiffened and shouted, "Logan!" The sound of his name on her lips pushed him over the summit. He shouted triumphantly as the climax rocked him.

He collapsed onto her, and she ran her hands down his slick back. He felt gloriously sated. After a moment, Logan shifted and looked at her with a smile. Neither spoke. Words didn't exist to top the experience they had shared. He had never felt this kind of physical and emotional synchronicity with a woman.

Stop it. Now was not the time to analyze what happened. Soon enough the harsh light of day would bring its complications. For the time being, he just wanted to enjoy this moment.

Sydney.

She reached up and wiped a bead of sweat from his temple.

He smiled sheepishly. "Sorry, I don't mean to crush you."

She wrapped her arms more tightly around him. "Don't move. I like you right where you are."

Logan smiled and relaxed into her body. *Did life get any better than this?*

When Sydney had stopped him earlier, he'd nearly had a heart attack. But when she mentioned birth control, he felt both relief that she wasn't having second thoughts and chagrin at his lack of forethought. He supposed he shouldn't beat himself up too much; after all, he hadn't had sex with a mortal since the 1800s. Besides, his Sydney was prepared.

His Sydney? He glanced down at her. Her eyes were closed, and a satisfied smile lingered on her lips, which were swollen from his kisses. *Yes, definitely his Sydney*, his heart said.

But his logical mind had other thoughts. For example, she had just given him her body without knowing he was capable of draining every drop of blood from her veins. Most women tended to be touchy about things like that. So even if he wanted her to be his, he knew he had no right to wish it. Besides, she had never said she was interested in a romance. In fact, she had said just the opposite the night he kissed her. No, he should just take advantage of the time he had while he could. But he knew the memory of this night would stay with him forever.

He looked at her. Eyes closed, she smiled the smile of the sated. Unable to resist, he bent down and kissed her again. "Wake up, Sleeping Beauty."

"Mmmm, you wore me out," she said, rolling into him.

For the next several hours, he proceeded to wear the hell out of her.

#

Logan woke suddenly. His mouth felt like a desert. His body called out for blood after the rigorous workout he and Sydney had shared. A quick glance toward the windows revealed the first rays of sunlight spreading over the sky.

Dawn. In addition to the blood, he needed the supplements that allowed him to function in the daytime.

Spooned against Syd's warm, soft body, he tried to ignore his need for blood in order to enjoy the feel of her a few moments more. When his stomach cramped viciously, he knew he had to get up. He leaned up to make sure she still slept. Then he gently backed away from her and crept out of bed. It was risky to feed with her in the house, but his thirst could not be denied. The longer he went, the more danger there would be to her.

He went into the bathroom and closed the door. First he went to his medicine cabinet to get his sun allergy pill. Shaking with hunger, he dropped the bottle onto the tile floor. He cursed softly under his breath. When he heard nothing in response to the clatter, he went to the closet and switched on the light. The refrigerator hidden behind a row of clothing beckoned him. He grabbed the first bag of blood, popped the pill in his mouth, and gulped down the contents in just a few seconds.

Ahhh, that was better, he thought. However, after his fight with the rogue and his lovemaking with Syd, his thirst was stronger than usual. He grabbed one more bag and poked his fangs into it. The scent and taste of blood consumed him as the liquid did its work to repair his body.

#

Sydney wasn't sure what woke her. Lethargy weighed down her limbs, so she snuggled deeper into her pillow. Hoping to find the warmth of Logan's body, she wiggled her rear end backward only to encounter more cool sheets.

She looked back over her shoulder to find Logan gone. She slowly sat up and looked around the room. A wool throw sat at the foot of the bed, so she grabbed it and wrapped it around her body.

Where was he? She looked at the windows and saw the pale beams of sun filtering through the windows. Thinking that perhaps he rose early and went to go make coffee, she got up to use the restroom. She walked slowly in concession to the tenderness between her legs. A secret smile played on her lips as scenes from her marathon lovemaking with Logan played through her mind. Never in her life had she experienced that many climaxes with a man. He was a sex machine, she mused with delight as she walked into the bathroom and flipped on the light.

At first she didn't notice the sounds coming from the closet. However, as she neared it she heard a groan and a shuffle of movement. The sound stopped her in her tracks, but then she realized it must be Logan. Deciding to surprise him, she crept to the doorway of the large walk-in closet. Then she leapt forward and yelled, "Gotcha!"

Her laughter died a rapid death as he whipped around. Her mind scrambled to make sense of the scene before her. Logan stood naked with a bag of liquid he had pressed eagerly against his mouth. His eyes widened, and he immediately dropped the bag with a thud. She looked from him to the bag and back again, her mouth agape in shock.

Then, as if in slow motion, he swiped at his mouth with the back of his hand. A red smear appeared on his wrist as he pulled it away from his mouth.

"What the hell is going on here?" she demanded. He only stared at her, looking as guilty as if she had walked in on him masturbating.

"What are you doing?" she asked again, her voice rising slightly. She had no idea what she'd walked in on, but instinctively understood it was something he hadn't wanted her to see.

"Uh," he said, looking from her to the almost empty bag on the floor trickling red onto the white carpet. "Syd . . . I, uh . . . shit!"

"What is that?" she asked, pointing a finger to the stain.

He stared at her for a moment, indecision clear on his face.

"It's blood," he said quietly.

She stared at him for a moment and then slowly said, "Blood?"

"Blood," he said again, watching her closely.

"Please tell me that is a code word for alcohol," she pleaded.

"Sydney, look, I have to tell you something. But you have to promise not to freak out. Okay?"

She stared at the bag at his feet as she nodded slowly. Then she looked at him and said, "I think you'd better talk fast 'cause I am starting to freak out."

"I think maybe you should sit down," he said and took a step toward her. She backed away quickly.

"Talk. Now," she demanded.

"Syd, I really think you should sit down for this."

"Talk!" she said, louder this time. She couldn't take her eyes away from the smear of blood next to his full mouth.

"Okay," he said. "It's kind of a long story, but the truth is . . . I am a vampire."

At his crazy announcement, she shook her head as if to knock some sense into it.

"You're a vampire? You're a vampire! Sure, Logan, and I am the goddamned Tooth Fairy! Vampires aren't real!" she shrieked.

"I know it's not something you expected to hear, but it's true. We are very real."

"But, but, but . . . no! You're one of those lunatic people who pretends to be a vampire, aren't you?" Fantastic, she thought. Just when she thought she'd found a great guy who was fantastic in bed, he turned out to be shit-house crazy.

"Syd, I promise I am not crazy. Vampires exist. See? I have fangs," he said and opened his mouth to reveal two sharp white incisors.

She squinted as she looked at them. They appeared real enough, but her mind refused to believe his asinine story.

"Logan, take those out. You're not fooling anyone. You need some psychiatric help."

"I can't take them out—they're real," he said and tugged at one of them with his fingers. When it didn't budge, she didn't even flinch.

"Okay, so you had some quack dentist implant fangs into your mouth," she said, starting to feel a little frantic.

"Sydney, if I had these implanted, don't you think you'd have noticed them before now? No dentist could create fangs that can expand and retract," he said and then suddenly the pointed teeth started rising into his gum line and were replaced by normal looking canines.

Quickly backing away, she pointed at him. "That's, that's not normal, Logan. What the hell is going on here?" The bathroom counter halted her retreat. He walked toward her, a pleading look on his face.

"Syd, I promise I'm not crazy. I *am* a vampire."

She held up a hand and demanded, "Stay where you are!"

He immediately halted. Grabbing a towel from the rack to his left, he quickly wrapped it around his waist.

"Logan?" she said, hearing the confusion and fear in her own voice.

Finally, he met her eyes. She saw the truth there and shook her head frantically. "No! Vampires sleep in coffins!"

"Sweetheart, if you'll let me explain, you'll understand that most of what you believe is just a myth," he said as calmly as he could.

"That's funny. Until about five minutes ago, I thought vampires were myths, too. So obviously some myths are true," she said. She didn't want to admit she believed him, but saw no other explanation. She began to scoot to her right toward the door.

"Syd, let's just calm down," he said.

"Calm down? Calm down! I walk in on the man I just had sex with drinking blood, and then he tells me he's a soulless fiend from hell, and I need to calm down? Not likely! Wait, you aren't going to suck my blood are you?" she asked a little hysterically.

He held out a hand to halt her retreat. She stopped immediately, fear rooting her in place.

"Syd, no. Think about it. I could have done that any time during the past week, and I didn't. If you'll think for a minute, you'll realize you walked in on me drinking from a bag of blood. I don't feed from humans . . . anymore."

"Anymore?" she whimpered. She had to get out of there. She turned and raced out the door, catching him off guard.

She heard him yell after her with a curse, but she kept running. Then she remembered her car was at the bar. Without transportation, her only hope was to barricade herself in one of the bedrooms. She ran into the first guest room she encountered and locked the door.

She realized if Logan was really a vampire, a simple doorknob lock wouldn't stop him. She looked around wildly, trying to find anything to barricade the door. On the far side of the room from where she stood by the door sat a large four-poster bed. Obviously, she could never move the heavy piece all the way across the room. Two wicker nightstands flanked the bed, and a rattan rocking chair sat near the room's window. Great, she had to pick the room with the least effective furniture on earth for barricading a door.

Then she saw it. To her right, sharing a wall with the door, stood a tall dresser. She went to the far side of the piece and shoved with all her strength. It budged a few inches. Luckily, it stood less than a foot from the perpendicular wall. If she could brace herself against the other wall, she might be able to get it close enough to the door. She started by bracing her feet on the wall and pushing the heavy piece with her back, but it began to tip over. Turning, she braced her rear end on the wall and lifted both feet to push the dresser. The heavy piece finally started to move closer to the door. But before she could get it all the way in place, her body lurched backward as the wall behind her caved in.

Crap!

She pried herself out of the wall as a shower of white plaster and sheetrock rained all over her and the floor. A butt-sized hole marred the once-pristine surface.

Freakin' great. She tried to fight the tears which threatened to fall. But then she heard Logan bang on the door.

"Sydney? Open up. We need to talk."

Adrenaline surged through her, and she slid the dresser home right before he rattled the doorknob.

"Go away!"

"Sydney," he started calmly. "Please let me in. There are things I need to explain to you. It's not what you think."

"Oh, really? It's not that you're a bloodsucking demon?"

"I am not a demon."

"Funny, I notice you don't deny the bloodsucking part."

"Well, it's kind of hard to deny when you walked in on me right after I had done it," his voice rose a bit.

"I repeat: Go away!"

"Dammit, Sydney, can't you just hear me out? I won't hurt you. Think about it. If I wanted to, I could have done so while we were making love."

"Oh, that's really comforting! And I definitely don't want to talk about that. Especially now!"

She heard a thump on the door. Then another.

It didn't sound loud enough for him to being trying to break down the door, but her knowledge of vampires was sorely lacking. For all she knew, he had changed into a bat and was trying to break in that way.

"What are you doing?" she asked, her voice rising an octave.

"I am banging my forehead on the door," came the muffled reply.

Oh God, he had changed into a bat. She ran over to the window and closed the curtains. She figured if he tried to get in that way as a bat, then he might at least get tangled in the fabric on his way in.

But wait. Could bats talk?

"Logan? Are you by any chance flying right now?"

"What?"

"You know. Flying. Wouldn't banging your head on the door mess up your sonar?"

"Woman, what the hell are you talking about?"

"Don't yell at me, Logan Murdoch. I just wanted to know if you changed into a bat yet."

Syd narrowed her eyes when no response came. She crept to the door and placed her ear near the crack. Then she heard it. At first muffled and low and then growing in volume.

"Don't you laugh at me! It's a valid question!" she yelled.

Damn him. She was the injured party here. He had lied to her, used her body, and then sprung the whole "I am the undead" crap on her. She knew she should be scared right now, but she was too angry with him to care.

The chuckles on the other side of the door abruptly stopped.

"I'm sorry for laughing. But if you'll just let me come in and explain. The stories you have heard are just myths."

"I think I'll err on the side of caution on this one," she replied. "Besides, I am really pissed at you right now."

"You have every right to be angry. But can you try to see it from my point of view? When exactly was I supposed to tell you about this?"

"Gee, Logan, I don't know—maybe before we slept together."

She heard him heave a sigh. "I promise I didn't intend to deceive you. And as for last night, you know as well as I do neither of us planned for it to happen."

If she wanted to be honest, she would admit he had a point. But she couldn't get over the idea she had been so blind to him. That she had let her emotions and libido override her logic, and look where it had gotten her. So, no, she didn't feel like being honest. She felt like hurting him as much as he'd hurt her.

"You're right. I know I certainly didn't plan it. In fact, I should be thanking you for this. 'Cause now I don't have to have the awkward post-one-night-stand conversation with you."

"What the hell is that supposed to mean?"

She squeezed her eyes shut and tried to keep her tone light. "Oh, you know, the 'Thanks for the orgasms, but I'm not interested in anything more,' talk."

CHAPTER TEN

Logan clenched his teeth as her words cut through him. Syd had been planning on dumping him anyway.

It was Brenna all over again.

Then he recalled Sydney's passionate responses the night before. No one could fake the intensity they'd shared—both physically and emotionally. His mother's words came back to him. Sydney wasn't Brenna. She was scared and on the offensive to shield herself from her fear.

"Bullshit," he growled. "You know we have something here. How can you lie like that?"

"The real question is how can *you* lie like that? Even if I had been interested in more, which I wasn't, the fact you drink blood is a major deal breaker. Not to mention you took me to bed under false pretenses."

"What false pretenses?"

"That you were human!"

Logan took a deep breath. Arguing with her would accomplish nothing. He had to get her to see reason.

"I am human. I just have different nutritional needs."

He heard her snort through the door. "And you can't go

into the sun."

"Yes, I can. I just have an allergy that requires medication," he said, trying to sound reasonable.

"But you're the walking undead!"

He took a deep breath for patience, reminding himself she had been raised on horror stories and myths about his kind.

"I promise you I am very much alive. Last night should have convinced you of that. I just have certain . . . skills that people don't have."

"So you're mortal?"

He hesitated.

"Well?"

"No," he said quietly. Obviously not quietly enough though.

"Jesus," she said.

He shook his head, knowing this conversation was not helping to calm her fears. He ran a hand through his hair in frustration. This situation qualified as worst-case scenario on his list of reasons he should never get involved with mortals. Feeling out of his depth, he decided it was time to call in reinforcements. Surely his mother could help Sydney see reason.

"I need to make a phone call. Don't go anywhere." He turned to walk back into his bedroom.

"Logan? What do you mean? Logan?" Her voice echoed down the hall behind him.

He had quickly thrown on a pair of jeans when Syd ran out, but went to his closet to retrieve a shirt. Then he went to the phone by his bed and dialed.

"Yes, I know what time it is, but we have a problem," he said after his mother answered.

"No, nothing with Raven. It's Sydney. She found out I am a vampire."

He listened for a moment.

"No, I didn't tell her. She walked in on me . . . It doesn't matter why she was here. What matters is she's freaking out." He briefly described the situation. Then he sighed. "Of course I tried to explain everything. But she refuses to come out . . . Yes, I think that's best. See you in a little bit."

He hung up the phone with a sigh. Bringing his mother into an already tense situation worried him, but he had no choice. His mother could influence Sydney's mind. He hated to resort to mind control, but, honestly, if he had the power himself, he would have already tried it. He knew she'd have to calm down before she would listen to reason.

He went back into the hall to check on Syd. When he pressed his ear to the door, the sound of quiet sobs reached him.

"Syd? Honey, are you okay?"

"Don't call me 'honey'! Where did you go? To find a victim for your next meal?"

He sighed. "No, I called my mother to see if she'd come over."

"*What?* Logan, how could you?" The sobs rose in volume.

"I thought you liked my mother. I thought she could help you calm down."

"That's the problem, you oaf. I do like your mother. But now she'll know I am a slut."

Logan's jaw dropped. Lord save him from women and their crazy logic.

"Honey, you're not a slut."

"Then please tell me how I am supposed to explain why I am sitting here in nothing but a small throw blanket at six in the morning in your house. Logan, she's going to know we slept together."

Logan wasn't too thrilled about his mother knowing, either, but it couldn't be helped. Besides, she would figure out the score the minute she walked in the house. Her mind reading abilities mixed with her heightened sense of smell made it impossible to hide. But despite that, he felt guilty for Sydney. The fact he was to blame for her tears tore at him. The last thing he wanted to do was cause her more pain.

He put his hand on the door, wishing he was touching her instead. He wasn't used to feeling helpless, but when it came to Sydney he found himself more and more at sea. He wanted to erase her pain or absorb it into his own body. He didn't know where to find the right words, so he focused on solving the one problem he could handle.

"Go into the closet. You should find some old clothes of mine. They're too big, of course, but better than a blanket."

He heard her shuffling around. Nothing but the sound of hangars and sniffles reached him for a few moments.

"Syd? Did you find something?"

"Yeah, I guess," she said. "Logan? I just thought of something. Does this mean your mother knows you're a vampire?"

He paused. She wasn't going to like his answer, but he knew he couldn't lie to her anymore.

"Uh, yes, she knows. You see, she's one too. Oh, Callum and Alaric as well."

"Argh!"

Grimacing, he spoke quickly, "I swear to God, none of us would ever hurt you."

"Oh, that's nice. A vampire swearing to God. Give me a break, Logan."

"So I guess you don't want to come out now." He put his ear to the door again when she didn't immediately respond. He held his breath, hoping she had calmed enough to emerge.

"Hell, no!"

He released his breath. She needed time.

"I understand. Can I get you anything else?"

"Some garlic and crucifix would be nice," she muttered.

#

Geraldine's head hit the tree trunk. She jerked up when the bark dug into her cheek.

"Damned surveillance is wreaking havoc on my skin," she muttered as she sat up and rubbed her face.

Without the promise of eternal life, she never would have sacrificed her beauty rest to camp out in the woods. She shifted on the blanket and put her back to the tree. She would have to go get a massage this afternoon. But her discomfort was worth it. The scene she witnessed in Logan's driveway guaranteed Raven's favor.

When she had called Raven and told her about Logan's comment implying he couldn't read Sydney's mind, her mistress had been elated.

"Ah, perhaps we have found the missing piece," Raven had said excitedly. Geraldine knew how important finding Logan's soul mate was to her mistress and was elated she was the one to figure out Sydney was the one all along. But when Geraldine had asked her mistress if she had finally earned the right to be turned, Raven had simply commanded her to stay put and report any new developments.

Geraldine tamped down the guilt she felt about spying on Sydney. She didn't like the idea that the girl could be hurt. She shook her head. It couldn't be helped. Sometimes a lady had to crack a few eggs to make a soufflé.

The sound of a car coming up the drive made her sit straighter. She grabbed the binoculars from the blanket and focused on the car.

Hmmm. Momma Murdoch is making an early house call.

Kira got out of the car and rushed up the steps. She entered the front door without knocking. Geraldine wished she could be a fly on the wall when Kira discovered her son *in flagrante delecto*.

Before she could work up a good mental image of a naked Logan, a red Ferrari zoomed up the driveway. Geraldine watched Callum Murdoch exit the car and rush into the house as well.

She grabbed her phone. But then put it back down when she remembered that Raven would be sleeping right now. She chewed on her lip for a moment. What to do? Should she risk trying to peek in a window? No, with the vampires' excellent hearing and mind powers, they'd surely discover her.

She decided there was no way she could find out what was happening in the house—for now. Besides, the sun was rising, and she loathed exposing her delicate skin to its harmful rays.

After all, if she was going to be immortal, she needed to keep herself looking her best. She packed up her gear and crept back through the forest. Her first stop would be the spa. After, she'd take a much-deserved nap. Then once the sun went down, she'd report to her mistress. Maybe tonight Raven would be so grateful for all of her hard work that she'd finally change her. She picked up her pace. Obviously, she needed to get the works at the spa. It wasn't every day a woman became immortal.

#

Logan heaved a sigh of relief when he heard his mother running up the steps. The cavalry had arrived.

Kira rushed up to the door. "How is she?" she whispered.

"She's made a request for garlic and a crucifix. Does that give you an idea?"

Kira laughed. "I like this girl."

Logan didn't respond. He liked her too—maybe too much. He just hoped he hadn't scared her off for good.

He looked up to see his brother coming up the stairs.

"What are you doing here?" Logan asked.

"I called him. I figured with my mother's instincts and Callum's good humor we could undo any damage you did."

Fan-freaking-tastic.

It was bad enough his mother was involved. But his brother would now have material to tease him with for the next few hundred years.

Callum walked up and put his hand on Logan's shoulder. Logan tensed, waiting for the first zinger.

"Don't worry, brother. We'll fix this."

Logan blinked, suddenly feeling guilty that he'd underestimated Callum.

"Thanks, I appreciate your help," he said sincerely.

Kira knocked softly on the door.

"Sydney, dear, it's Kira. Will you open the door for me?"

Logan heard Syd moving around behind the door.

"I'm sorry, but I can't," came the muffled response.

Kira pulled Logan further from the door.

"Darling, I think I am going to need to influence her. Don't worry. I just want to calm her down enough to open the door and listen," she said.

Logan thought about it for a moment. He worried about

trying to manipulate Sydney into compliance. On the other hand, maybe it would help her to relax a little. All this stress couldn't be good for her.

He nodded. "Okay, but just calm her down. Don't try to convince her to blindly accept the situation. I want her mind clear so she can understand when we explain everything."

His mother nodded and went back to the door. To Logan's surprise, his brother said nothing. He merely sent Logan an encouraging smile.

Kira focused on the door as if she could see through it.

"Sydney, dear, open the door. You're safe here. No one wants to hurt you," Kira said, her voice calm but commanding.

They all listened as something bumped against the door. Logan held his breath.

"I can't," came Sydney's monotone reply.

Kira glanced at Logan, confusion clear in her eyes.

"Why not, dear?"

"Dresser."

"Could you repeat that?" Kira asked, shooting another confused look at Logan, who merely shrugged.

"Dresser in the way."

Kira nodded and said, "Step away for a moment, dear."

Kira lifted her hand, and suddenly the sound of the dresser scraping against the door could be heard. The brothers shared a look. They each had impressive skills, but their mother's age gave her a much larger bag of tricks.

"Sydney, the dresser is gone now. Please open the door."

Silence. Logan started for the door, impatient to get to Syd. Kira's hand grabbed his arm.

"She's very strongwilled, Logan. Forcing her will only serve to complicate things. Give her a moment."

Just then, the lock clicked, and the door swung open. Syd stood calmly just beyond the threshold. Logan drank in the sight of her. Her hair, still mussed from their encounter earlier, tumbled down around her face. The halo of fiery red and gold stood in sharp contrast to the dark blue terrycloth robe that engulfed her. He longed to drag her back to bed, but shook the improper thoughts from his head.

Syd gazed at Kira for a moment, and then she looked in his direction. Suddenly her eyes widened, and she started to slam the door. Luckily, she was no match for his mother's preternatural speed, and Kira stopped the door before it moved more than a few inches. Syd blinked and shook her head.

"What the—? I don't know what kind of vampire mumbo jumbo you just used on me, but I refuse to talk to *him*," she said, pointing an accusing finger in Logan's direction.

"Looks like she needs a little more convincing," his mother said wryly. "You two go downstairs. We'll be down in a few moments."

"Mother, I—" his words were cut off when Callum put an arm around his shoulder.

"Come on, big brother. Looks like they need to have some girl talk."

Logan looked from the patient gaze of his mother to the defiant one of Sydney.

"All right, I'm going. But you remember what I said about not influencing her reactions," he said to his mother. Kira nodded. He cast one last glance at Sydney, who looked everywhere but at him. Heaving a weary sigh, he turned to go. Hopefully, his mother would just calm Syd down and not try to interfere. *Yeah, right.*

#

Syd suddenly realized she was in the hallway with Kira. "How in the hell did I end up out here? Last thing I remember I refused to come out."

"Sorry, dear. I'm sorry afraid I had to use a tad bit of hypnosis on you. We all need to have a serious talk, and trying to converse through a door is just silly."

Syd stared at her for a moment while she took stock of her physical and mental state. She felt oddly relaxed given the situation—being along in a house full of vampires didn't normally give one a sense of peace.

"So you're saying you can control my thoughts?"

"If I wanted to, yes. I can also read them."

"Oh, that makes me feel better."

Kira chuckled softly. "Sydney, I know you have been through a lot tonight. I just wanted you to calm down enough to be able to listen to what we have to say with an open mind. I know you're confused and anxious, but really this is all a silly misunderstanding."

"Silly? I am food to you! Call me crazy, but I don't find that silly at all."

Kira sighed. "You have every right to be angry, but you have to believe we would never hurt you. After spending time with Logan for the last week, can you honestly say he's done anything to make you feel threatened?"

The woman had a point, Syd admitted to herself. She actually felt very safe around Logan. The fact he had gotten into a fight protecting her proved he cared about her well-being. No, Logan didn't threaten her safety—just her heart. She winced inwardly, thinking about the night they had just shared. Best not to think about that now.

"Sydney, darling, you know I am right. And as for the events earlier tonight, I think you and Logan should talk about that after he has had a chance to explain about being a vampire."

Syd's eyes widened when she remembered Kira could read her thoughts. She abruptly cleared her head, hoping the woman didn't get too clear a picture of her and Logan doing the deed.

"Dear, please don't worry. It's nothing I haven't seen before."

Eeeew.

"Now, will you please come downstairs with me and give Logan a chance to explain?"

Syd tapped her foot as she considered Kira's suggestion. Either she could stay in this room indefinitely, staring at the hole she put in Logan's wall, or she could go downstairs and get this over with. Deep down she knew none of them would ever hurt her.

"Okay, I'll go listen. But I want your word you will not influence my mind in any way."

Kira smiled. "I promise I won't influence you."

Syd held up a finger to indicate the woman should wait a moment. Then she ran to the closet to grab something she had seen earlier. When she emerged, Kira looked as if she struggled not to laugh.

"Planning on a spot of tennis?"

Syd clutched the two tennis rackets together so the handles formed a cross.

"No, it's a cross," Syd explained. "Wait. Why aren't you backing up?"

"Oh, sweetie, I'm afraid you've been watching too many movies. Crosses have no effect on us."

Her shoulders drooped. Even though she trusted them not to hurt her, she really was powerless against them. Kira's gaze turned sympathetic.

"No, you're not, dear. I'm sure the rackets would cause a nasty bump if you hit one of us on the head. Now, come along."

She knew Kira was using mental suggestion on her again, but she welcomed the sense of calm that descended. Kira seemed genuinely concerned with making Syd feel comfortable. Dropping one racket but still clutching the other, she followed Kira out the door.

"And don't worry dear, I won't mention the butt through the wall incident to Logan," Kira said with a smile in her voice.

Stopping in her tracks, Syd was about to remind Kira about her promise not to read her mind. But before she could speak, Kira explained.

"No, dear, I promised not to influence you," the woman calmly explained. "I never said I wouldn't read it."

Grimacing, she mentally kicked herself for giving the woman such a loophole. Her only option right now, short of starting an argument she had no patience for, was to get better at controlling her thoughts. She stuck her tongue out at Kira's back as a test.

"Darling, that gesture is so unbecoming of a young lady." Kira sounded on the verge of laughter, but Syd couldn't see her face as they descended the stairs.

Crap.

"And such language."

Abruptly clearing her mind, she focused instead on the remaining few steps. At the bottom, they walked toward the living room where they'd all met the night before.

Immediately her gaze collided with Logan's. Her step faltered. Now that she was down here, she wasn't sure she could face him.

"Sydney, dear," Kira's calming voice cut through her turbulent thoughts. Syd took a deep breath and continued into the room.

She took the seat farthest away from him. She despised feeling vulnerable, so she decided to go on the offensive.

Clutching her tennis racket, she looked Logan straight in the eye. "So, anything else you've been keeping from me? Like—oh, I don't know—you're married to the Blair Witch?"

CHAPTER ELEVEN

"**I** suppose I deserved that," Logan said, his mind alternating between relief she didn't seem scared and annoyance at her sarcasm. "But tell me, would a monster have saved you from the attack last night?"

Syd maintained her stubborn posture, but conceded a small shrug.

"I appreciate that, but it doesn't excuse the fact I walked in to find you consuming blood. That's just not normal, Logan!"

He ran a hand through his hair. "You found all this out in the worst way possible. If I ever thought this would happen, I would have told you."

"Why didn't you tell me?" she asked.

"What was I supposed to say? 'Boy, I sure could go for a tall glass of blood right about now. Could you pass the salt?' That would have gone over really well," he said, not able to keep the sarcasm from his tone. Then he looked her straight in the eye, needing to reassure her he hadn't deceived her on purpose.

"Honestly, I didn't think I'd ever need to tell you. I didn't plan on . . . things progressing like they did."

Her pink cheeks reflected his own discomfort about

discussing the topic in front of his mother and brother.

"I don't mean to interrupt," Callum said. "But perhaps this is a discussion you two should have after we leave."

Logan sent a grateful look to Callum. Perhaps once he explained the reality of being a vampire to Syd, she would be more receptive to discussing their future. Or lack thereof. Shaking off the melancholy that thought produced, he mentally switched gears. Syd still looked upset, but also seemed relieved at the idea of changing the subject.

"Okay," he began and then cleared his throat. "I am sure you have some questions."

She looked around at all of them for a moment as if gathering her thoughts. He would give anything to know what she was thinking right now so he could know exactly what to say.

"How old are you?"

Logan grimaced; he had hoped to cover other areas before easing her into this subject. After all, what woman wanted to find out she slept with a man who was more than four hundred years her senior?

"I am 437."

Syd's mouth dropped open. He sat up straighter, feeling vulnerable all the sudden.

She looked like she wanted to ask something else, so he raised his eyebrows, dying to know what she thought.

"Wait! You're the Hot Scot!" Syd exclaimed. "Like really, really him!"

"Yes," he said. "My father, Cornelius, painted it as a gift to my mother." He glanced at Kira and saw the pain in her eyes at the mention of his father. He regretted making her sad, but knew he had to be honest with Sydney.

Her eyebrows drew together. "But you said his name was Royce."

"Royce is my first name, but I go by my middle name."

Her mouth formed into a silent "oh" as she struggled to process the implication of his admission. He worried she might get mad again at this latest deception, but her next words eased his mind.

"Well, I guess this makes proving the authenticity of the painting easier," she said with a laugh. "I can't believe it was you the whole time."

He shrugged. "Well I couldn't very well walk in there and tell you it was me, could I?"

"No, I can see why you made up the ancestor story. How was it stolen?"

"We were visiting family in France at the time and left a very small staff in place to watch the keep. Upon our return, we discovered the staff dead and many of our valuables gone. A group of foolhardy villagers believed they could scare us into leaving their region," Kira explained. "You see, we were . . . different then. We didn't have bagged blood for sustenance. I am afraid the people didn't like having us as neighbors."

Logan spoke then. "As for what happened to the painting, I believe it was probably sold for profit."

Syd shook her head. "That doesn't make sense. Remember, the anonymous donor did not provide any provenance with the painting. It is unlikely someone back then would have wanted a portrait of an anonymous man. It was only in more recent times this type of work became popular to collect. Therefore, surely a record of the sale would exist. Yet I found nothing about it.

"Even though the donor wanted to be anonymous," she continued, "they could have given us sales records if they had bought the painting if for no other reason than to prove its authenticity. No, my guess is it passed down through a family. That would explain the lack of paper trail."

Kira nodded. "That would also explain why we could never find it despite decades of hunting for it."

"Well, that's one mystery solved," Callum said.

Syd looked at Logan in awe. "I still can't believe you were alive in the seventeenth century. You're like a walking history book."

"Nah, if you think he's old, you're going to freak when you find out how old mother is," said Callum with a chuckle.

"Thanks, son," Kira said with a rueful smile. Syd raised her eyebrows in question.

"Seven hundred-ish," Kira admitted.

"Seven—? You're kidding! Well I guess the whole vampire thing explains why you look so young. I thought you had just spent a fortune on plastic surgery," Syd said.

Kira chuckled. "When I was turned I was still quite young by today's standards. But in those days I was already considered past my prime at the age of eighteen."

"Wait, you said you were turned. So you were all made into vampires?"

"No. The boys' father, Cornelius, turned me. Callum and Logan were born vampires."

"Vampires can give birth?"

"Yes, dear. I think you'll find we're much more like mortals than you think. The only difference is vampire children take longer to reach their prime, and then they stop aging."

"This is so weird," she said, sounding more confused than judgmental. "I thought people only became vampires when they were bitten by another one."

"That's a fallacy perpetuated by Hollywood. In fact, a turning involves an exchange of blood, not just a bite," said Logan.

"Have you ever turned anyone?" she asked.

"No, turning a mortal is allowed only in certain cases."

"Allowed by whom?"

"The Brethren Council, a governing body of elder vampires. We have laws, just like mortals, that govern our behavior. But I think before we delve into the intricacies of our culture, we should start with the basics."

Logan tried to focus on her eyes, but when she bit her lip in thought, his attention strayed to her luscious mouth. The mouth he had kissed mere hours before. He gave himself a mental shake. Now was not the time for those thoughts.

"How do you get your blood?" she asked, not really sure she was ready for the answer.

"We actually have not fed from human sources for decades," Logan replied. "Bagged blood made feeding off mortals unnecessary."

"And Logan is in the process of developing a synthetic blood product to completely break our dependency on human blood," Callum added.

"Really? Is that the big project you have been working on?" she asked.

"Yes, I call it Lifeblood. Synthetic blood has existed for years for mortal uses, but my formula is specifically for vampire nutritional needs. We are working on including all the supplements we already take into the Lifeblood."

"Supplements? That was the bottle I saw earlier?"

"The stories about vampires not being able to go in the sun are true. However, the real reason is we have an extreme allergy to it, not because we combust when exposed to sunlight. In addition, the paleness and gaunt look people associate with us is the result of acute anemia, so we also need a large amount of iron."

"That makes sense," she said, her brows furrowed. "But what about the whole damned-for-eternity part?"

Logan sighed. He glanced at his mother. She smiled encouragingly from her spot next to him on the couch.

"We are immortal, but not because of a curse. Our bodies are just able to heal quickly, and we have immunity to the illnesses that plague mortals."

Syd raised her eyebrows in question. "But where did you come from?"

"Honestly, no one really knows. Some vampires like to believe we are like gods; they even have a bible of sorts filled with vague prophecies and myths. But they are in the minority. My theory is we are the result of a genetic mutation that occurred thousands of years ago. I believe a virus caused extreme changes to our DNA, which resulted in a stronger race."

"Okay, but if that's true, then why the anemia and the sun allergy?"

He smiled at her quick mind. "An excellent question. I believe the weaknesses are Mother Nature's way of keeping checks and balances."

"I suppose that makes sense. How do you explain the mind control and psychic skills?"

"Have you heard it said that mortals use only a small portion of their brain?"

"Yes, I read somewhere we only use like ten percent of our minds."

"I believe the mutation allowed vampires to tap into the other ninety percent, allowing us to read minds and influence our surroundings."

"Speaking of which," she said in a suspicious tone. "Did you influence me?"

When he didn't respond, Syd narrowed her eyes and leaned forward menacingly, obviously assuming his silence indicated guilt.

"Of all the rotten . . . You creep!"

"Sydney, dear, sit down. Logan can not influence your mind."

Logan sent a glare to his mother.

"I'm sorry, darling, but we can't leave her under the impression you have been controlling her against her will."

He knew she had a point, but he really didn't want Sydney to learn the whole truth.

"But why not? How could you influence me, but not Logan?" Syd addressed his mother. Logan was about to launch into an explanation when his brother cut in.

"Sydney, sometimes there are exceptions—mortals we cannot touch mentally. Mother is older and stronger than most vampires. There are very few, if any, she cannot read."

"So you can't read my mind either?" she asked Callum. He glanced at Logan, his apology clear in his eyes.

"Uh, yeah, I can read it," he grudgingly admitted.

"But aren't you younger than Logan?" she asked.

"Yes, I am 314. But in this instance, age has nothing to do with why I can read you and he can't."

Logan's blood pressure rose. He didn't know if he should forcibly shut up his brother or launch into an explanation to

Sydney.

"Okay, what aren't you guys telling me?" She looked at Logan, her eyes narrowed into slits.

He knew she wouldn't stand for excuses now, not after everything else. But he honestly didn't know how to explain the soul mate issue to her when he himself didn't know if it was true. The scientist in him demanded that a more rational explanation must exist. And the man in him didn't want to face the idea that this woman, whom he had come to care for, might laugh in his face if he told her how he felt, especially given her skittishness about the vampire issue.

"Sydney, dear, we believe the real reason—"

"Mother," Logan interrupted in warning tone.

"What? She deserves to know," Kira said to him. Then she turned to Syd. "As I was saying, we believe you and Logan share a special . . . connection that prevents him from being able to influence you."

Logan couldn't look at Sydney. While his mother hadn't actually come out and said "soul mates", the implication had to be clear to Sydney.

"A connection? You mean like chemistry or something?"

"Yes, sometimes when there is chemistry between a vampire and a mortal it interferes with the vampire's ability to influence the mortal's mind."

Logan dared a glance at Sydney. Luckily, she didn't look appalled. Instead, she looked at him quickly before staring down at her shoes. But despite her attempts to hide it, he saw the blush spread on her cheeks. The fact she didn't deny the chemistry between them gave him some hope everything might work out. But he wasn't fool enough to hope they were out of the woods.

"Syd, the truth is we don't know for sure why I can't read your mind. But I promise you I have not influenced any of your actions since we met," he said.

"No, dear, he couldn't read your mind either," Kira said.

Syd's head snapped up. "Stop that! Anyone else reads my mind and I am out of here."

"Mother," Logan said, a warning clear in his tone.

Callum chuckled. "Don't worry, Syd. We won't tell him anything. It is far more fun to see him squirm."

Syd's frown wobbled, and then a small smile peeked from the corner of her full mouth. Logan wanted to be mad at his meddling relatives, but seeing Syd relax made him feel decades younger.

"It's so bizarre. You guys seem like such a normal family. Well, except for the blood drinking, immortality, and psychic abilities."

Kira chuckled. "Thank you, dear."

Logan allowed himself a smile.

"Wait," Syd said as if something had just occurred to her. "The other night you said your father died. If you are all immortal, then where is he?"

Logan's smile disappeared. He glanced at his mother, who suddenly looked ill. Callum stood and came over to sit on the arm of the couch next to her and placed a comforting hand on her shoulder.

Syd glanced at the uneasy faces around her and said, "Oh dear, I'm sorry if I upset you."

Kira smiled wanly at Syd. "That's all right, dear. I know you didn't mean any harm. And it's understandable you would be confused."

"We are not impervious to death. Stakes, bullets, knives and other weapons can kill us if it hinders our blood flow to an important organ and body part. Also, our bodies can't repair something as extreme as decapitation," said Callum.

"Unfortunately, my father made enemies in the vampire community," Logan explained. "Being vampires themselves, they knew his vulnerabilities and attacked him one night when he was traveling alone."

"I'm so sorry. How long ago did this happen?"

"It was just after the Scottish rebellion. My father suggested that we organize and lend our strength to the Jacobite cause after the massacre at Culloden. However, many of our kind at the time vehemently opposed interfering in mortal affairs," explained Logan.

"Wow," Syd said quietly.

"Now you understand why we fled Scotland. We traveled first to France, but we cut our time there short when the French Revolution started brewing. Luckily, across the Atlantic, the Americans had just established their own government. We moved to North Carolina in 1788, and the rest is history, so to speak," Logan said with a grin.

"My family didn't come over until the late 1870s from England, so I guess that makes you more American than me," she said, an adorable lopsided grin on her face. "And that goes a long way to explain why your Scottish accent isn't stronger."

"It was a hard time for us, trying to find a new home," Kira said with a sad smile as she looked at her sons. "But we're proud to call ourselves Americans, although we do try to visit Scotland as often as possible."

Callum cleared his throat and patted his mother's hand.

"I think we could all use a break. How about a drink?"

Syd's eyes widened, and her hand went to her throat as she shrank back in her seat. Logan mentally cursed his brother. Obviously, she thought blood was on the menu.

"Syd, relax. He means a regular drink."

"Oops, sorry," said Callum, looking chagrined. "I meant like a soft drink."

Syd relaxed. "Do you have anything stronger?"

Kira laughed and said, "Of course we do—we're Scottish. What you need is whisky."

#

Syd smiled at Callum when he handed her the snifter. She took a tentative sip. She saw Logan frown at his brother, but ignored it to take her first sip. The fiery spirit blazed a trail down her throat.

"Smooth," she croaked, causing her companions to chuckle.

"You'll get used to the burn," Kira said, taking a drink from her own glass.

Syd nodded and took another sip. This time she savored the smoky flavor of the whisky.

"This raises another question," she said, feeling more mellow as warmth spread through her midsection. "Can you get drunk?"

Logan chuckled. "Yes, but it takes quite a bit more for us to feel the effects of alcohol or drugs than it does for mortals."

"And do you need to eat and drink for sustenance?"

Logan nodded. "The nutrients in food are beneficial, but we do not need it to survive."

Syd watched him as he spoke, taking in his relaxed posture. She gazed at his hand, which cradled his own snifter of whisky—the same hand that just hours before had brought her to the edge of ecstasy and beyond. The hands that caressed her face and made her feel cherished and safe. She didn't know how to combine the Logan she knew then with this Logan—the one who drank blood and was old enough to be her great-great-great-etc. grandfather.

"Sydney?"

"Hmm," she said looking up to his face.

"I think you zoned out for a minute," he said with a smile.

"Sorry, I was just trying to process everything. This is all so . . . I don't know," she finished lamely.

"Poor dear," said Kira. "You must be exhausted."

"No, I'm fine. It's just a lot to take in."

"You're doing great, considering," Logan said.

"Thanks," she said and smiled at him. Their eyes held for a moment. She felt something indefinable pass between them. But before she could name it, the connection was broken when Callum spoke.

"Yes, you have been very brave," Callum said supportively.

Then she laughed. "Oh, I don't think barricading myself in a room is brave."

"Nonsense," said Kira. "Your reaction was quite normal. After all, I am sure you had quite a fright."

"I have to admit it was a shock. I thought Logan was injured at first."

She saw Logan flinch at the reminder. She wasn't sure what to think about everything she'd learned tonight, but she knew he felt horrible about the scene in his bathroom. She also believed they wouldn't hurt her.

Even though their explanation went a long way to dispel the myths about vampires, she didn't know what to do with the information. Or what it meant for her feelings for Logan.

"Syd, I cannot apologize enough for that," Logan said quietly. She nodded to acknowledge the apology because she had no idea what to say.

"What exactly happened?" Callum asked. Syd saw the devilish sparkle in Callum's eye and knew he was baiting his brother. It was odd seeing centuries-old men act like regular brothers.

"I was distracted and accidentally ripped a bag of blood."

"I bet you were," Callum said, sending a significant glance Sydney's way.

"Is there anything else you want to know, dear?" Kira asked quickly when Logan's eyes narrowed and leaned toward his brother menacingly.

"Honestly, I don't think my brain can handle any more right now."

Kira smiled. "Perhaps a good rest will help you sort through everything."

Syd suddenly had to stifle a yawn. She'd been sleepy before but not this exhausted.

"Yes, Syd, that's probably best. Why don't you go lay down in the guest bedroom?" Logan suggested.

"I was kind of hoping one of you could give me a ride home," she said.

The other three exchanged uneasy glances.

"What?" she asked.

"It's probably not a good idea for you to leave right now. You've been through a lot. Besides, I am sure you'll have more questions after you've rested," Logan said.

"I can always just call you," Syd said, not liking where this was going.

"Dear, you've had a shock. We're worried that once some time has passed you might become agitated again," Kira said.

Syd fought another yawn. Her eyelids suddenly felt like lead weights.

"Maybe you're right. I am dead on my feet."

She flinched.

"Pardon the pun," she said, her words sounding slightly slurred to her own ears.

"I'll help you get settled," Logan said. He stood and helped her out of her seat. Her knees nearly buckled when she stood. Luckily, Logan moved quickly and wrapped an arm around her waist.

"Good night, Sydney," Kira said. "We'll talk again later."

"Sleep well," Said Callum.

"G'night," she said and allowed Logan to lead her out of the room.

He helped her up the stairs and to the doorway of the same bedroom she had barricaded herself in a few hours before.

"Do you need any help?" he asked as he paused at the threshold while Syd continued into the room.

"Hmm?" she murmured as she turned to look at him.

"Do you need anything before you go to sleep?"

She shook her head and plopped down on the bed. She looked up at him as he hesitantly walked into the room. Even in her tired state, she appreciated the view. She didn't say anything as she let her gaze roam over his body.

He cleared his throat. "Yes, well, um, I guess I'd better let you get some sleep."

She nodded but continued to stare at his mouth. She slowly licked her lips.

"Logan," she said quietly.

"Yeth," he whispered back.

She looked up suddenly. "Did you just say *yeth*?"

CHAPTER TWELVE

Logan's hand flew to his mouth.

"No," he mumbled. "Lithen, I need to get back downthairs."

She narrowed her eyes at him. "There it was again. What's up with the sudden lisp?"

Her eyes widened as a thought occurred to her, "Your fangs are out aren't they?"

He shrugged. "I gueth."

She stood quickly, her instincts telling her to get the heck out of there.

"Thyd, no, I would never bite you," he said, holding up a hand to calm her.

"Sorry, it just caught me off guard," she said, staring at his mouth. "Can I see them?"

He scowled and shook his head.

"Come on, Logan. Just a peek?"

He shook his head, but something caught his attention to her right. He paused and then walked toward it. She glanced over and froze.

Crap! She'd totally forgotten about the hole.

"Uh, Syd?" he began, the lisp gone. "What happened here?"

"What?" she asked, playing dumb. She wanted the floor to open up right then.

"The large hole in the wall," he said, pointing to the crater.

"It's not that large!" she said, absentmindedly putting her hand on her rear end.

Then she caught herself, "I think it was here before I came in here."

His eyes narrowed as he looked at the hole again. Then he looked at her. His shoulders suddenly began to shake.

"Shut up!" she said. "That dresser was heavy! And I was scared."

Instantly he sobered. "God, Syd, I'm sorry you were so afraid. Please tell me what I can do to make it up to you."

She dropped on the bed again, her fatigue returning in full force.

"I don't know, Logan," she said.

He nodded and shifted his weight. "I promise you're safe here."

"I know," she said, feeling too worn out to talk anymore.

"I guess I'll let you sleep then," he said quietly.

"Okay," she said. He turned to go.

"Logan?"

He turned back and raised his eyebrows. She saw the lines of strain bracketing his mouth, and her heart went out to him. Underneath all the turbulent emotions the night had caused, she genuinely cared for him.

"I—um . . . good night."

He nodded and held her eyes for a moment.

"Good night," he whispered. He flipped the light off and closed the door.

#

Logan tried to put his game face back on before he returned to the living room. His talk with Sydney had left him feeling more defeated than ever. Just when he'd thought there was hope, his damned fangs came out. But worse, the hole in the wall had reminded her of the terror she'd felt earlier. Terror he'd caused. Who was he kidding? He didn't stand a chance with Sydney now.

"How'd it go?" Kira asked.

He shrugged. "She should sleep for a while. She could barely keep her eyes open when I left."

"That's not what I meant," she chided.

"I know," he said and sat in the leather club chair next to the fireplace. His mother and Callum exchanged uneasy glances.

"Son, you mustn't blame yourself. None of us could have predicted she would find out like this."

"Oh, really? I did! I told you from day one having a mortal in this house was a mistake," Logan said.

Kira sent him a disapproving frown. "Young man, I know you are upset, but I will not let you pass the buck here. Need I remind you that the two of you had not been engaged in research when this happened?"

Logan didn't respond. What could he say? He never should have acted on his feelings for Sydney. Making love to her was a mistake, and now he was paying for it. In spades.

"Mother, I think we need to focus on what comes next instead of harping on how we got here," Callum said. Once again, Logan was shocked his brother would pass up an opportunity to tease him.

"Yes, you're right," Kira said with a sigh. "Logan, how do you want to proceed?"

Logan took a deep breath. What he wanted was to go back in time and do everything differently. Unfortunately, his wants weren't an option.

"I think we need to just let her go," he said.

"What do you mean?" Callum asked.

"I think she's been through enough. I say we just clear her mind from yesterday evening on."

"I thought you didn't want us to tamper with her mind," Kira said.

"I know, but I think it's easier this way," Logan said as he rubbed his eyes.

"Easier on whom?" Kira said, her implication clear.

He dropped his hand and demanded, "What do you suggest, then?" He didn't mean to take this out on his family, but he didn't know how to deal with the emotions he felt.

"Son, Sydney is a big girl. She will eventually accept everything we have told her and decide how to deal with it. I think we should keep her here for a few days until she gets used to the idea."

"Mother, I will not make her a prisoner," Logan shot back.

"Of course not, darling. But I think she needs time to ask questions and become used to this new reality. Besides, if we let her go before she is ready, she might go to someone and reveal the truth. The time is also for us to be sure she can be trusted to keep our secrets."

"I don't think she'd tell anyone," Logan said.

"Darling, did you see her tonight? She's in shock. Otherwise, she would have been unable to joke with us. Once it wears off, she will be angry or scared again—probably both. We need to help her through that."

"Logan, she's right. It would be unfair to send Sydney on her way without helping her accept the truth. Besides, there's also Raven to deal with. If she finds out how deeply Sydney is involved with all this, she could try to use her against us."

Logan lowered his head to his hands. He didn't know if he could face Sydney once the shock wore off and she realized she found him repulsive. But he couldn't risk her safety. Resigned, he nodded his agreement.

"Besides, darling, you two have some issues to work through," Kira said.

Logan laughed bitterly. "Mother, I think what we have goes way beyond the normal relationship issues. But you're right. I suppose we do need to talk."

"It's decided then. Syd will stay here for a few days. Callum and I will check in periodically."

"What should we do about Raven while this is happening?" Logan asked.

"I'll take over the search. Our sources have come up with nothing so far, but I have a conference call with the Brethren

Council this afternoon."

Kira nodded. "I'll call her boss and explain we have asked Sydney to go to our estate in Asheville to do some additional research. That should cover her absence for a couple of days. I'll also run by her apartment and gather some clothes for her. She'll be more comfortable with her own things."

Logan sent a grateful look to his family. "Thanks, both of you, for all of your help. I'll call Alaric this morning and ask him to continue work without me for a couple of days."

"Darling, I know this is difficult. But please try not to worry. Everything will work out as it should. Now, you should grab some sleep too. If you need anything, call us."

She and Callum said their good-byes and left. Logan called Alaric and filled him in quickly. His friend had questions, but Logan had no energy to explain everything. He promised to call the next day with more details.

When he went upstairs, he paused briefly outside Sydney's door. With his keen senses, he could hear her soft sleep sounds through the door. He turned away, his shoulders slumping, and went to his room. This time, he locked the bathroom door when he fed. Then he collapsed onto his own bed and prayed for sleep to give him a reprieve from his troubles.

#

Syd jerked awake. She couldn't remember the nightmare, but she felt relieved to have her eyes open. The thick curtains prevented her from knowing the time, but she felt as if she had slept for days. She sat up slowly and rubbed the sleep from her eyes. She needed coffee. But her mind kicked in, and she realized that to get it, she'd have to face Logan.

She got out of bed and went to listen at the door. She heard vague noises from below. Then the intoxicating scent of coffee mixed with the smoky aroma of bacon caused her to inhale deeply. Her traitorous stomach growled. How could she just walk downstairs and eat a civilized breakfast with a vampire?

Suck it up, Sydney, she chided herself, wincing at the bad pun. She knew from their talk last night Logan and his family were not monsters. No, it wasn't fear keeping her in the room, but uncertainty.

None of her previous experience with men prepared her to deal with finding out her current lover was a vampire. She knew she should be more concerned with finding out vampires even existed, but take away the drinking blood and immortality, and the Murdochs seemed almost normal. Her logical mind balked at the idea, but her instincts told her she was right to trust them. However, she had no idea what these developments meant for her relationship with Logan. Her stomach growled again, and she decided to take her cues from him and go from there. Perhaps not the most mature attitude, but it worked for her purposes.

She tightened the belt of her robe and followed the breakfast smells to the kitchen. She found Logan standing at stove with a dish towel thrown over one shoulder as he cooked. His damp hair glistened in the morning light. He wore a white polo shirt and faded blue jeans that hugged his firm rear. He turned toward her on bare feet with a frying pan in one hand and a spatula in the other. He looked so handsome and domestic that for a moment she longed to wake up to this scene every morning.

"Good morning," he said with an uncertain smile. "Did you sleep well?"

She nodded. "What time is it?"

"It's two in the afternoon, but I thought you might like breakfast," he said. "Why don't you sit down, and I'll get you some coffee."

She hesitantly walked past him toward the bistro table on the far side of the kitchen. She sat with her back to the large bay window so she could watch his graceful movements as he poured the coffee.

"I'm surprised you can cook. Most bachelors just order take-out," she said, trying to fill in the silence.

He smiled crookedly. "I've had a few years to learn."

"Oh, yeah, sorry," she said, feeling stupid for forgetting how old he was.

He walked to the table and set a steaming mug in front of

her. Then he knelt beside her and looked into her eyes.

"Syd, don't worry. I know this all takes some getting used to."

His nearness made her fidget. She had so many questions to ask that she didn't know where to begin. So she decided to concentrate on her coffee instead. She nodded to acknowledge his comment and then reached for her mug.

He stood and went back to the stove, where he piled two plates with scrambled eggs, thick-cut bacon, and buttered toast. The he set her plate in front of her before taking his own place across the table.

She inhaled the delicious aroma of the breakfast. "Logan, this looks wonderful. I'm starving."

"I thought you might be. Scotch whisky tends to give one a mean hangover," he said with a wink.

She chuckled. "It does pack a punch. But I meant I haven't eaten since last night." She immediately regretted her words. The last thing she wanted was to get into a discussion about last night's events.

She decided to cover her unease by digging into her meal. Logan took her cue and began eating as well. The next few moments passed quietly. She scrambled for something to say to break the tension hanging over the table like a dense fog.

"So—" she began.

"My mother—" he said at the same time. They both laughed uncomfortably.

"You first," Syd said because she had no idea what to say.

"Okay. My mother went by your apartment and brought back some clothes for you. We thought you'd be more comfortable with your own things."

"That was nice of her, but honestly, I'd prefer to just go home after breakfast. Did she get my car too?"

Logan suddenly became engrossed with his eggs.

"Logan?"

He glanced up at her and then quickly reached for his own mug.

"Actually, we thought you should have a couple of days to

adjust to things before you went home," he said and then took a sip.

"What?"

"Syd, you've had a major shock. You need time to adjust before you go back to your life," he explained calmly, as if explaining something to a child.

Her eyes narrowed. "Where is my car?"

"We haven't picked it up yet."

She set down her fork with deliberate slowness. "Are you telling me I am a prisoner here?"

"You are not a prisoner. It's for your own safety."

"Are you trying to convince me I am safer in a house full of vampires than in my own apartment?"

"Well . . . yes. Look," he said quickly when she started to rise. "Raven is still a threat. If she finds out you are helping us, she might decide to come after you. If that happens, you are safer here with us than on your own."

"Raven. You mean the head of the mysterious extremist group?"

Logan sighed. "I am sorry I sent you on that wild goose chase. But at the time I thought it best to limit your involvement."

"And now?"

He ran his hands through his hair. "And now, unfortunately, you are smack in the middle of a vampire feud."

Syd took a moment to digest this newest development. "I think you better start talking."

"Raven is the head of a sect of rogue vampires called the Sanguinarians. Most of her activities have been more of a nuisance than a threat, but for some reason she's targeted my family and me. I don't know what she has planned, but stealing the painting was a bold move on her part."

"Sanguinarians?"

"It means 'blood thirsty,'" he explained. "Raven believes that vampires should adhere to the old ways. If it were up to her, we would all feed off humans and pretend we're some sort of gods to rule over humans. She doesn't want us trying to fit into the mortal world. Other rogue groups exist, but the Raven is organized. She even has mortal helpers who assist her."

"But why is she targeting you?"

"I developed many of the drugs we use to make us more like mortals. With Lifeblood, our dependence on human sources will be gone. I think she wants to prevent me from succeeding. I don't know what her plan is, but Syd, I can't risk her involving you."

"But how would she know?"

"She has to sleep during daylight because she refuses to use the sun allergy remedies. However, her minions spy for her during the day. We have no idea how much she knows at this point."

"So basically I am trapped here until you figure out what she has planned? What about my job. Logan?"

"We called Stiggler earlier and told him we sent you to our Asheville estate for more research."

Syd couldn't believe what she was hearing. "So now not only can I not leave, but you're lying to my boss. Logan you had no right!"

He held his hands up in a placating motion. "We were just trying to help. It's not every day a person finds out vampires really exist. We thought you could use a break from your work to get used to everything."

Syd stood, unable to talk to him anymore without shouting.

"Syd? Where are you going?" he asked as she turned to leave the room. She stopped halfway to the door and turned slowly around.

"I am going to go shower and dress. Then I am going to find my cell phone and have Jorge come pick me up."

Logan was out of his chair and in front of her before she could blink. She took a step back, shocked by his display of power.

"I can't let you call Jorge. Syd, no one can know about us. Please, just give it a couple of days."

"What would you do in my shoes? Would you just meekly accept that a group of people seem bent on controlling your life?"

He sighed. "We aren't trying to control you."

"Bullshit."

"At least give it the rest of the day. You are overworked, and on top of that you've had some major shocks over the last couple of days. Your job can wait."

"Logan, that job is all I have left. I won't have you blowing it off because it doesn't serve your purposes."

"That's not what I meant. I know your job is important. But please don't pretend it's the real reason you want to leave."

She stared at him for a moment. Then she said, "What do you mean?"

"Look, we have to talk about last night. You can't run away from what happened."

She crossed her arms defensively. "I can't talk about that right now."

"I know you've been through a lot, but I think we both know until you found out I am a vampire things were getting . . . intense between us."

"Logan, it's not like I found out you had an annoying habit or something. You drink blood. You're immortal. Those are pretty big issues for me!"

He ran his fingers through his hair. "I know it's big. But tell me this: if I wasn't a vampire, would you want to be with me?"

She cringed at the vulnerability in his eyes. She didn't want to hurt him. Vampirism aside, he really had gotten to her heart. But telling him that wouldn't change anything.

"I don't know," she whispered.

He nodded slowly. "At least admit last night was more than just sex to you."

Syd looked away. They both knew it was more than sex. A lot more. Syd had never felt that kind of connection physically or emotionally with any man. What she didn't know was if it mattered now.

"Syd?"

She took a deep breath and looked up. "Logan, I can't do this now. You have to give me some time."

"Fine."

She flinched at the edge of steel in his tone. "Can I go shower now?"

He closed his eyes for a second as if praying for patience. "Will you promise me you won't call Jorge?"

She thought about it for a moment. Maybe she did need some time. After all, this was a big house. Surely she could find something to occupy her time so she could avoid Logan. Being around him was close to physical pain as she battled with the disappointment of what could have been.

"Yes, I promise I won't call Jorge." He let out a relieved breath, but she held up a hand. "I won't call him today. But I suggest you have someone get my car because I can't promise I won't leave tomorrow."

She turned again to go, leaving him staring after her. Only this time she had run out of the burst of adrenaline her earlier outrage had provided. Her feet felt heavier with each step she took away from Logan. She knew their relationship discussion wasn't over. But for now, she would pretend the big pink elephant wasn't hanging around in the house, dodging her every move.

CHAPTER THIRTEEN

Logan shook his head as he watched Sydney leave the kitchen. All he'd ever wanted was to work in his lab and help make life easier for his kind. Then he had let his mother talk him into going to the museum. Now everything had gone to hell.

What he wouldn't give to be able to handle his personal problems like he approached science—with logic and reason. But those skills were wasted in the current quagmire that was his life. For too long he had avoided social interaction, and his personal skills were beyond rusty. Again he wished for a glimpse into Sydney's mind. Then he could quit saying things to make her angry.

He sighed and gathered the breakfast dishes. As he straightened the kitchen, he tried to make sense of his conflicting emotions. He realized he could no longer deny his feelings for Sydney, but their recent conversation underscored his original concerns about getting involved with her to begin with. Once again, he found himself ready to admit feelings to a woman who wasn't interested. Maybe he had blamed his vampirism too long. Perhaps the truth was no woman—mortal or vampire—could love him.

While there had been plenty of lovers over the years, few stood out as meaningful relationships. Before Brenna, he had gone through a string of vampire mistresses—sowing his youthful oats. And after Brenna, he had approached his lovers with cynical detachment. An arrangement that suited his female vampire companions just fine.

Now an auburn-haired spitfire had him tied up in knots. He knew she needed time, but his impatience made him edgy. Her reaction to their lovemaking had been genuine. A man wasn't sexually active for three centuries without learning to read a woman's response in bed. But for some reason, he suspected that her reservations stemmed from more than him being a vampire. She had not acted scared of him this morning. Hell, she'd even yelled at him. How many mortals would have the courage to yell at a vampire? He would have smiled at her audacity if he didn't find it so damned frustrating.

But what other reasons could she have to fight her attraction? He knew she was worried about her job, but he couldn't see how pursuing their relationship would hurt her career. No, she was using it as a shield to cover something else. He just had to figure out what.

The phone rang as he loaded the last cup in the dishwasher.

"Logan, darling."

"Hello, Mother," he said, not bothering to hide his lack of enthusiasm.

"I take it from your tone things aren't going well."

"Well she hasn't run away. Yet. But she isn't too thrilled with the situation."

"That's to be expected. Give her some time. I was calling to suggest the three of us have dinner tonight."

"Might be a good idea. After our last conversation we could probably use a referee around here."

"Oh dear, what did you do?"

"Nothing! She just got irrational," he said defensively.

"Logan, please tell me you didn't dictate to the poor girl."

He grimaced. "I suppose I could have been a tad more sensitive, but give me a break. I am doing the best I can here."

"I know you are. At least you didn't try to have a relationship talk with her too," Kira said with a small chuckle.

He flinched but didn't respond.

"Logan, you didn't!" Kira exclaimed. "Didn't I teach you anything about women? Bringing up that subject when she's already feeling confused and overwhelmed is guaranteed to push her away."

"And when exactly did you give me this lesson, oh great relationship master?"

"Don't get sarcastic with me, young man. What did you expect so soon after dropping the vampire bomb on her? The girl has to learn to trust you again before she'll give you her heart."

"You're wrong. She said she wasn't interested in a relationship before she found out I drink blood."

Kira mumbled something that sounded suspiciously like "idiot man."

"You are both so confused right now neither of you knows what you really want. Now promise me you won't broach the relationship issue again until after everything has settled down."

"No problem," Logan said adamantly. He certainly wasn't eager to go through that again.

"Good. I'll be by around seven. I'll bring pizza. It's Syd's favorite."

Logan frowned as he hung up the phone. He didn't know pizza was Syd's favorite food. How could he not know that? Or her favorite color. Or about her family, other than she didn't speak to them. Perhaps he should take advantage of their proximity over the next couple of days to learn about her past. Maybe then he could get to the bottom of her resistance to admitting her feelings.

He smiled. He would give her some space this afternoon, and then he'd subtly work some questions into their conversation after dinner. It seemed fair that she talk about her past after he had to delve into his the night before.

He walked out of the kitchen, on his way to the lab, when the doorbell rang.

"This place is Vampire Central Station," he muttered to himself as he went to answer it.

When he opened the door, Alaric stood on the porch with a grin almost as bright as the afternoon sunshine.

"You're in a good mood," Logan said.

"You're about to be, too, my friend. I finished the clinical tests."

"That's great!" He held up his hand to the high five he knew was coming. Alaric might be a hundred years old, but he acted like a college kid half the time.

"I figured you could use a break and might want to go over the results with me."

He started to nod, but narrowed his eyes instead. "My mother sent you here, didn't she?"

Alaric's smile faded. He quickly held up his hands. "Dude, I promise I was already on my way over when she called on my cell. But she did say you might need a distraction."

Logan eyed his friend suspiciously, knowing he wasn't getting the full story. Alaric lasted five seconds before he caved.

"All right, she also said I needed to keep you out of Sydney's hair for a few hours. Something about giving her time to think," he admitted.

Logan started to respond defensively but stopped himself. It wasn't Alaric's fault his mother was a seven-hundred-year-old busybody. Besides, they did need to discuss the formula.

"Okay, come on in," he said. Alaric let out a relieved breath.

"Man, I thought you were going to let me have it there for a second."

"I would have, but I need an ally around here. I am surrounded by women out to make me crazy."

"Dude," Alaric said, nodding sympathetically.

"Let's get to work," Logan said, suddenly feeling optimistic now that something seemed to be going right.

#

Syd heard the doorbell ring as she stepped out of the shower. Wrapping a plush towel around her body, she went to the bedroom door to listen. She recognized Alaric's voice echoing in the foyer. Hopeful the two men would lock themselves in Logan's lab for the rest of the afternoon, she returned to the bathroom.

As she towel dried her hair, she thought back on the events of the last few days. She would bet money no other museum curator in the history of the profession had ever spied on a client, then made love to him, and then found out he was a vampire all in one night. Hell, she probably was the only woman in the history of women to accomplish all that in one evening.

Leave it to me to fall for the dead guy.

She reminded herself Logan wasn't dead. In fact, according to him, unless someone chopped off his head or stabbed him in the heart, he couldn't die. She giggled, suddenly feeling a little hysterical.

She sat on the toilet lid and began combing her hair. The rhythmic motion calmed her a bit, but her mind still raced.

Logan was immortal. For some reason that fact bothered her more than the blood drinking. Perhaps the fact he was creating a synthetic blood made it less icky. But the immortality? How was a woman supposed to wrap her mind around that one? Even if they could work through everything else, she couldn't accept the idea of growing old while he remained gorgeous. She could just picture him looking hot and strong and young as he helped her maneuver a walker across a street.

She remembered Logan mentioning mortals could be turned into vampires. Her mind screeched to a halt before she would allow herself to entertain the notion. It was one thing for a woman to daydream about marrying a guy. It was something completely different to think about becoming a vampire, not to mention committing herself for eternity to a guy. Even if she felt more connected to Logan than to any other person on earth. Even if touching him felt like coming home.

Lord, next she'd be picking out crystal patterns to use on special occasions. Except while most couples toasted with champagne, they would use blood. *Eeeeew!*

Okay, maybe she wasn't totally over the blood thing—

synthetic or real.

Determined to shake off her crazy thoughts, she went to the bedroom. She rummaged through the bag Kira had packed for her. She thanked her lucky stars Kira went to her apartment instead of one of the men. The woman remembered every essential Syd could possibly need—underwear, matching outfits, hand lotion, makeup, a hair dryer, condoms . . .

Syd held up the box of condoms for inspection. She had bought a small box of condoms earlier in the week—four of which she had used the night before. However, the box in her hand was an economy-size assortment pack. Her eyes widened at the variety contained therein: glow in the dark, flavored, ribbed for her pleasure, lubricated, nonlubricated . . . even the spectrum of colors was mind-boggling.

It appeared Kira's errands had extended beyond going to Syd's apartment. Syd's shock gave way to chuckles. The woman was something else. Obviously, Kira supported the idea of Sydney and Logan being . . . intimate. But how many mothers went so far as to buy enough condoms for an entire army? Sydney was still new to the whole concept of vampire families, but surely even a seven-hundred-year-old vampire would know some boundaries.

Syd guessed she should be shocked or offended, but honestly, the comedic value of the situation was a welcome distraction. She collapsed onto the bed and allowed herself a good laugh. After a few moments, she realized tears of mirth had given way to real sobs. The thought she'd never be able to make a dent in the ridiculously large box with Logan depressed her.

She swiped at the tears on her cheeks, chalking her wild mood swings to hormones. *Sure, hormones*, her mind scoffed. She stood and grabbed the box and stuffed it at the bottom of her bag. No use leaving it around for Logan to find. She grabbed some clothes from the pile on her bed and went back to the bathroom to change. While she dressed, she lectured herself to forget about what could have been and focus on getting through the next few days with her sanity intact.

She debated putting on makeup and doing her hair, but then decided to go with a quick blow-dry and a dab of lip gloss. She pulled on her comfortable faded jeans and a large white button-down shirt. If Logan was forcing her to bum around his house for the next couple of days, she'd be damned if she was going to put any effort into looking good for him.

Now that she was dressed, she looked around for something to do. She wasn't used to inactivity. She usually worked every day, even on the weekend. The museum always had something going on, so even if she wasn't conducting research, she was leading tours or attending events.

She had not taken a vacation since she'd started at the museum. Before that, she was so busy finishing her masters' degrees and doing her student teaching that she never had time for a break. Until now, she had not given much thought to the fact she seemed to do nothing with her life but work.

Her experiences with her family and friends after she broke her engagement with Cole made her wary of trusting anyone. But who could blame her for keeping people at arm's length? When she tried to explain her reasons for breaking the engagement, her own mother called her ungrateful and spoiled. Now she understood that her parents couldn't fathom her desire to marry someone who respected her for her ambitions. Not when their own marriage was essentially one of two strangers living in the same house and showing up to the same social functions. Even her former girlfriends didn't understand. In fact, she recently heard one of her bridesmaids was now engaged to Cole. *Better her than me*, Syd thought.

Despite the trials of the last few years, Syd had mainly felt optimistic about her life. She was proud of her decisions. But recently the lack of companionship got to her more and more. However, she still found herself pulling away when someone tried to get close to her. She was too used to being alone, and too afraid that once she got to know someone they would push her away like her family did. After all, if she couldn't rely on her own family to stand by her, then whom could she trust?

Logan, her mind whispered. She shook her head. Logan had

done nothing but lie to her from the moment they'd met. She understood why he hadn't told her sooner about the vampire thing, but still, if he could hide something like that, what other secrets was he hiding? No, her decision to distance herself emotionally from him was a good one.

She headed downstairs, hoping to find a book to keep her mind occupied. Luckily, she found a note from Logan telling her he'd be in his lab and that Kira was coming over for dinner.

Good. At least we won't be alone tonight.

In the library she scanned the shelves. She grabbed a book by Dan Brown she had wanted to read but never had the time. She was mildly surprised a vampire included best sellers in his book collection but figured even vampires could enjoy a good book.

A cozy leather club chair next to the fireplace beckoned her. She settled in and sighed contentedly as the action of the book swept her in from the first page. She couldn't remember the last time she had read something for pleasure. Maybe this forced vacation would do her some good after all.

#

"As you can see, Lifeblood is compatible with the samples of the elders' blood we tested. Now, we just need to gather our group of test subjects to drink the blood in real life situations and report back. Once that formality is done, we can release it."

Logan smiled. "Great work, Alaric. I know the council will be thrilled with our progress, especially given the delays we've had recently."

"Any news on Raven?" Alaric asked.

Logan shook his head. "Callum will check in if he finds something. The good news is if her goal was to distract us so much we couldn't finish Lifeblood, she failed," Logan said, glad something seemed to be going his way today.

Alaric nodded and began putting the Lifeblood samples he had brought with him into the refrigerator under the counter.

"So, how are things with Sydney?"

Logan sighed. "She seems to be handling the fact we're vampires pretty well. She's not too thrilled with me, however."

Alaric frowned. "What did you do?"

"Why does everyone keep asking me that?"

Alaric chuckled. "Sorry. But you have to admit that sometimes your people skills leave a lot to be desired."

"I talk to people," Logan said defensively.

"You talk to your family and me, Logan. All vampires. Mortals are a different breed. You have to finesse them a bit."

"Easy for you to say. Admit it; you've gotten so used to reading mortal's minds that if suddenly you couldn't, you'd be as clueless as me."

"I guess you're right." Alaric shrugged. "Although I have the advantage because I was mortal. I know how their minds work. You, my friend, are a True Blood. You've never known the concerns mortals face."

"That's true, but Callum doesn't seem to have any problems in that area, and he was born into this too."

"Yes, but you have also spent the last couple hundred years in a lab. Callum has always been more social. Even before Murdoch Biotech was created, he always had a more public role in the family."

Logan frowned. Had he spent too much time with test tubes and not enough being around people? He knew the answer was yes, but honestly, after four hundred years on the planet, he had lost his patience for socializing.

"I suppose I have become a bit of a recluse," he said.

"Hey, man, don't sweat it. You're doing fine. You just need to remember Sydney's different from us. She has mortal concerns that drive her. Your only interaction with women in the last couple of centuries, and that was even limited, was with vampire females. They lack the vulnerability mortal women have. Try to be more sensitive."

"Lord, help me. If you say I have to recite poetry, I am going to gag."

Alaric laughed and playfully punched his friend in the arm. "Nah, you just need to listen to her. Really listen. You can't analyze everything she says using logic. You have to see underneath her words to the subtext."

"What the hell are you talking about? Have you been watching Oprah again?"

"Hey, Oprah rocks! But seriously, women don't always come right out and say what they really mean. You have to read her body language. Watch her when she doesn't know you're looking."

Logan groaned. "Can't you just read her mind for me and report back?"

Alaric slapped Logan on the back. "Sorry, dude. Gotta work through this on your own."

"Traitor," Logan said, knowing he sounded petulant but not caring.

"Consider it a personal enrichment exercise. You're growing."

"That's it. No more Oprah."

"You can't stop me, man. I've got TiVo."

Logan chuckled, but he respected Alaric's opinion. Maybe tonight, when he approached Syd with his questions, he'd try the whole sensitive guy thing. Hell, he couldn't mess up any more than he already had.

#

Syd jerked awake when the doorbell rang. She rubbed her eyes. She vaguely remembered the hero of the book running through the streets of Paris. Apparently, the suspense in the book couldn't compete with her body's need for sleep.

The doorbell rang again. Guessing Logan was still in his lab, she got up and headed for the door. Spying Kira through the peephole, Syd opened the door with a smile.

"I have come bearing pizza," Kira announced. She held up an armload of pizza boxes.

"My savior," Syd responded with a grin.

"I hope you're hungry. I brought enough to feed an army."

"Pizza's my favorite."

"I know," Kira said with a wink. She walked into the foyer, bringing with her the intoxicating aroma of spicy sauce and fresh-baked pizza crust.

This was one time Syd appreciated the woman's skill at mind

reading. Her mouth watered as she followed Kira to the kitchen.

"I assume the boys are in the lab," Kira said.

Syd nodded. Kira placed the boxes on the center island and went to the wall intercom.

"Logan, Alaric, put down those Bunsen burners and get up here. Pizza's getting cold."

She turned from the wall and sent Sydney a conspiratorial smile.

"The doorbell is wired to ring in the lab, but sometimes nothing can coax Logan out. Luckily, Alaric is a fool for pizza, so he'll drag Logan up here."

"How did you know Alaric was here?"

"I called him earlier. He said he was on his way over."

"Oh," said Syd, feeling silly. She assumed Kira had sensed his presence or something.

"Don't feel silly, dear. I can sense him. However, I was telling the truth. We did speak earlier. And to answer your next question, no, vampires cannot read each other's minds. Only mortals'."

Syd didn't know what to say, so she just went to the fridge and grabbed a soda.

"How are you holding up, dear?" Kira asked as she pulled plates from the cabinet.

"Oh, you know," Syd said evasively.

"Yes, dear," Kira said with a sympathetic smile. "I do know. But if you need to talk, I am here for you. I know Logan can be ... well, a man ... so if you need girl talk, I am a good listener."

Syd smiled. She really liked Kira, but she had no idea where she would even begin to talk about her feelings. And she was afraid she felt so comfortable around Kira that once she started she'd never stop. Before she knew it, she'd be asking for love advice from Logan's mother.

"If it would make you feel any better, I could pretend he's not my son while we talk," Kira said.

Syd's head snapped up. *Drat!* She'd gone and thought in front of Kira again. She really needed to stop doing that.

"Uh, would you be offended if I asked you to stop doing that?" Syd asked.

Kira laughed. "Of course not, dear. I apologize if I was being intrusive. I am afraid old habits die hard."

Syd nodded. When she heard footsteps coming down the hall, her heart leapt.

"Chin up," Kira said, her tone sympathetic and commanding at the same time.

Syd smiled gratefully at Kira and decided not to chide the woman for reading her mind again. But as she uncrossed her arms and forced the tension in her neck muscles to relax, she realized it wouldn't take a mind reader to see she was nervous. She walked to the other side of the island from the door just as the two men strode through it.

Alaric, leading the way, was the first to notice Syd.

"Hey, Sydney, how's it hanging?"

She chuckled. "Hi, Alaric. What's new?"

"Oh, you know, trying to stay out of trouble," he responded.

"And failing as usual," Logan joked as he walked up to the island across from her. Syd laughed and looked at Logan. He caught her eye and smiled back.

Alaric cleared his throat, breaking the moment. "So, uh, are we gonna eat?"

Soon everyone was seated with their meals, Sydney across from Logan, thanks to maneuvering from Kira.

"Logan, how is the research coming along?" Kira asked.

"Very well," he responded with a smile. "We're ready to begin the real world tests."

Sydney watched his eyes light up as he discussed his work. She found his dedication admirable. Of course, she had already witnessed his dedication to his family. He might pretend to get annoyed with them, but the love he felt for them was obvious.

Seeing him joke with his family now, she suddenly felt like an outsider. Sometimes she wondered if she would ever have a family like this of her own—people who cared about her work and who wanted to know all about the things that mattered to her. She knew the chance of reconciliation with her family was impossible. The only way she could have that type of relationship was to find a partner and create her own family. She glanced at Logan again as he continued to speak, suddenly sad to her bones that Logan could never be that partner for her.

"Sydney, are you all right, dear?" Kira's asked with concern.

Looking up at three concerned faces, she shook off her thoughts. Two of those faces had *carte blanche* access to her thoughts. She grimaced, hating herself for not being more vigilant around these people.

"Yes, I'm fine," she said, forcing a smile. Kira and Alaric nodded right along with Logan. Syd smiled at them, thankful they didn't call her on her lie.

"You've been awfully quiet," Logan said. "I'm sure this science talk must be boring for you."

"Oh, no, Logan, it wasn't that. I guess I'm just tired," she said quickly.

"That's understandable, dear. Perhaps you should get to bed early," Kira said. "We were just about to leave. Weren't we, Alaric?"

Alaric looked up. "We were?"

Syd bit back a smile as Kira sent the man a pointed look. He looked longingly at the pizza boxes on the counter before sighing. Syd heard a thump under the table. Alaric's head whipped around to look at Kira.

"Um, I mean yes, we were," he said staring Kira down. The pair stood and began clearing the table.

"I guess I'll hit the sack," Syd said and started to stand too.

"No!" Logan suddenly exclaimed, making everyone look at him curiously. "I mean, I thought you and I might enjoy the fall weather on the patio for a while."

Syd looked at him curiously. Why would he suddenly want to spend time together after they had both avoided each other all day?

"You did?"

"Uh, yes," he said, sounding unsure. "It's too nice a night to waste going to bed early."

Syd continued to look at him, her mind furiously trying to

figure out his motives.

"We'll get out of your hair and let you two figure things out," Kira said, dragging Alaric behind her. "Don't bother seeing us out."

Syd glanced at Alaric, who shrugged. Everyone seemed determined to give them some time alone. She turned to see Logan still looking at her. When their eyes met, he raised his right eyebrow in question. He looked so earnest she found it hard to deny him his simple request.

"Okay, fresh air sounds nice actually," she said with a hesitant smile.

He seemed to let out a relieved breath. "Great. I have a bottle of wine we can open. I'll meet you on the patio."

Syd nodded and headed to the French doors that lead from the kitchen to the patio. Outside, she wandered to the edge of the veranda and took a deep breath. The smoky scent of burning leaves and the sharp tang of pine in the air soothed her. The crisp, cloudless night boasted a canopy of twinkling stars and a crescent moon.

After being cooped up all day, the slight chill had an invigorating effect on her. She decided Logan's suggestion was a good one. After their argument earlier, perhaps spending some time relaxing would ease the tension that crackled between them.

She turned when she heard Logan. He carried two glasses and a wine bottle to the table.

"What an amazing night," he said, taking a deep breath as he picked up the corkscrew.

"Yes, fall is my favorite season," she said, accepting the glass he offered.

Now that they'd covered the weather, she had no idea what to talk about. She avoided his gaze as she took her first sip. The smooth, oaky taste of the wine warmed her instantly.

"This is good," she said as she took a seat facing the large backyard.

Logan took a sip from his own glass and sat next to her. For a few moments, they enjoyed the flavor of the wine. Syd wondered what Logan was thinking. He sat twirling the stem of his glass between two fingers as he gazed into the yard beyond the veranda. He seemed so lost in his own thoughts she started when he finally spoke.

"So, you were pretty mad at me this morning, huh?"

CHAPTER FOURTEEN

Smooth, Logan chastised himself as soon as the words left his mouth. He wanted Sydney relaxed and willing to talk. Reminding her of their argument didn't fall into the category of relaxing subjects.

Her soft chuckle helped eased the tension in his shoulders.

"Actually, I've had some time to think about that today, and I want to apologize. You were trying to make the best of the situation," she said.

"Syd, you don't have to do that. You were right. I was being a tad autocratic," he said. "I apologize for my actions."

"And I mine," she responded, stubborn to a fault. "Let's just call a truce, okay?"

He took in her smile and responded with one of his own. Alaric was wrong—this relating to women stuff wasn't so hard after all.

"I'd like that," he said.

Silence descended again for a moment before Syd spoke.

"How long have you known Alaric?"

"Seems like forever." Logan chuckled. "But it's only been

eighty years in reality."

Syd laughed. "Eighty years sounds like a long time to me."

"I guess that's true for a mortal," he said. "But in my case, eighty years goes by like a blink of the eye."

She didn't say anything but looked thoughtful as she took a sip of wine. He watched a single drop glisten on her bottom lip. What he wouldn't give to lick it off for her. He shook himself mentally.

Mentally undressing her probably wasn't on Oprah's list of sensitive behavior.

He cleared his throat, trying to remember what they had been discussing. Luckily, Syd saved him.

"How did you two meet?"

He frowned slightly. He was supposed to be asking the questions here. But maybe if he opened up a little, she would feel more comfortable when he started probing her. He mentally slapped his head at his choice of pun.

Probe her, indeed. Focus, man!

"Callum and I found Alaric in an alley after he was attacked by a rogue vampire in Los Angeles. We were able to save his life, but we were too late to prevent Alaric from being infected with the virus. He was disoriented and violent. We subdued him and then brought him home to help ease him through the transformation. He adjusted quite well to the changes, and we all got along so well that he never left. I realized pretty quickly he had an exceptional mind, and he was eager to help me in the lab."

"Wow, that's amazing. I guess you've been through a lot together," Syd said. "If I didn't know better, I'd think you two were related."

"He's like a brother to Callum and me. I'm sure you've seen my mother treat him like a son, too."

"You know, it's so odd. I never thought vampires would have close-knit families," she said.

"Actually, not all of us have families. I guess it's a lot like mortal families," he said. He hoped his segue was more subtle that it sounded to his own ears.

"Hmmm, I suppose," Syd said.

"What's your family like? You said you don't speak to them." *So much for the subtle approach.*

She took a long gulp of wine. She wouldn't meet his eyes, and her crossed arms clearly said "keep out." He hated to upset her, but he needed to understand what made her tick, even if he had to hit a few nerves to get her to open up. So he waited silently for her response. He'd found over the years most people couldn't stand silence, so they'd start talking just to fill the void in the conversation.

"No, we don't speak anymore," she said. Clearly, she wasn't going to volunteer anything.

"How long has it been since you spoke to them?"

She looked up then. Gone was the at-ease Sydney who suggested a truce. Replaced was a woman with shuttered eyes and a defensive posture.

"I really don't want to talk about them," she said. "I'm tired. I think I am going to go to bed now. Thanks for the wine."

As she stood to leave, Logan scrambled for something to say to make her stay. He stood quickly and gently grasped her arm to halt her retreat.

"Syd, I'm sorry. If you don't want to talk about your family, you don't have to. But please don't leave," he pleaded.

She turned around slowly. When she met his gaze, his heart nearly broke at the sadness he saw there. What had happened with her family? It didn't matter anymore what caused her skittishness about a relationship, although her reaction certainly indicated he had found the source. He just wanted to hold her and prove to her she could trust him.

He tentatively wrapped one arm around her shoulders. She slowly turned into him, as if longing for the contact but not trusting it. He wrapped the other arm around her, reveling in her softness and the subtle vanilla scent he now associated with Sydney. She held stiff for a moment, but relaxed gradually as he stroked her back.

"I'm sorry I upset you," he whispered into her silken hair. He inhaled a breath of her vanilla-scented shampoo.

THE HOT SCOT

"Shh," she said. "I don't want to talk anymore. Just . . . hold me for a minute."

He could tell the request cost her. He suspected Syd wasn't used to appearing this vulnerable in front of anyone. He felt lucky she would choose him to lean on, even if for only a brief moment.

She stirred in his arms. He reluctantly leaned back and tipped up her chin with a finger. He noticed she hadn't let herself go enough to cry, but her eyes glinted with unshed tears.

"You okay?" he asked softly.

She nodded. "Thanks," she said quietly. A slight blush rose to her cheeks, and he suspected their moment of connection was about to be broken.

"Guess I'm hormonal or something," she said.

Yep, the moment was definitely over, he thought. Leave it to Syd to make a joke when things were getting deep. He knew it was a joke because his heightened senses told him she was just about to ovulate. He shook his head. If Syd was upset his family could read her mind, imagine what she'd say if she found out they all could sense her cycle as well.

"That's fine. I shouldn't have pushed," he said. "But if you ever want to talk about it, I'm here for you."

She shifted away from him a bit. He missed the physical connection immediately. "I know. I'm just not ready yet."

He nodded. "If I promise not to be nosy anymore, will you stay out here with me?"

She stifled a yawn. "Honestly, I am really wiped out. I think the wine exaggerated the effects of the week."

He stifled his frustration, knowing he was being selfish. She obviously needed to rest.

"That's fine. I have some work I can do in the lab anyway," he said truthfully.

She glanced around the patio as if stalling for time. "Do you want me to help you clean this up?"

He glanced at the two glasses and bottle and then sent her a wry smile. "Thanks, but I think I can handle it."

Her laugh sounded forced. "Yeah, I guess a big scary

vampire like you can handle a few dishes, huh?"

All humor fled as he turned and looked at her.

"I hope you aren't scared of me," he said, his voice soft with an undertone of intensity.

Her smile faded as she put a hand on his arm. "Oh, I didn't mean it like that."

"Good. I'd rather die than hurt you," he said. He gazed directly into her eyes, trying to convey his sincerity through his pupils. He slowly lifted a hand and brushed a few stray strands of hair behind her ear, using the motion as an excuse to caress her ivory skin.

"I know that, Logan," she whispered. "I trust you with my life. I just can't trust you with my heart."

His hand dropped impotently to his side as she turned and walked away. He felt stunned by her admission. He originally thought she wasn't interested; instead, she was afraid he'd break her heart.

Well, doesn't that beat all? We're both scared of the same thing.

#

Syd woke up the next morning feeling as if she had a hangover and PMS combined—in other words, tired and bitchy. But she knew the intermittent bouts of tossing and turning combined with erotic dreams about Logan were to blame for her current funk.

Of course, her embarrassing display of emotion in front of him didn't help the situation. However, instead of aiming her anger inward, as she probably should do, she decided to blame Logan. After all, if he hadn't suggested the wine to start with, none of that would have happened.

She threw back the covers and grunted at the cheerful sunshine spilling through the open curtains. She mentally added forgetting to close them last night to her list of things that were Logan's fault.

She stalked to the bathroom and frowned at her reflection. The bags under eyes were large enough to store loose change. Her hair looked like a nest of rats had taken over. And worst of all, the Mt. Kilimanjaro of pimples had sprouted on her chin.

She didn't know whether to scream in frustration or just curl up in the fetal position on the floor. Her more rational brain stepped in and suggested a compromise. So, she sat on the toilet seat cover and cried.

She cried for her job, which seemed almost impossible to salvage at this point. She cried for herself because it felt good. She cried for Logan and for things she could never share with him. She even cried for Jorge, who would probably lose his job because of her.

After crying herself dry, she blew her nose and stood in front of the mirror again. The crying jag had done nothing to improve her appearance. She stuck her tongue out at herself, hating the self-pity she couldn't shake.

Steeling her resolve, she decided a shower and some time away from this house was just what the doctor ordered. She didn't look forward to the confrontation with Logan over her decision, but so be it. It was time to take back control of her life.

Armed with a plan, she felt more confident as she dressed. Soon she was ready to face the enemy. Marching out her door and down the stairs in search of Logan, she felt calm and composed. Surely if she presented her case in a rational way, he would understand her concerns. And if he didn't, she'd just call Jorge and get him to sneak her out.

She wandered through the downstairs rooms but found no sign of Logan. She knew he was awake because his bedroom door was open when she passed on her way to the stairs. Deciding he must be in the lab, she headed for the door down the hall from the kitchen.

Unsure of how to proceed since she had never been in his lab, she knocked. When nothing happened, she turned the knob. To her surprise, the door swung open to reveal a set of well-lit carpeted stairs. For some reason, she had pictured the corridor leading to lab as more of a dark, cobweb-filled passageway lit by torches. She chuckled at her silliness as she started down the steps.

At the bottom, she found a small room with a door. At first

glance, it seemed like a normal door, but on closer inspection, she could see it was only painted to look like wood. She placed her hand on it and felt the cold bite of steel beneath her palm. Set in the wall next to the door was a small panel. When she opened it, she whistled low at the keypad with a thumbprint scanner. She knew Logan took his experiments seriously, but seeing this gave her a whole new respect for the importance of his work. She put her ear to the door to listen for any movement on the other side, but of course heard nothing. She bit her lip. Knocking on a reinforced steel door seemed silly. But without another option, she lifted her hand and rapped a couple of times on the panel.

Suddenly, a whoosh of air hit her as the door swung open to reveal Logan wearing an amused grin.

"You make a horrible spy," he said.

"What do you mean?" she asked, sounding defensive to her own ears.

He pointed behind her, and she turned to see a video camera in the upper corner near the stairs.

"I have been watching you since you were in the foyer," he said with a chuckle.

"Hey, you were spying on me," she accused.

"It's my house. I have a right to observe what goes on here. Especially when it involves a woman with a history of snooping," he said with another grin and opened the door to the lab wider. "Welcome to my lab."

She walked past him into the room and her mouth fell open. The lab was larger than her entire apartment. Shelves of microscopes, glass flasks and other paraphernalia she couldn't name lined two walls. Several computers sat under the shelves on wide counters. Papers and other equipment covered a large island in the center of the room. On the far wall sat a massive desk with a black ergonomic chair.

"Well, what do you think?" he asked from behind her.

"Is that a centrifuge?" she asked, pointing to the corner of the room where a large machine stood.

"Yep, this room is a replica of our labs at Murdoch Biotech, only smaller."

"Smaller?" she asked.

"Yes, our labs at the company have five to ten technicians working in them. It's usually just Alaric and me here, so we only have the basics," he explained.

"Holy smokes, I had no idea you had this kind of set up down here."

"It's not something we advertise. A lot of espionage happens in my business. We wouldn't want anyone breaking in to steal our secrets."

"I guess that explains the security," she said. She wandered farther into the room cautiously. She didn't want to break anything important. She couldn't believe this cold room was where he spent his days.

"So, did you need something, or is this just a friendly visit?" he asked, taking a seat on one of the stools next to the island. She walked up and gingerly leaned against the surface.

"Syd, relax. There's nothing in this area you can hurt," he said.

She allowed herself to relax enough to sit on the stool next to him. Now that she was here, her bravado from earlier had fled. Logan wore a white lab coat and seemed perfectly at ease in the sterile environment. She, on the other hand, preferred the colorful and noisy chaos at the museum to the antiseptic feel of this room. She felt her hands grow sweaty and knew she'd get claustrophobic if she had to be there for too long. She decided she'd best say her piece and leave.

"I need to go to the museum today and wondered if Callum had brought my car back yet," she said, trying to sound nonchalant.

Logan's eyes flashed for a moment. Then he calmly said, "I thought we already discussed this."

"We discussed it yesterday. Today I want to go and get some work done," she responded.

"I see," he said and began to rub his chin contemplatively. "Well, to answer your question, yes, Callum brought your car over late last night."

When she started to smile and speak, he held up one hand to stall her.

"However, I must reiterate the dangers of you leaving. Callum reported last night that the Brethren Council has heard that Raven is planning something big. We don't know what it is, but we should not take any chances right now."

"Logan, I know you want to protect me, but I can't neglect my life. I have a job, for now at least, and I need to go in for a couple of hours. Besides, I am going stir crazy here. I need to get away for a little bit," she said.

"Syd, I would be happy to escort you anywhere you want to go," he said reasonably.

She hesitated and avoided his knowing gaze.

"Oh, I see. You need space from me. Is that it?" he asked, sounding hurt.

"Logan, it's not that. I just need to have some time in familiar surroundings to sort through everything," she said.

"I don't know . . ."

She decided she needed a compromise. After all, he wasn't dictating she stay, and he had valid concerns about her safety.

"Okay, how about this? I will promise to be gone no longer than three hours. I'll even check in with you every hour," she suggested.

"Make it two hours and check in every thirty minutes," he countered.

"Logan, that's ridiculous. It will take me an hour just to get to the museum and back. Three hours and you can call me every thirty minutes," she said.

He thought about it for a minute. Syd hated having to haggle for a few hours of free time, but she didn't want to fight with him anymore.

"Deal," he began. She smiled and jumped up. But he held up a hand. "Not so fast. First, I insist you take my car. No offense, but that car of yours couldn't outrun a dog. You'll be faster in the Porsche if something happens. Second, you go straight to the museum and back here. No side trips. Third, I want you to stay near Jorge while you're there. Make sure he knows where you are at all times."

"Okay, I think you're a little desperate if you want Jorge to play protector," Syd said.

"Syd, I'm serious. Raven may sleep during the day, but her minions might be watching this house as we speak. You have to be on guard. If you can't promise me you'll be careful, then I won't let you go."

"Oh no, don't pull that macho alpha-male crap on me, Logan Murdoch. You aren't the boss of me. I am a big girl and can take care of myself," she said, her voice rising.

Logan sighed. "We don't need another argument. Just promise me you'll be safe."

She took a deep breath. "You're right. I'll be back in no time. Don't worry, I promise I'll be careful."

"I still don't like it, but you're right. I have no right to play lord and master here. I just worry about you. If anything happened, I couldn't forgive myself."

Syd stood and rubbed her hands together. "I'll be fine. Now, where are the keys to the Porsche?"

#

Ten minutes later Logan stood on the front porch watching the dust rise behind his car as Syd sped away. He ran his hands though his hair. His gut told him this was a mistake, but he found he was no match for Sydney once she set her mind to something. Actually, she reminded him of the other stubborn female in his life. No wonder his mother and Sydney got along so well.

He turned to go back inside after the car disappeared around the bend. Maybe he'd use the peace and quiet to get some work done. He had some reports to look over and then had to map out the plan for the rollout of Lifeblood.

Who was he kidding? He knew he was going to spend his afternoon waiting by the phone. *Was it too soon to call her?*

CHAPTER FIFTEEN

Syd gunned the engine on the open stretch of road, feeling freer than she had in a long time. Once she was out of Logan's sight, she pulled over and lowered the motorized convertible top. The wind wiped through her hair and made the bright leaves on the roadside swirl through the air like confetti. She cranked up Aerosmith's "Sweet Emotion," which had just come on the local classic rock station. She sang loudly as she drove, leaving her worries behind.

Too soon, she turned into the museum employees' parking lot. Checking her reflection in the rearview mirror, her cheeks blossomed with color. However, her hair looked exactly like one would expect after driving way too fast with the top down. She reached into her purse to grab a brush. When she pulled her hand out she found she had grabbed her cell phone instead. She winced—four missed calls.

Crap. Logan must be frantic.

She hit the Send button. The first ring barely finished before Logan's angry voice blasted from the earpiece.

"Where the hell are you?" he yelled so loudly she had to hold the phone away from her ear.

THE HOT SCOT

"Logan, I'm fine. Besides you called before the thirty minutes we agreed upon."

"Why didn't you answer your phone?" he demanded.

"I had the top down and the radio on. I couldn't hear it," she said defensively.

"Did we or did we not discuss the possibility of you being followed? How are you supposed to notice if you're out taking a joy ride?"

"Believe it or not, it is possible to enjoy oneself and be aware of the surroundings. I kept an eye on the mirrors the whole way here. I'm sorry you were worried, though."

She heard his put-upon sigh clearly through the connection.

"All right, but I want to reiterate that I think this is a really bad idea," he said.

"Taken and noted. Now, I just pulled into the museum, so let me get to work. I'll talk to you in half an hour."

"Fine, but next time I call you better pick up on the first ring," he demanded.

"Aye, aye, captain," she said mockingly and hung up before he reminded her to be careful again. After gathering her bag, she headed to the employees' entrance, making sure to keep an eye out for anyone suspicious. She had no idea what a minion looked like, but she suspected they were a lot like the Goth kids she'd seen hanging out at the mall in their "The Cure" T-shirts and black fingernail polish.

However, she'd recently learned a lot of her assumptions about vampires were dead wrong. With that thought in mind, she made one last survey of the parking lot. When she caught herself eyeing a blue-haired museum volunteer suspiciously, she decided Logan's doomsday attitude was starting to wear off on her.

She took the employee elevator to the third floor, where the staff offices were located. Since it was Monday, the museum was closed to the public. But the staff would be hard at work preparing for a new week of programming.

Syd walked down the corridor toward her office. She waved to a few coworkers and stopped to chat with another curator. It felt great to be back in her element, on familiar ground. She stopped outside her office and looked at Jorge's empty desk. She shook her head. Her whole world had been turned upside down in the last week, but she could always count on Jorge to stay the same. She shrugged, figuring he was either chatting up one of the museum guards or taking a two-hour-long coffee break.

She opened the door to her office and shrieked. Jorge's corresponding shriek echoed off from where he sat on top of her desk barefoot in the half-lotus position.

"What in the hell are you doing in here?" she demanded.

"You gave me a stroke," he said at the same time.

"What?"

"Just when I was about to achieve inner peace, you barge in and throw off my chakras," he accused.

"Jorge, get off my desk. Have you done any actual work since I've been gone, or can your chakras not stand the strain?"

"Duh," he said as he untangled himself. "Of course I've been working. I was just taking my meditation break."

"Meditation break? Since when do you meditate?"

"Since today. I owe it all to my yogi, Fred. He has opened a whole new world to me," he said with a faraway look in his eyes.

"Wait, what kind of yogi is named Fred? And since when do you take yoga?"

"You mock what you do not understand. I started yoga on Saturday. You remember my friend Pierre? You met him at the Christmas party last year. Anyway, he told me about the hot instructor at his yoga studio, so I decided to check him out. Fred is a yoga god. You should see the positions that man can twist his body into . . ."

"Okay, enough. I get the picture."

"No, Syd, I am telling you this is love," Jorge said.

"Well, I am very happy for you and Fred," she said, trying to keep a straight face. She'd missed Jorge.

"Thanks, girl. Hey, what the hell happened to you? I've been calling you for two days. You look like death warmed over," he said.

"Gosh, Jorge, stop it. You're going to make me blush with all the compliments."

"Sorry. But seriously, girl, you look ragged."

"Things have been . . . interesting," she said.

"Oooh, do tell. Oh lord, please tell me those bags under your eyes are the result of playing marathon hide the salami with the Hot Scot all weekend."

Syd laughed but didn't really want to discuss Logan's salami with Jorge. She decided to go with the story Logan gave Stiggler.

"No, nothing as interesting as that. They sent me to Asheville on Saturday night to check into their archives there," she said.

Jorge narrowed his eyes. "Really? And you drove four hours to Asheville on Saturday night and fours hours back last night? Boy, that must have been some speed research you were doing," he said.

She looked away, knowing she was busted. Stiggler might buy anything any the Murdoch's were selling, but Sydney had never been able to get anything by Jorge.

"Okay, look, things have been a little weird over the last couple of days, but I don't want to talk about it," she said.

"Hmm. Given your appearance, I'd say you've been through the wringer. Just tell me one thing, and I'll drop it. Did anyone hurt you?" he asked, suddenly serious.

She smiled at him, grateful for his friendship. Besides the thwarted attack in the alley and some damage to her heart, she hadn't truly been harmed. Therefore, she looked Jorge straight in the eye when she responded. "No one has hurt me. I just have some things to work through."

"All right, I assume this has to do with Logan. I know you don't want to talk about it now, but if you ever do, I'm here okay? And if he ever does hurt you, I'll damage his salami for you," he stated loyally.

"Thanks, Jorge. You're a good friend," she said and hugged him.

"You're a pretty righteous babe yourself," he said and hugged her back.

"Miss Worth, why is it I am constantly finding you throwing yourself at men around here?" Stiggler's grating voice asked from behind Sydney. She slowly turned to face him. "Although in this instance I use the term *man* loosely."

"Mr. Stiggler, I resemble that remark," Jorge said and sent Syd a wink before slinking out of the office.

"Mr. Stiggler," she said, trying to mask the distaste his presence inspired.

"I see you're back from Asheville. I trust you are here because you have wrapped up the Murdoch issue."

"Not exactly. I came in to catch up on some other work. I am afraid I don't have the proof yet," she said.

"What's the hold up, young lady? The police are following leads on this theft even as we speak. By the time they find the portrait, we need to have this matter settled," he said.

"I understand the gravity of the situation. All I can say is I am doing the best I can. In fact, I have neglected all of my other work to focus solely on this case," she said, hoping he'd take the hint and let her get back to her job.

"Yes, don't think I haven't noticed the neglect. I am watching you, Miss Worth. Once this Murdoch fiasco is over, you and I are going to have a long talk about your future at this museum. Or should I say your lack of future?" he said and sneered.

Syd stared at him for a moment, struggling not to take the bait. Her fighting side wanted to get into it with him right then. She had had enough of his crap. But to go there would guarantee she'd be fired before the end of the day. All she could do for the time being was to be professional and appeal to the museum board later on to keep her job.

"Mr. Stiggler, if you have complaints about my performance, I suggest you document them. But for now, I have work to do," she said as calmly as she could.

"I have already begun a file," he said. "Rest assured the board will be receiving a full accounting."

"Until then, I have a job to do. Please excuse me," she said and walked to the door, giving him a not-so-subtle hint to hit the road.

He continued to stare at her in what she guessed he thought was a menacing manner and then finally left. She closed the door firmly behind him, feeling proud of herself for remaining calm. After dealing with vampires, Stiggler was about an intimidating as a kitten.

A knock on the door broke into her thoughts. Hoping Stiggler hadn't come back for round two, she opened it. Jorge stood there with a huge grin.

"Girl, that was awesome! Way to go," he said and held up his hand for a high five. Syd halfheartedly slapped his palm and turned to sit at her desk.

"Why aren't you doing the happy dance? You put the pig in his place," Jorge said, taking a seat in the small chair opposite her.

"I have too much to do to start celebrating yet. Besides, he basically said after I finish the Murdoch case I am going to be unemployed."

"Come on, Syd. There's still hope. You still have the museum board behind you," he said.

"I know. I am just tired of dealing with everything. I think I need a vacation," she said.

"Oooh, girls' trip. We should go to this great little island in the Caribbean that Pierre told me about. Hot guys as far as the eye can see," he said with a dreamy look in his eye.

"First of all, what happened to Fred? And second, I doubt those kind of hot guys would have any interest in me."

"Syd, I'm in love, not dead—I can still look. And as for you, I thought you just needed to relax. What better place to relax than an island where none of the men will be trying to get in your pants?"

Syd laughed. "Maybe you have a point. But first I have to sort through all this mail," she said, gesturing to the huge stack on her desk. Apparently, Jorge had been too busy meditating to do his job.

"Ooh, look at the time. I need a coffee break," he said and stood to leave. "Have fun with that."

Before she could stop him and order him to help, he was gone. Her cell phone rang from her purse, which she had dropped by the door. She bolted out of her chair and grabbed it as it hit ring number three.

"Don't yell. I had to dig through my purse," she said by way of greeting.

Logan's deep laugh filtered through the line. "That's okay. I am calling fifteen minutes later than I said I would. I decided after my last call I was acting like a mother hen."

Syd chuckled back. She felt comforted by his rich voice. "I thought you were going to sprout feathers."

He chuckled again. "So how's it going?"

Syd sighed. "I have used up almost an hour of my allotted three and have gotten no work done. But on the bright side, I had a run-in with Stiggler."

"Do I need to call him?" Logan said, suddenly sounding protective again.

"No, I handled it. For now. I was just about to dive into a week's worth of mail when you called."

"Okay, I'll let you get to it. Listen, it seems silly for me to call you again when you're so busy. Why don't you just give me a ring when you leave?"

"Thanks, sounds like a good plan. I am probably going to just lock my office door for the next hour and a half and focus on work anyway. But I'll call you when I leave," she said.

She hung up the phone after their good-byes feeling slightly better. Odd that the only thing she wanted to do earlier was get away from him, but now she just wanted to get her work done and go home. She paused.

Home?

No, she didn't mean home. She meant Logan's house. And she only wanted to go back there because . . . Well, she didn't know why exactly. Best not to think about it now. She glanced at her watch. She had one hour and fifteen minutes before she had to head out. Time to get cracking.

An hour later, Syd had sorted through her mail, returned eight phone calls, reviewed the plans for an upcoming exhibition, and gotten an update from Jorge on all the museum gossip. After all that she decided she deserved a restroom break. Jorge knew where she was headed. Not because she volunteered the information in the name of caution, but because, being Jorge, he asked.

After doing her business, she went to the sink to wash her hands. The door opened, and Geraldine walked in. The woman paused in midstride when she saw Syd. Her mouth gaped for a second, but she recovered quickly.

"Sydney, I didn't expect to see you here," she said.

"Did you think I used the men's room?" Syd joked.

Geraldine looked confused for a moment, and then her face cleared, indicating she got it.

"No, I meant here at the museum. Mr. Stiggler said you were in Asheville," she said.

"Oh, uh, yes, I just got back and decided to come in and catch up on some work," Syd replied.

"How long are you planning on being here today?" Geraldine asked. Syd frowned at the woman's nosiness. She wondered if she was spying for Stiggler.

"Actually, I am leaving in a little bit," she said.

"Oh, good," Geraldine said, sounding relieved. At Syd's questioning look, she quickly added, "It's just I know you must have a lot of catching up to do since you've been working on that project for the Murdochs."

Syd assumed Geraldine was spying for Stiggler and didn't answer. She watched the woman fidget for a moment.

"If you'll excuse me," Geraldine finally said. "I just remembered I have to make a phone call." She scrambled out the door, leaving a confused Syd behind.

That was weird, Syd thought as she tossed her paper towel into the trash. Syd knew Geraldine was a bit eccentric, but her behavior just then had been downright odd.

As Syd made her way back to her office, Logan's warnings briefly flitted through her brain, but she shrugged them off.

Geraldine was harmless, and Syd's initial hunch was probably right—the woman had just been snooping on Stiggler's behalf. She pushed Geraldine from her mind and concentrated on wrapping up for the day.

Twenty minutes later, Syd turned off her computer and picked up her cell phone.

"Hey," she said when Logan answered. "I am about to leave."

"Are you in the car?"

"No," she said stifling a yawn. "I am heading there now."

"Why don't you call me when you're in the car so I know you made it okay?"

"Logan, I'm fine. What could happen between my office and the car?"

He sighed that long-suffering sigh of his. "Fine, but if you're not here in the next thirty minutes, there will be hell to pay."

Syd chuckled. "Okay, then. That just means I'll have to drive really fast in that hot car of yours."

"Just wear your seat belt," he said, but she heard the smile in his voice.

"Yes, sir. See you in a bit," she said and hung up.

She grabbed her bag and made one last pass through her office to be sure she wasn't forgetting anything. Then she went out to give some last minute instructions to Jorge.

"Headed back to Maison d'Murdoch?" he asked.

"Uh, yeah," she said, hoping he wouldn't grill her.

"Are there a lot of boxes left to go through?" he asked innocently.

She heaved a mental sigh of relief. "Yes, a few. Look, I really need to get going. You can call my cell if anything comes up. I'll check in with you tomorrow."

"Okeydokey, boss lady," he said with a friendly smile.

"Have a good day. Tell Fred I said hi," she said with a wave as she turned to go.

"Will do. Oh, and Syd," he said.

She paused and turned back with her eyebrows raised in question.

"Don't forget to use a condom," he said with an evil grin.

She felt her cheeks heat as she recalled the econo-sized box sitting in her suitcase. Knowing she looked guilty as hell, but not knowing what else to do, she just turned and walked away. Jorge's laughter followed her as she hurried to the elevator.

All the way to her car, she could only think about condoms and Logan and how she was on her way back to his house. She lectured herself that given the current state of affairs, the last thing she needed was to muddy the waters by sleeping with Logan. Again.

The memory of their first encounter nudged its way to the front of her mind. Maybe the fact he was a vampire was to blame for their explosive lovemaking. After all, the same heightened senses and strength that gave him an edge over mortals in everyday life had to translate into bedroom activities as well. She decided that must be the reason he was the best lover she had ever had. Granted, her list of lovers was brief, but he definitely took the cake.

Looking at it that way, she rationalized, maybe using more condoms wasn't such a bad idea. After all, she should take advantage of his special skills while she still had access to them. Because she knew soon she would go back to her life, and he would continue with his. Eventually, she would be old and grey and he would still be beautiful. Who knew? Maybe by then he'd settle down with some vampiress.

She frowned at the thought. If her attraction to Logan was only physical, then why did she feel ill at the thought of him with another woman? After all, it wasn't like she loved him or anything.

Right?

She stewed as she approached the Porsche, which gleamed in the late afternoon sunlight. She reached for the door, but stopped when a red Corvette pulled up alongside her. Geraldine got out of the car and came around to where Syd stood.

"Hi, Geraldine, what's up?" Syd asked, trying to hide her lack of enthusiasm over the woman's interruption.

"Syd, I am so glad I caught you," the older woman huffed,

out of breath.

"Did you need something?" Syd asked.

"Actually, yes," she replied, her eyes darting nervously around the empty parking lot.

"Well," Syd said, wanting to get this conversation over with and leave.

"I need you to come with me," Geraldine said quickly.

"Where?" Syd asked. Feeling uncomfortable, she started to back away.

"I can't tell you, but please Syd, just get in the car," Geraldine pleaded as she took another step toward her. When the woman reached into her purse for something, Syd's instincts went on red alert, and she decided it was time to get out of there.

"Geraldine, I'm sorry but it's been a long day. I really need to get going," Syd said as she started to reach for the car door.

"I really didn't want to do this, but you leave me no choice." Geraldine suddenly pushed a rag in Syd's face and held tight while she struggled. "It would have been so much easier if you had just come along nicely. But no, you had to be difficult about it."

Syd swiped at the woman's hand, but Geraldine had a surprisingly strong grip. She had no time to question why Geraldine would be doing this to her. She tried to hold her breath, but soon she was gasping from the combination of the struggle and fear. The smell of chemicals hit her like a ton of bricks. Suddenly, she felt lightheaded, and her strength seemed to desert her.

After dragging her to the Corvette, Geraldine shoved her into a low seat. Her head lolled to the side, and her eyelids felt heavier by the second. She felt rough hands on her chin as her head was turned.

"Still awake, huh? Jeez, you're stubborn. Don't worry. You'll be out before you know it."

Syd tried to speak, but only managed a small croak. She slowly licked her lips. "Why?" she finally managed to whisper.

"It's nothing personal. I just need you to help me gain

immortality," Geraldine said. "Now we gotta get out of here, so pass out already."

Geraldine closed the door and raced around to the driver's side. Another rag was shoved in Syd's face. She gagged and struggled to fight the dense fog taking over her brain. But her adrenaline and her strength ran out. The world went black.

CHAPTER SIXTEEN

Logan paced in the foyer as he waited for Syd. He glanced at his watch for the seventh time in as many minutes—ten after five. His fingers itched to call her, but he convinced himself that she probably got caught in traffic on the Beltline. He'd give her five more minutes, and then he'd check in.

He paced for two more minutes before giving in and dialing her cell. He cursed when the phone went straight to voice mail.

Trying to remain calm, he hoped she got caught up at work after she phoned. He quickly dialed her office number.

"Sydney Worth's office, Jorge speaking."

"Jorge, it's Logan Murdoch. Is Sydney around?"

"Well, helloooo, Logan. No, Syd left about an hour ago. I thought she was on her way to your house," Jorge said.

"So did I," Logan said, dread pooling in his stomach. "Did she mention needing to make any other stops on her way here?"

"No, she seemed to be in a hurry to get back to your house. But you never know. She could have stopped by her apartment. Why don't you give her a shout there?" Jorge suggested.

"Good idea. Thanks, Jorge," Logan said.

"No problemo. Listen; while I have you on the phone, I feel

it is my duty as Sydney's friend to warn you: If you break her heart, I will personally make your life a living hell."

"Take a number," Logan said and hung up.

He shook his head as he dialed Syd's home number. If he didn't find Syd soon, Jorge's warning would be the least of his worries.

"Dammit," he exclaimed as her home phone switched to voice mail too. He left another message and hung up.

Sydney would know he'd be worried. She wouldn't have run some frivolous errand without calling him. As much as he fought it, he knew he had to face the possibility Raven had gotten to Sydney. He struggled with his rising panic and decided to rally the troops. Even if Raven didn't have Sydney, he might need help trying to track her down.

Then a thought occurred to him, and he dialed the museum again.

"Jorge, it's Logan again. I need a favor. Can you go down to the parking lot and see if there's a black Porsche there?"

"Um, sure. Can I ask why?"

"I can't really get into it now. Can you just call me back after you've checked?"

"Yes, but if this involves Sydney, I expect an explanation when I call back."

"Fine. Please hurry," Logan said and hung up.

He prayed the car wasn't there, but his gut told him the museum was the obvious place for Raven's people to get at Syd. While he waited for Jorge to call back, he called Callum.

"Syd's missing," Logan said without preamble after his brother picked up.

"What? How?" Callum asked, his voice concerned.

"She went to the museum a few hours ago to do some work and never came back. I expected her half an hour ago, and I can't reach her at any of her numbers."

"Raven?"

"That's what my gut tells me. Have you located her hideout yet?"

"Not yet," Callum said, sounding regretful. "She's hidden

herself well this time. Have you called the others?"

"Not yet. You get on the phone and call in every favor until you find that Italian psycho. I'll call Mom and Alaric. Get here as soon as you can, okay?"

"Got it. Logan, don't worry. She probably just needed to run an errand," Callum said.

Logan said good-bye and hung up. He didn't believe the reassurances anymore than Callum did, but he appreciated the effort.

His phone rang.

"Logan, the car you described is still in the parking lot. I also found Syd's purse lying next to it," Jorge said, sounding frantic. "What the hell is going on?"

Logan's stomach fell at the confirmation of his worst fears. Jorge deserved to know at least part of the truth. "I believe she has been kidnapped by the group that stole the painting."

Jorge's horrified gasp came across the line. "We have to call the police!"

"No! We can't have the police involved," Logan said sharply.

"Bullshit. I am going to call them right now," Jorge said. Logan cursed and wished his mind control powers worked over phone lines.

"This group is unpredictable. The police will only get in the way," Logan said. His mind scrambled for a way to get Jorge to listen to him. "Why don't you come over here? My family is on their way over as we speak. Maybe you can help us think of a way to rescue her."

"You're sure you can get her back?" Jorge asked, sounding unsure.

"Jorge, I promise you if going to the police would get her back, I would be on the phone already. I can get her back faster without them. Will you help us?" Logan said.

"I'll be right over," he said and hung up.

Logan heaved a sigh of relief that one catastrophe had been averted. He wasn't worried about Jorge finding out more than he should because the mortal didn't stand a chance against four vampires. They'd simply implant a cover story in Jorge's head and make him take a nap while they rescued her.

Assuming they could find her. He shook off that thought and called his mother and Alaric. Now all he could do was wait.

#

"Wake up!" a female voice commanded, breaking through the haze surrounding Syd's brain. She tried to open her eyes, but they felt gritty, and she had trouble focusing. Her mouth felt wrapped in gauze, and she had a splitting headache. When she attempted to lift her hands to run over her eyes, she discovered she was bound to a ladder-back chair. She pulled at the bindings but only managed to abrade the soft skin of her wrists.

A contemptuous laugh echoed in the room.

"Don't even try it. You'll only wear yourself out."

Syd blinked rapidly, trying to regain focus. After several attempts, her vision cleared. But she blinked again at her first glimpse of the creature before her.

Striking a pose not two feet from her stood a woman who appeared to have raided Elvira's closet.

"Raven?"

"Ah, I see my reputation precedes me," Raven said with a smirk, her blackberry lipstick accentuating the dazzling white of her smile. The silky length of her ebony hair cast her skin with a milky glow. The cat-like green eyes were even more exotic with a thick border of kohl. She wore a skintight black sheath with a plunging V-neck and slit up to her thigh that left little to the imagination.

Down to the black velvet cape and the slight Italian accent, Raven appeared to be the embodiment of the undead femme fatale. Except for the battered combat boots.

"Hey, these boots are comfortable. And I resent the Elvira dig," Raven said, sounding offended.

Syd flinched at the reminder that Raven could read her mind. She shut down her thoughts, not wanting to give the woman ammunition against her.

"Don't bother," Raven said with a casual wave of her hand.

"I already know all I need. Besides, you're such a typical mortal. All of your thoughts are clearly written on your face."

"Why am I here?" Syd demanded.

"Well, duh. You're a pawn in my bid for ultimate power," she said with an evil laugh.

Syd eyed Raven nervously. The woman obviously had a few screws loose.

"Just kidding. Don't look so nervous. I won't bite," Raven said with a laugh.

"Well, you are a vampire, so the thought crossed my mind," Syd replied.

Raven sighed. "Sydney, Sydney, Sydney. I don't bite normal mortals. I only feed off of criminals. Besides, I already ate tonight. I adhere to a strict no-snacking-between-meals rule. Have to watch my girlish figure," she said, patting her flat stomach.

Syd had absolutely no idea what to say to that, so she remained silent.

" I am not going to hurt you. I just need you for a little spell I want to cast to stop Logan," Raven said.

"I won't help you hurt Logan," Syd said, not knowing how she could stop Raven, but needing to put up a brave front.

"I'm not going to hurt him, silly. I am just going to control his mind for a bit so he won't release Lifeblood onto the market."

"But why?" Syd asked.

"I know you've been hanging out with the Murdochs. I am sure they filled your mind with all sorts of nonsense about how they want vampires to assimilate into mortal culture. But I say why should we? We're the superior race. We're faster, stronger, and we're immortal. Your kind should be worshipping us," Raven said, her voice rising with the passion of a zealot.

"You want to take over the mortal race?"

"No. Your kind calls us evil because we feed off of you. But we only do that for survival. I say mortals are more evil. Look at the atrocities you have perpetuated against each other. You use religion or politics or money as justification to commit genocide. Not even counting those cases, look at the corruption rampant in your society. We should aspire to that? Ridiculous. No, mortals should worship us, not the other way around, as the Boredom Council would have it."

Syd didn't want to get into a debate with Raven about the moral decay of society. She focused instead on figuring out Raven's motives. "Then why aren't you going after the Brethren Council instead of Logan?"

"I have been protesting the Brethren's dictates for decades, ever since they outlawed feeding off humans in favor of bagged blood. I mean I understood their reasoning to an extent, but it's a slippery slope. Then they said to take supplements to let you live in the daylight. Now Lifeblood. And there have been a dozen other smaller developments along the way. They are trying to take away our identities, to make us ashamed of the very things that make us different from mortals," she said as she paced.

"But from what Logan said, you are just another species of human," Syd countered.

"Logan is a scientist. He wants to believe there is a scientific explanation for our existence. But many of us don't buy his genetic mutation bunk. I for one believe we were blessed by the goddess Diana, who in her wisdom gave us the need to drink blood and the inability to go in the light as tests."

"Tests?" Syd asked.

"It's not so different from the debate your own race has about evolution versus creationism. I just don't want to lose the magic of our existence in favor of sterilizing it through science."

Syd blinked.

"What, you didn't think I knew big words?"

Syd shook her head.

"Whew, okay. I'll get off my soapbox. Now, I am sure you're wondering how you fit into this plan of mine," Raven said.

Syd nodded. The woman was obviously crazy. She didn't want to say anything that might make her go off again.

"Tsk, tsk," Raven said. "If you're going to insult me, at least have to guts to say it out loud."

Syd blushed. "Sorry."

"That's okay. I know you're brainwashed by your lust for Logan. I don't expect to make you a convert. I just need some of your blood," Raven said.

"*What?*"

"Oh, please, I know you're Logan's soul mate. Even if Geraldine hadn't heard Logan admit he couldn't read your mind, your pathetic lovey-dovey thoughts for him are clear to me," Raven said. "And don't worry about the blood part. I just need a little bit."

Syd stared at Raven in open-mouthed shock. Her mind felt like it was going to explode.

"Wh-what did you say?" she whispered.

"I just need a little blood, just a small prick on your finger should do," Raven said with a dismissive wave of her hand.

"No, the s-soul mate part," Syd said.

"Oh, that. Everyone knows vampires can't read the minds of their soul mates. They say it has something to do with the chemical reaction to each other being so strong it blocks the receptors. Or something. Anyway, as I said, even if I wasn't privy to that little tidbit, I knew the minute I saw into your mind that you're crazy for the guy. It would be kind of sweet if it didn't make me want to puke," Raven said, the soul of sensitivity.

Syd could only stare at the lunatic while her mind struggled with the information. Logan had admitted he couldn't read her mind, but he said he didn't know why. Did he lie about it because he didn't want her to know about the soul mate issue? She shook her head. It didn't matter. They didn't love each other.

"Wait, you didn't know you loved him? Mortals," Raven said with a sigh. "You're so wrapped up in your neurosis you don't even know your own minds."

"I do not love him. I mean I care about him, but there's no way he's my soul mate," Syd said, finally getting her facilities back in order.

"Why not?"

"He's a vampire. My soul mate can't be a vampire," Syd said, her voice rising an octave.

"You can't choose your soul mate. According to my beliefs, everyone's mate was chosen for them before birth. It's easier for vampires to recognize their soul mates because of the mind reading thing, but for mortals it's harder to see sometimes. Regardless, though, you can't mess with the goddess's plan," Raven countered.

Syd still felt like her world had shifted on its axis. Could Raven have been telling the truth about Logan being Sydney's soul mate? She hesitated to believe anything the crazy woman said, but why would she lie about it?

Syd had never given the concept of soul mates much credence. But after everything she had seen and heard over the last week, she decided she couldn't dismiss the concept outright. Whether or not Logan was her soul mate was another issue. And even if he was, what did that mean? Was she supposed to give up her career and become a vampire? The mere thought made her shudder. It was hard enough thinking about Logan as her boyfriend, much less the idea of spending eternity with him. Once she got out of this predicament with Raven, she needed to take a long, hard look at what she wanted. Because right now, she had no idea.

Syd tried to release the tension in her shoulders but it didn't work. She imagined Logan's face in her mind. How had this happened? A little over a week ago, she was an unappreciated curator, and now a crazed vampire wanted to use her blood to hurt Logan, who may or may not be her soul mate.

"Are you done with your internal monologue now?" Raven asked with a raised eyebrow.

"Soul mate or not, I am not going to help you hurt Logan in any way," Syd said.

"Aw, that's sweet—but silly. You can't stop me. Now I just have to wait a few hours because the spell will only work at midnight," Raven said.

Just then, the door to the storeroom opened, and Geraldine

walked in.

"Mistress," she said respectfully and bowed before Raven. When she looked up again, she met Sydney's gaze.

"You," Sydney said, putting all of her hatred into that one word. Geraldine quickly looked away but not before Syd saw the guilt written clearly on her face.

"C'mon Syd, don't blame Geraldine. She was just following orders. Although the homemade chloroform was her own idea. Genius," Raven said, patting the older woman on the arm. "Now, what is it you need, minion?"

"Mistress, I wanted to discuss my performance with you before the ceremony. I was hoping . . . well, I was hoping you might turn me tonight," Geraldine said with downcast eyes.

"Why on earth would I do that?" Raven asked, her tone filled with venom.

Geraldine looked up quickly.

"Well, I, uh—that is, you promised you would turn me once I proved myself," she said. She suddenly seemed to gain some confidence. "After all, I am the one who told you about the painting. I brought Sydney to you when no one else could. I spent an entire night in the cold, spying on Murdoch's home. I even did your laundry. Surely I have done enough to prove myself."

Raven laughed so hard she doubled over and slapped her knee.

"That's great," she said, wiping tears of mirth from her eyes. "Whatever gave you that idea?"

Geraldine frowned. "I am quite serious. During my orientation, you promised you would turn me."

Raven sobered instantly at Geraldine's defiant tone. "Enough, minion! You will never be worthy. To think I would turn you, a pathetic mortal, into a goddess just because you did some laundry and snitched on your coworker is preposterous."

Geraldine's shoulders slumped at Raven's cold words. "But you promised," she tried again, sounding like a whining child.

"Well, I lied. Now be gone from my sight. I can't stand your sniveling any longer."

Raven turned her back on Geraldine. The woman stood rooted to the spot, stunned. She slowly looked up to meet Sydney's eyes. Despite Geraldine's treachery, Sydney felt a measure of sympathy for her. Knowing Geraldine's vanity stemmed from her insecurity about aging, she assumed the woman saw becoming a vampire as the only way to retain what was left of her youthful appearance.

Syd tamped down her pity and mouthed, "Help me!"

"She can't help you, Sydney. She's just pathetic old hag," Raven's steely voice cut through the silence. Tears glistened in Geraldine's eyes just before she hardened her jaw and stormed out.

Syd tried to remain calm as her only means of escape abandoned her. Her only hope now was that Logan could find her before Raven completed the spell.

As Sydney struggled with her fear, Raven sighed and plopped down on a crate. "It's so hard to find good minions these days."

#

Geraldine barely noticed the chill as she stalked into the night with hot tears streaking her face. She knew her eye makeup was ruined but was too pissed off to care. What was the use, anyway? That heartless she-devil had shattered her dreams.

When she thought about all of the time she had wasted running errands for Raven, her blood boiled. She had betrayed Sydney, whom she had always admired, for nothing. Anger was replaced with guilt, which ate at her midsection as she stalked to her car.

She had momentarily considered going back in and telling the other minions about Raven's duplicity, but decided to let those idiots find out for themselves. Most of them were kids anyway. They would have plenty of time to recover once they figured out Raven's duplicity.

She got into her 'Vette and started the engine. The rearview mirror caught her gaze. She looked, really looked at herself for the first time in months. Even with the black streaks from her eye makeup, she looked pretty damn good. What had gotten into her?

She thought back to the beginning of this whole fiasco—her fiftieth birthday. Something snapped in her when she woke up that morning and realized how much of her life was wasted. Having been through two husbands—both of whom she married for money—she'd never relied on her own talents to survive. Her looks had been her only currency. But the men who used to faun over her were now chasing younger women, and suddenly the temporary job she took at the museum to hold on until she found another husband had become a necessity. She couldn't stand the idea that for the next twenty years she might be working for the Marvin Stiggler's of the world.

On that fateful day, instead of going back to school or trying to enrich herself from the inside, she had become obsessed with restoring her appearance.

Briefly she considered plastic surgery, but one of those horrible shows on television that showed what happened during those surgeries had ended that train of thought. She might be vain, but she wasn't a masochist.

It originally seemed Raven appeared in her life by chance. Geraldine had been sitting depressed and desperate at the Chanel makeup counter when Raven approached. It seemed one minute she was discussing the proper application of foundation (upward strokes) with the gorgeous young woman, and the next she was at the warehouse listening to a spiel about gaining eternal life. Later, she realized Raven had used mind control on her, but by then she was sold on the idea of becoming a vampire.

"Stupid fool," Geraldine said to her reflection as she swiped angrily at the black streaks on her cheeks. Her vanity had been her downfall. What was worse, because of her, poor Sydney was a pawn in Raven's scheme and could be in danger.

Taking a deep breath, Geraldine decided she had to do something to make everything right. She had to find Logan.

She put the Corvette in gear and sped toward his house. She

would help him save Sydney. Then she would get to work on fixing her life.

#

Logan struggled to remain calm as he listened to his brother talk on the phone. Callum had reached the end of his list, and no one knew where Raven's hideout was located.

He reminded himself Raven wasn't known for harming innocent mortals and ignored the voice in his head that said her recent behavior hinted at desperation. He itched to get in his car and beat down every door he came across until he found her. But he needed to keep a clear head.

"Logan, I'm sorry. No one knows where she is," Callum said after he hung up and walked over to sit next to Logan.

"Anyone have any other ideas?" Logan asked.

Four sympathetic faces looked back at him.

"This is ridiculous! How can Raven elude us like this?"

"Darling, she doesn't want to be found. You know as well as I do our kind can be very skillful at going to ground when we need to," Kira said.

"Um, what do you mean 'our kind'?" Jorge asked hesitantly from his chair by the fireplace.

"Jorge, darling, you didn't hear that. Why don't you take a nap?" Kira suggested with a wave of her hand. Immediately Jorge's head fell back and his snores filled the room.

Kira sent an amused glance to Logan. "There."

Logan ran his hands through is hair and stood to resume his pacing. "I can't just sit around waiting anymore."

"Son, I know you are worried. We all are. But you can't get yourself too worked up. We'll find her."

The doorbell rang, causing Logan's retort to die on his lips. He stopped pacing and looked around at his companions.

"Are you expecting anyone?" Callum asked as he stood.

"No," Logan said. He began walking to the foyer, followed by his family. He tried to remain calm even as his mind hoped Sydney waited on the other side of the door.

He opened the door to find a woman he had never met standing there. One look at the four people staring at her and the woman took a step back.

"Uh, hi, you don't know me. But I know where Sydney is."

CHAPTER SEVENTEEN

"Who are you? Did Raven send you?" Logan fired at the woman who stood defiantly on his doorstep. Despite the dark smudges under her eyes, she was an attractive woman. Wearing a pink twin set with pearls and black slacks, she didn't look at all like one of Raven's minions.

"My name is Geraldine. I work with Sydney. And no, Raven, definitely didn't send me."

Logan scanned her mind and knew she told the truth. He also noted the woman was sending off some major hatred vibes in relation to Raven's name. He still didn't trust her though. The woman obviously knew Raven. It could be a trap.

"Logan, let her in. I think we should hear her out," Kira said, placing a hand on his arm.

"Fine, but I am warning you. If you lie to us, we'll know immediately. You won't like the consequences," he said.

Geraldine looked at the four vampires staring her down. "I know who you are and what you're capable of. I am here to help Sydney. I owe it to her after what I did."

"You better come in and tell us what's going on," Kira said, reaching around Logan to guide Geraldine into the house.

The three men followed the women into the living room. Logan stood at the mantel while the others sat. He noticed Geraldine ring her hands anxiously as she refused his mother's offer of a drink.

"Okay, where is she?" he impatiently demanded, ignoring his mother's scolding look. He didn't care if he was being rude. The only thing that mattered was getting Syd back unharmed.

"What did you do to Jorge?" Geraldine asked, sending a curious look at Sydney's drooling assistant.

"He insisted on helping us find Sydney. But he doesn't know about us, we so couldn't have him asking questions. He's resting peacefully," Kira explained.

"Makes sense," Geraldine said, seeming to take the information in stride.

"Where's Sydney?" he repeated.

Geraldine took a deep breath. "Raven has her in a warehouse downtown. She is planning on using Sydney's blood for a spell to gain control of Logan's mind."

"What?" Callum asked. "A spell?"

"Yes. Raven got her hands on some ancient book, *Blood Grimoir* she called it, and found a spell to control other vampires' minds. That's why she's been harassing you. She needed the blood of an elder vampire, an image of the vampire whose mind she wants to control, and the blood of his soul mate to complete the spell," Geraldine explained.

"I'll kill her" Kira asked.

"She thinks if she can control Logan she can prevent Lifeblood from hitting the market. As for the soul mate aspect, I spied on Logan and Sydney," she admitted, sending Logan an apologetic look. "I heard him say something about wishing he could read her mind the night they fought in the driveway. I'm so sorry. This is all my fault."

Logan held himself back. Geraldine's admission made him want to punish her for her hand in all of this, but without her they'd never find Raven.

"What is your role in all this?" Callum asked.

"I am—was—one of Raven's minions. She said she would

turn me so I could stay young if I helped her. I didn't know she never intended to keep that promise until after I betrayed Sydney. We have to stop her before she completes the spell."

"That's ridiculous!" Logan exclaimed. "Even Raven isn't idiotic enough to believe a spell can give her control over me. In the old days many believed in its magic and saw it as a kind of bible, but these days how can anyone take it seriously?"

"Logan, you know Raven believes in the old ways. That's the whole reason she fights the advances we have made over the last hundred years. She honestly believes we're gods and that our powers have a magical source," Kira said.

"Her plans really don't matter. We're going to stop her. Even if she doesn't really plan on hurting Sydney, kidnapping her is unforgivable. Sydney must be terrified," Logan said.

"Actually, kidnapping her was my doing. Raven would have settled for some of her blood, but I panicked and kidnapped her." Geraldine cringed as if waiting for Logan to attack her.

He just stared at her.

"I'm so sorry. I was an old fool. You have to go get her and punish Raven. I know she has hurt your family, and she is leading all those kids who follow her like the Pied Piper. They have no idea they're all pawns."

Kira put an arm around Geraldine. "You did the right thing coming here. We'll save her," Kira said.

"Tell us where this warehouse is," Logan said.

"Actually, I was hoping I could show you. I have a few things I want to say to Raven," Geraldine said as she stood. Her resolute stance convinced Logan to take her. His experience with stubborn women told him arguing would only delay the inevitable. Besides, they needed to get moving.

"You can come. But stay out of our way until we say it's safe," Logan said.

"I will," she promised.

"Let's go," Logan said, rallying the troops.

"Uh, Logan, whose car should we take? Raven's spies might be on the look out for any of our cars. Besides, I don't think any of us have enough room for five." Callum said.

He looked at Geraldine for confirmation.

She shook her head. "Corvette."

"Shit," Logan said, tired of the constant complications. "I guess we're going to have to pile into Sydney's Focus."

"Shotgun!" Kira announced and headed out the door.

Logan grabbed the keys from Syd's purse, which Jorge brought with him from the museum. Now that he knew where to find her, he couldn't wait to take her in his arms and keep her safe. Once he had her back, he wasn't sure he'd be able to let her go. Ever.

Soul mate or not, Sydney meant everything to him. Whether it was fate or chemistry that created their connection, he needed her in his life. His panic and longing for her over the last few hours convinced him that no matter what he had to convince her to be with him. It felt as if his own heart was missing with her. Once he had her back safe, they were going to have a long talk.

He shook his head, watching his four companions squeeze into Sydney's small car.

"Mother, quit fighting with Callum over who gets shotgun, and get in the damned car," he said as he got in.

"Logan, I know you're worried about rescuing Syd, but there's no cause to be rude," Kira said as she shoved Callum and dove into the front seat.

Callum glared at her for a moment before folding his tall frame into the backseat. Alaric had the other window seat, and Geraldine was sardined in the middle. If Logan wasn't so worried, he would have laughed.

When he imagined swooping in to rescue Sydney, it seemed a bit more romantic than this. A compact sedan filled with his misfit family was a far cry from swooping in wearing shining armor on a trusty steed. But as long as he got Syd back, he didn't care.

#

"Miss Worth, it's time. Come with me, please," said the Robert Smith look-alike that came to get her. His love of the band The Cure was apparent from his black T-shirt. So pale his skin almost glowed, Syd wondered if he ever went out in the sun.

"Can I ask you a question?" Syd said, stalling for time.

"I guess," he said with a shrug. Syd guessed he wasn't a day over sixteen.

"Why do you want to be a vampire?"

His dull eyes lit up. "It would totally rock. First, I'll, like, never die. Also, no one will be able to beat me up anymore. But the best part is I'll have all the chicks I want. Not that I don't get tons of babes now. But once Raven turns me, no woman will be able to resist me. Especially those snotty cheerleaders at my school."

Syd felt sorry for the guy. Obviously, he saw becoming a vampire as his escape from being a geek.

"And you really believe Raven is going to turn you?"

"Of course. She promised," he said belligerently.

"I'd get that in writing if I were you, kid," she replied.

"Whatever. You gotta come with me now. Can't keep the mistress waiting." He reached down and untied her from the chair. Shaking out her hands, Syd grimaced as pins and needles shot through her fingers. She knew she'd never be able to overpower the kid, especially when he grabbed her arms roughly behind her and guided her forward.

"Listen, what would it take to convince you to let me go? I'll do anything," Syd said in a desperate attempt for freedom.

He paused. "Anything?" he asked with a hopeful note in his voice. Syd immediately caught his train of thought.

"Except sleep with you," she amended.

"Then no deal," he said and shoved her forward again.

"How about money?" she pleaded.

"Huh-uh. My dad owns a bank and stuff," he grumbled.

Deflated, Sydney shuffled her feet to slow their progress. He pushed her out of the storeroom and into the dimly lit, open warehouse area. Crates and palettes littered the walls, and the stale smell of abandon permeated the air. Her eyes scanning the space, Syd stumbled at the scene in the center of the room.

Someone had draped a stack of crates with a length of

crimson velvet. Large pillar candles stood at the corners of the platform and cast an eerie glow around the makeshift altar.

Raven stood next to the platform. In deference to the ceremony, she had changed into blood-red leather pants that clung to her like a second skin. Her black silk halter top made it obvious the woman held no special affinity for bras. The dominatrix-inspired ensemble was completed with a black satin cape and stiletto boots. Syd thought it a strange choice for ceremonial garb, but who was she to question the fashion choices of a lunatic?

"Tsk, tsk, Sydney. After all, are you really in a position to judge fashion?" Raven said, gesturing to Sydney's outfit.

She looked down at her jeans and sneakers. "Hey, it's not like I woke up this morning and thought to myself, 'I might end up a sacrifice in a crazy vampire's blood ceremony tonight, so maybe I should dress up.'"

Raven chuckled. "Don't worry. I have another outfit for you. Here." She handed Syd a garment bag.

"Go behind the crates over there and put these on," Raven demanded.

Syd had no idea what Raven was up to, but she figured anything that delayed the ceremony was better than nothing. At least she thought that until she opened the bag and got a peek at the joke of an outfit Raven wanted her to wear.

"Not just no—hell no," Sydney exclaimed, waving the red leather Princess Leia Return of the Jedi bikini monstrosity in the air.

Raven's laugh echoed in the cavernous room. "Come on Sydney. Where's your adventurous spirit?"

"I left it in my other pants," Syd replied. "There's no way on God's green earth you're getting me in this get up."

Raven squinted her eyes and growled, "Put it on."

"No," Sydney replied, crossing her arms.

Raven sighed. "Pretty please?"

"Huh-uh."

"Damn. Oh well. I just wanted to see if you'd do it. You've got spirit, Sydney. I like that. If you want to wear those frumpy clothes, it's no skin off my nose," she said.

"You are a freak," Sydney said, meaning it.

"Thanks," Raven replied. "Now, it's almost midnight. Time to hop up on the altar."

"Before I do anything, I want to know what's going to happen," Syd said, stalling again.

Raven sighed. "You know, I miss the good old days when mortals jumped to do my bidding. Now you're all 'Why?' and 'What's in it for me?' It's sad really.

"Okay, here's the deal. I need to mix a few drops of your blood with the old fart vamps' blood I stole from Logan. Then I drop that mixture onto the painting while reciting an incantation."

"Hold it. You can't put blood on the painting. It's a valuable piece of art," Syd commanded, cringing at the mere mention of defacing a painting.

Raven strolled over to the painting, which stood on an easel near the makeshift altar.

"This old thing? Please. We both know its real value is sentimental. Once Logan is under my control, he won't care if it has a few stains on it," Raven said.

"Raven, please, why are you doing this? You know as well as I do that if your spell worked, Callum or Alaric could handle the release of Lifeblood."

"Not if I blackmail them," Raven replied in a singsong voice.

Now Sydney was getting angry. Not only did Raven want to take Logan's life's work away from him, she wanted to use him to blackmail his family. Syd might be conflicted over her feelings for Logan, but she cared about the Murdoch family. She couldn't let Raven hurt them.

"I take it back. You're not a freak—you're a bitch," Syd said.

Raven laughed. "Sticks and stones, Sydney. I've been called far worse. Now, if you're done playing the loyal girlfriend, we'll get started."

"No, I won't let you do this!" Syd said and started to back away. She frantically searched the room for an escape route. But minions blocked every exit. She wasn't really intimidated by the gangly crew of misfits, but she knew Raven would catch her before she could make it five feet.

Raven heaved a deep sigh. "Sydney, enough horsing around. Just be a good girl and this will be over quickly. I really don't want to hurt you. But if I have to, I will. I've worked too hard for this for some mortal chick to give me lip."

Syd backed away another step, preparing to sprint for the nearest exit. Raven was on her before she could make it two feet. She flinched, waiting for an attack. But Raven just dragged her back to the platform with a huff.

"Now, sit," Raven commanded.

Seeing no other options, Syd did as she was told.

"Good girl," Raven said. She grabbed a golden goblet from the altar. Into it, she poured the vial of elder vampire blood she had pointed out to Syd earlier. When Raven grabbed a double-edged blade with a black handle from the velvet, Syd immediately tensed. Raven had promised not to harm Syd, but that wicked-looking knife gave her second thoughts.

"Relax," Raven ordered. "This is my Athame. It is for ceremonial purposes only."

Syd watched as Raven walked in a circle around the platform and the painting as she chanted in a low voice.

Syd had never felt so helpless in her life. Fighting Raven was dangerous, and Syd had no idea how to stop a magic spell. She could only pray Logan and his family would get there in time to stop Raven.

Syd glared at Raven as she approached the altar. Reaching beneath the drape, she retrieved a long needle and grasped Sydney's hand.

"This will only hurt for a moment," Raven said as Syd began to struggle. Suddenly she jabbed the tip into the fleshy pad of Syd's middle finger.

"Ouch!" Syd yelped.

"Quit being such a baby. It's just a flesh wound," Raven said. She gently squeezed Syd's finger to coax a few drops out to fall into the goblet.

Raven let go of her hand and swirled the goblet a few times.

"Time for the magic," she said quietly. Syd heard nothing but the sound of her own ragged breathing as Raven approached Logan's portrait.

Standing slowly, Syd began to inch her way toward Raven. A concrete plan eluded her, but she knew there had to be a way to sabotage the ceremony. Raven's trance-like chant covered Sydney's movements.

"*Ex cruor of vetus quod pectus pectoris of amor. Ex is imago of immortalis. Tribuo mihi ops imperium suus mens. Ego queso vos valde dea!*"

Sydney reached for Raven as she raised the goblet. Suddenly a crash reverberated through the room. Raven, startled by the commotion, dropped the goblet on the floor.

"No!" she shrieked as she looked helplessly from the splash of crimson on the concrete to the group of vampires bearing down on her. "You ruined it!"

Syd spun around to see Logan, looking like an avenging angel, speed into the room, followed closely by Callum, Alaric, and Kira. Minions scattered the instant the foursome of powerful vampires broke through the door.

"Back away from the painting, Raven," Logan commanded. Obviously knowing the odds were against her, Raven took a few hasty steps back.

"Hey, Logan, what's new?" she asked nonchalantly.

When Logan reached Sydney, she let out a relieved cry as his strong arms wrapped around her. He pulled her a few feet away from the commotion around the painting.

"Logan, thank God! You stopped her just in time!"

"Are you all right? I swear if she hurt you . . ." he said as his hands traveled over her checking for damage.

"No, I'm fine. I'm fine," she said, tears of relief stinging her eyes as she looked at his beloved face.

He wrapped her in a fierce hug and kissed her forehead. She heard him swallow audibly and looked into his eyes. The wetness she saw in the corners of his eyes shocked her. Her questions were cut off by a loud string of Italian expletives coming from near the painting.

Callum and Alaric each held one of Raven's arms as she struggled against them.

"Raven Coracino, I am taking you into custody on behalf of the Brethren Council for the crimes of mortal abduction, larceny, and disorderly conduct," Callum said.

"Oooh, I love it when two virile vampires manhandle me," she cooed. Then she turned serious. "Boys, is this really necessary? No one got hurt. Ask Sydney. She'll tell you I treated her well."

Syd felt Logan tense as he took a step toward Raven, anger radiating out of every pore.

"She had better not have one scratch on her, or I will personally come after you," he growled.

"Logan," Sydney said and grasped his arm. "I'm fine, really. Just a little scared."

He turned his head to regard her. "That doesn't excuse her actions."

"I know, but let the council handle this. Can we leave now? Please?" She put her hand on his face, trying to soothe the savage expression on his face.

"Just a moment," said Kira.

Syd looked at Kira, who gestured to the doorway. Geraldine stood just inside, waiting to be summoned.

"Geraldine, I believe you have a few words for Raven." Kira said.

Syd watched as the woman squared her shoulders and marched toward Raven. The momentary shock on Raven's face when she saw Geraldine was quickly replaced with disgust.

"You! You lead them here," Raven accused. "How could you?"

"How could I? You have no honor, no loyalty to anyone or anything but yourself. I am ashamed I once wanted to be like you. Luckily, I learned my lesson before it was too late. I only hope that helping those who have been harmed by my stupid vanity will begin to make up for the pain I caused them," she said, stealing a glance at Sydney before returning her accusing glare back to Raven.

"You have no conscience. You use children to do your dirty work. Then you shun them, not caring who you hurt with your misguided plans."

"Please, you are nothing but an aging mortal. How dare you judge me?"

Geraldine sadly shook her head. "Good-bye, Raven. I hope one day you learn a lesson from all of this."

She turned and walked toward Sydney.

"Sydney, I cannot apologize enough for the pain I have caused you," she said sincerely.

"You helped them find me?"

Geraldine nodded. "I was a fool for thinking Raven was the answer to my problems. I am just glad I learned my lesson before it was too late."

Tears formed in the woman's eyes. Syd wanted to stay angry at her for her betrayal, but knew she couldn't blame Geraldine for everything. She knew Geraldine had learned her lesson the hard way and seemed genuinely remorseful.

"Don't come near me with chloroform again, and we'll be fine," Sydney said to break the tension. Everyone but Raven chuckled.

"Agreed. Now, I am going to get out of here and let you guys deal with her," Geraldine said and turned to go.

"Geraldine?" Logan said. She paused and looked back. Logan wrapped an arm around Syd as if needing to touch her to ensure she was really safe. "Thanks."

She smiled, and with a wave, she left. Syd nestled further into the crook of his arm. She looked over to see Kira approach Raven.

"Do you not see the pain you cause? Your selfish actions show you are nothing but a child."

"Whatever." Raven sneered.

"How sad that all of your centuries have not taught you any lessons," Kira retorted.

Raven turned to look at Callum. "Can we go now? If I have to sit through one of her lectures, I might throw up."

Callum nodded. "I called the council on the way over. They were sending a car to pick us up. It should be here by now. Councilman Orpheus is looking forward to having a nice long chat with you."

Raven blanched, making Syd wonder who this Orpheus was and why the mention of his name seemed to cow Raven when nothing else had. But the worry on Raven's face was quickly replaced with defiance.

"Bye, Raven. We'll be sure to have front row seats to your trial," Logan said.

"I'll wear something special just for you, Logan," Raven said and blew him a kiss.

"Let's go," Callum said. He and Alaric pushed Raven into motion.

"I'll go with you," Kira said and followed the trio. She sent Logan and Sydney a smile as she passed.

Once they were alone, Logan turned to Syd. She saw an array of emotions swirling in his deep blue gaze.

"Are you really okay?" he said softly as he caressed her face with one strong palm.

"I really am," she said, turning her face into his touch.

"God, I was so worried. I don't know what we would have done if Geraldine hadn't found us," he said.

"Honestly, I don't believe Raven would have actually hurt me," Sydney said. "She seemed more intent on her crazy scheme to control your mind. I am just glad you got here in time to stop her before she completed it."

"The spell would not have worked, Syd. That book she found it in is useless. Just a compilation of myths and legends," he said, seeming unconcerned.

"But—" she began.

"Syd, it doesn't matter. We stopped her, and you're safe. That is all I care about," he said. He wrapped his arms around her again and kissed her forehead. She couldn't remember the last time she had felt so safe. Then she realized the last time was when they had made love.

The memory triggered heat that began in her belly and

radiated outward. She met his gaze, suddenly longing for more than a chaste kiss on the forehead. Her intent must have been clear because his eyes widened. He leaned in, and she met him halfway. The kiss began softly but quickly intensified as their tongues met. Syd didn't think about the problems they faced. She just focused on his hot mouth and warm body as he tightened his hold. She angled her head to gain better access, feeling the need to absorb him into herself. With his hands on her face, she felt precious and cherished.

He eased back on the kiss slowly. Then finally he pulled away. She slowly opened her eyes. When she saw his protruding fangs, she gasped and started to retreat.

"Don't," he said raggedly. "Please, don't be afraid of me."

She heard the raw pain in his voice and made herself stop. He had proven again and again he wouldn't harm her.

"I'm not. I just wasn't expecting to see . . . Do they always extend when you're . . . excited?"

The side of his mouth quirked up. "Yes."

"Why didn't they prick me when we kissed?" she asked, growing bold enough to take a step toward them.

"Syd, I was born with them. I learned how to work around them over the years," he said with a smile. She thought she detected a hint of relief in his expression. Obviously, he was concerned about her reaction.

"But the other night you were lisping," she said.

"I wasn't expecting to become . . . aroused by our conversation. When they extended I wasn't expecting it and I, uh . . . I bit my tongue," he said sheepishly.

Syd laughed.

"Hey, it hurt!" he said with mock offense.

"Oh, sorry, big bad vampire. I didn't mean to make fun of your serious injury," she joked back.

He laughed with her for a moment. Then he put his arm around her again. "Let's get out of here," he said.

"Yes, I think I have had all the excitement I can stand for one evening. Take me home," she said.

He paused. "You want to go to your apartment?"

She immediately realized her mistake. She felt unsure about how they would proceed and didn't want him to think she considered his home hers.

"No, I meant take me to your home if you don't mind," she said. "That way I can . . . uh . . . get my car and my things."

His frown grew at her words. "Well, your car is here. If you want, I can take you home and send your things to your apartment later."

It was Sydney's turn to frown. She wondered if he was trying to get rid of her. She really didn't want to be alone, but she also didn't want to intrude if he didn't want her around.

"Um, I guess it's okay if that's what you want to do," she said.

He stared at her for a moment. She squirmed inside as she tried to appear nonchalant on the outside.

"Look, Syd, I am not good with this whole male female double-talk thing. Since I can't read your mind, I am having trouble understanding what you really want. So you're going to have to tell me," he said honestly.

She took a deep breath, relieved he wanted to speak plainly but nervous about his reaction.

"Honestly, I don't want to be alone tonight. Can I stay at your place?"

Logan's frown turned into a smile. "Of course. I want you to come back with me, but I thought you wanted to be alone."

Syd laughed, relieved she didn't have to go back to her apartment alone. "Okay, then."

He grabbed her, and he turned toward the door. But then he paused.

"What's wrong?" she asked.

"I forgot the painting. Be right back." He turned around and grabbed the painting off the easel. Syd knew it would have taken two mortal men to carry it, but with Logan's enhanced strength, he lifted it effortlessly.

"I can't believe that after everything we went through to get this thing back, I almost forgot it," he said with a laugh.

"I guess we need to figure out how to handle this with the

museum," she said.

"Let's not worry about that now. We can talk about it later," he said.

She nodded. She was exhausted yet wired at the same time. Putting off worrying about anything else seemed just fine to her. She just wanted to go to Logan's house and relax.

"By the way, I should warn you in advance: Jorge is passed out in my living room," he said as they walked.

CHAPTER EIGHTEEN

"What did you do to Jorge?" she demanded.

"Relax, he's fine," Logan said as he put the painting into the backseat of her car. "He insisted on helping us, but we couldn't have him finding out we're vampires. So Mother made him take a little nap. He should wake up soon," he explained.

He opened the door for her, and she collapsed into the seat with a sigh. Once he had taken his own place in the driver's seat, she glanced over at him.

"Logan, thank you for coming to get me. I know you must have been worried when I didn't show up this afternoon," she said.

He started the car to give himself some time to compose his thoughts. Remembering the hours he had spent not knowing if she was hurt or how to get to her made his stomach clench. He wanted to tell her that he never wanted her out of his sight where he couldn't protect her again. But he knew it was impossible.

"I should have gone with you today," he said gruffly.

"Logan, this isn't your fault. If it's anyone's fault, it's mine for insisting on going and not listening to you," she said.

"No, it's neither of our faults. There was no way either of us could have known Geraldine was involved. We should just put it behind us. Raven is the council's concern now," he said.

Syd sighed. "I hope they're not too harsh on her."

He turned to look at her. "I would think you of all people would want her punished. After all she did kidnap you," he reminded her.

"I know, it's just—Logan, she might be eccentric and misguided, but she wasn't violent. She honestly believes in her cause. She doesn't want your kind to lose your identity in favor of blending into mortal life."

Logan snorted. "Did she brainwash you?"

"No, she didn't. Maybe you two have more in common than you think. You're only interested in the science behind being a vampire, while she focuses on the supernatural aspects. Perhaps there is a middle ground where your approaches can meet."

Logan thought for a moment. Then he shook his head. "I believe in tangible facts. Perhaps if Raven wants us to take her views seriously, she should try to find evidence instead of pulling pranks and attempting to inspire rebellion against the Brethren. Until she does that, I will continue to see as nothing other than a fanatic."

"What do you think the council will do to her?" she asked.

"I honestly don't know. Perhaps they will banish her to an uninhabited area until she learns her lesson," he said. "Then she would be forced to use synthetic blood to survive. At least that's what I'd do. A little poetic justice."

"I think she needs some therapy. She obviously has some issues," Syd said.

Logan laughed. "That'll be the day."

"What? You don't think therapy would help?"

"Sydney, vampires don't see shrinks."

"Well, why not? If mortals have emotional baggage during our short lives, you guys have to have an entire semitruck full."

"That's ridiculous."

"What, Logan, you don't have any issues?"

"No," he said, knowing he was lying but not wanting to

admit any weakness to her.

"Bullsh—," she started but was cut off when Logan's cell phone rang. He shot her an amused glance as he answered. *Saved by the bell*, he thought.

He talked to his mother for a few minutes. When he hung up, he was laughing. Syd raised her eyebrows in question.

"That was my mother. She had Callum drop her off at my house to get her car. She ran inside to check on Jorge while she was there," he said.

"And," Syd asked impatiently when he paused.

"He was awake. She found him in the kitchen eating left over pizza. He seemed a little confused about how he ended up at my house alone after midnight. It seems mother accidentally erased his memory of you being kidnapped when she put him to sleep. So she convinced him we were at my house drinking to celebrate finding the painting. He thinks he passed out and that you and I went to get more alcohol."

Syd laughed. Kira's solution was perfect.

"So where is he now?" she asked.

"Mother was on her way to take him home when she called. He decided he was too drunk to drive," he said and chuckled.

"Well, at least we don't have drive around looking for an open liquor store to prove your mother's story," she joked.

A few minutes later they pulled into Logan's driveway. Logan let them into the house and they went to the kitchen.

"Are you hungry?" he asked.

"I am starved. I haven't eaten since I grabbed a candy bar at the museum for lunch," she said. "Did Jorge leave us any pizza?"

Logan nodded as he pulled the box from the fridge. Syd grabbed some plates and headed to the table. He made sure she had enough and then spoke.

"I need to go take care of something. Will you be all right for a few minutes?"

Syd looked up. "Is everything okay?"

"Yes, I, uh, have to go . . . check on something," he said evasively. He didn't want to admit he hadn't fed in hours. He felt drained and weakened from the day and needed to go grab a couple of bags of blood. Being near Syd when he was this hungry was dangerous. He had already caught himself staring at her neck more than once. He must have been doing it again because she reached up a hand and self-consciously rubbed her neck.

"Logan, it's okay if you need to go feed. I understand," she said.

"You do? I didn't want to upset you," he said.

"Well, if it's a choice between you drinking a bag of blood or biting me, I'd prefer the former," she said with a shaky laugh.

"Syd, even if I was dying from lack of blood, I would never bite you," he said.

She nodded. "I know. You just kept staring at my neck."

He felt himself blush. "Sorry. It's an instinctive response. I'll go take care of it now."

He sent her a reassuring smile and left.

#

Syd drew a shaky breath after he left. She had tried to put on a brave front while he was there, but honestly, the whole feeding thing freaked her out. Logically, she understood he needed blood to survive, and he didn't feed off mortals. But when she saw his gaze return to her neck repeatedly, she got a serious case of the willies.

She took a bite of pizza, hoping the food would calm her. As she ate, she wondered why every time she managed to forget that Logan was a vampire, something happened to make her face the truth again. How could she date a man who drank blood? Could she handle seeing his fangs every time they were intimate? She wasn't sure. She did know that the idea didn't bother her as much as it did when she had first learned he was immortal. But she still wasn't sure.

A few moments later Logan walked in. When she saw him, she couldn't believe the change. When he left the kitchen, he'd looked pale and a little weak. But now he seemed to glow with vitality.

"Feeling better?" she asked.

"Much. How about you?" he asked as he took a seat next to her.

"The pizza hit the spot," she said. She pushed back a bit from the table.

"Do you want to go to bed?" he asked.

She paused, staring at him. Tension hung in the air for a moment before he spoke again.

"I meant are you tired?" he asked, a slight flush staining his cheeks.

"I'm too wired to sleep," she said, hoping he'd take the hint.

"Okay, what do you want to do then?" he asked.

Make love to you.

"I don't know. What do you want to do?" she asked instead.

His gaze turned molten as he took her hand and held it. "Syd, I want to make love to you more than just about anything in the world right now," he replied. Struck mute by his honesty, she merely nodded.

"But," he said, regret clear in his voice. "I think we need to talk."

Syd let out a breath she hadn't realized she'd been holding. Talk about a let down. Here she was ready to throw herself at him, and he wanted to talk? She really didn't like the sound of that.

"Can't we talk later?" she purred, caressing his hand with her thumb.

He took a deep breath. "Sydney, I know that you have been through a lot. And maybe this is the wrong time to have this discussion. But I can't in good conscience take you to my bed again without clearing things up between us."

Damn him for being logical, she thought.

"Oookay, shoot," she said, dreading the conversation to come. She didn't know exactly what he planned to say. However, if he turned down sex to say it, she figured she wouldn't like it.

"I need to know where we stand," he said.

"What do you mean?" she asked, stalling for time.

"I need to know if what is happening between us is more

than just sex to you. The last time I asked you, you practically ran out of the room before answering," he said, staring into her eyes.

She took a deep breath. So much for easing into the conversation. "Logan, I was upset and confused then."

"Yes, but your nonanswer spoke volumes. I don't know if you were protecting yourself or if it is true. And I noticed you didn't answer again just now. So I'll ask one last time: Do you think there is a future for us or not?"

She took her hand back and stood. She stalled by going to the fridge to grab a drink. Her mind worked furiously to come up with an answer. When she came back to the table, she had worked up a good amount of anger at him for putting her on the spot, causing her to lash out at him.

"What does that mean, Logan?" she demanded as she put her soda down with a thud.

He rubbed his hands over his face. "I need to know if you can accept the fact I am a vampire."

She stared at him, dumbfounded by the vulnerability she saw on his face. She was so wrapped up in her own concerns she forgot he had a stake, pardon the pun, in all this too. Logan wasn't at all like the monsters portrayed by Hollywood. He wasn't the eccentric creature of the night Raven aspired to be. Instead, he was a brilliant man who loved his family. She asked herself: Was it the vampirism that held her back? No.

"Logan, I think I could get used to the vampire stuff . . ." she began. He leapt out of his seat and hugged her before she could continue.

"God, I am so relieved," he said and kissed her hard. Syd gently disentangled herself from him and held up a hand.

"Logan, wait. There's more." His smile faded, and he sat back down.

"I might be able to get used to the things that make you a vampire, but there are a few things you neglected to mention the other night," she said.

His brow furrowed. "Such as?"

"Why can't you read my mind?" she demanded.

His jaw dropped. When he recovered he said, "What do you mean?"

"Raven seemed to think you couldn't read my mind because we are soul mates. Did you know that?"

He couldn't meet her eyes. "Yes," he admitted.

"Hmm, that's interesting. Didn't you tell me you had no idea why you couldn't read my mind?"

She didn't wait for him to respond. "You lied to me! Again. First, you lied about the painting, then you lied about being a vampire, and now you lie to me about this soul mate thing. How can I trust you Logan?"

His head whipped up. Every trace of remorse fled his expression. "We've already covered the first two, so let's not drag them into this discussion. As for us being soul mates, I thought it might be a little too much for you to take right after you found out you had slept with a vampire. Besides, at that time I wasn't sure I believed it myself."

"You weren't sure of what?" she asked.

"For years I have heard old wives' tales about soul mates. But I chalked it up to superstitious nonsense. Then when I met you and couldn't read your mind, I was nervous. As a scientist, the very idea of a mystical connection between two people seemed ludicrous."

"And now?"

He walked over and put a hand on her shoulder. "Now it doesn't matter. Fate or not, I believe we *should* be together. I don't know how it happened or why, but I believe in it. In us. I love you, Sydney."

His words hit like an electric shock. The last thing she expected was for him to say . . . what he'd said. She looked in his eyes and saw his emotions bared for her view. She believed he meant . . . what he'd said. But she battled with her own feelings.

If they were really soul mates, then fate had decided their match long before they were born—they had no choice. Sydney's whole adult life was built on the idea that she decided her destiny. Isn't that what she had done when she walked away from her family to pursue her dreams?

If it wasn't fate, then she had to decide if she believed they had enough going for them to make a leap of faith. A leap that involved more sacrifice for her than it did for him.

She turned and walked a few feet away as she struggled with her thoughts. She hugged her arms to herself, and when she spoke, she heard the pain in her own voice.

"What would the future hold for us, Logan?"

He seemed crestfallen that her words were not the ones he wanted to hear. But he recovered enough to say, "Whatever we want."

"Is that true, though? Wouldn't I have to agree to give up my life and become a vampire if I wanted to be with you? Or could you handle being with me for a few decades and watching me grow older each day until I died?"

"You could take some time to get used to the idea of turning. You're still young. There's no hurry," he said reasonably.

"So you wouldn't want to be with me if I didn't become a vampire?"

"Of course I would, but why would you chose that over immortality? You wouldn't have to worry about being sick or injured. You wouldn't even have to work anymore. I have enough money to keep us happy for many centuries," he said.

"So, let me get this straight. You want me to give up my life—the life I have worked so hard to build—to be with you? To lose my identity? What do you lose Logan? What do you have to give up? Nothing. Yet you ask everything of me," her voice rose and pain ate at her insides like acid.

"Sydney, that's not true. You would be gaining a partner, a family. You would live forever. Why are you fighting this? Can't you even admit that you love me too?"

Syd clenched her teeth as tears spilled down her cheeks. She felt torn in two as her mind warred with her heart. In the end, her sense of preservation, honed by her hard-learned lessons in life, won out.

"No," she whispered. "I can't tell you that."

Logan flinched at her words. "Syd, don't do this to us. Just talk to me. We can work it out," he pleaded.

She shook her head. "I need to go."

Reaching for her, he said, "No, we're not done."

Syd backed away, shaking her head. "Don't. Can't you see? It will never work." She turned to go, needing to escape.

"Syd, I love you. Don't run away. We can work through whatever is worrying you," he pleaded again.

She stopped and turned to look at him one last time. "Good-bye, Logan."

Stifling a sob, she ran through the house, not realizing she could never escape the pain she felt because it was inside her. A part of her very being. She didn't stop running until she got to her car. Within seconds she was speeding away from the house. Away from Logan.

A few minutes later she pulled the car over, unable to drive as tears clouded her vision and sobs wracked her body. Minutes felt like hours as she cried herself dry. Finally, she calmed enough to swipe at her eyes and nose with a crumpled tissue from her glove box and a let out a deep, shuddering breath. Feeling calmer, she glanced at the rearview mirror. Part of her was disappointed she didn't see Logan's car bearing down on her. Then she remembered the Porsche was probably still at the museum.

She convinced herself she felt relieved he couldn't follow her. The last thing she wanted was another confrontation with him. Her bruised heart would surely break in two if she had to face him again. When she remembered the devastated expression on Logan's face when she'd said good-bye, more tears threatened to fall. Another swipe with the tissue and a deep breath dammed the flow. Pulling her car back onto the road, she thought the more distance between them right now, the better. Now if she could just convince her heart it was true.

#

As Logan watched her run away, he fought the urge to chase her and make her see that he loved her. See they were made for each other. See that he had not truly lived until she was in his life. But she was past seeing reason. He would not make her stay, so he had to let her go.

How had this happened? He berated himself for trying to talk to her in the first place. Talk about horrible timing. The woman just gotten home from being kidnapped by a lunatic vampire, and he had tried to have a relationship talk with her?

I'm a fool.

But he couldn't blame everything she said on stress. If she loved him, wouldn't she at least be open to talking about a future together? Wouldn't she try to listen to him? But no, she just spouted nonsense about giving up her life.

Obviously, the vampire issue was the real reason for her refusal. After all, she never said she loved him. She only said she wouldn't become a vampire.

He punched the counter, not noticing the pain. He had done it again, ignored his instincts and had his heart pulverized. How could he have believed a mortal woman could love a man like him anyway? He was a freak of nature. He would be better off finding a female vampire who understood him. His bravado failed when his mind reminded him that he didn't want a female vampire, or any other female for that matter—except Sydney.

She doesn't want you, his merciless brain reminded him.

His anger turned into defeat as the truth sunk into his bones. Syd was gone. She didn't love him. He had never minded being a loner until she came into his life. Now he was going to spend eternity tormented by the memory of her—her smile, her bravery, her passion for life.

He felt a tear fall down his cheek. The last time he'd cried was the day his father died. Now he cried because his hopes for a happy future had died.

The phone rang. Racing to answer, he prayed Sydney had come to her senses.

"Sydney," he said, his voice rough with emotion.

"No, dear, it's your mother. What's wrong?"

Logan's shoulders dropped as disappointment crashed down on him.

"I can't talk right now," he said, not caring if he was rude.

"Royce Logan Murdoch, you tell me what is happening right now, or I am coming over," she commanded.

Logan groaned. The last thing he needed was his mommy coming over to fuss over him.

"Let's just say the whole soul mate theory is a load of bullshit," he said.

"Oh my. Darling, what happened? Are you okay?"

"No, I am not okay. I told her I loved her and she ran. I told you from the beginning it wouldn't work. I'm a fool," he said.

"No, you're not. I don't know what happened, but I know that girl loves you as much as you love her. You can't give up," his mother said.

"I already did," he said.

She tsked. "I did not raise my son to be a quitter. Now, did you find the envelope I left for you?"

"What envelope?" he asked suspiciously.

"You'll see. You can thank me later."

Logan sighed and banged his head against the wall next to the phone. What had she done now?

"Good-bye," he said and hung up.

He knew he'd get hell from her later for his rudeness, but right now it was for the best. If he stayed on the phone, he probably would have just taken his anger and frustration out on her.

He just wanted to go to his lab and lose himself in his work. It was all he had left. But first, he had had an envelope to find. Part of him knew exactly what he would find in it. If he was right, his mother might have given him the perfect way to give himself some closure with Sydney.

#

Syd groggily opened one eye as pounding came from somewhere in her apartment. She glanced around with bleary eyes, realizing she had fallen asleep on her couch. Her head ached, and her neck felt stiff. Then she remembered crying on her couch all night until she had finally passed out. She pulled herself up off the couch. Stumbling, she immediately tripped over an empty tissue box and knocked over two empty pints of

Ben and Jerry's New York Super-Fudge Chunk.

"Well, that explains the nausea," she said aloud as she righted the dripping ice cream containers. She looked up when the pounding resumed and realized someone was at the door.

She immediately worried Logan had come to talk but threw out the idea. Why would he bother? She had put the last nail in that coffin the night before.

When she looked through the peephole and saw Kira staring hard at the door, she groaned and considered pretending she wasn't home.

"Sydney, I know you're standing there. Open up," Kira demanded.

Shit! She knew Kira well enough to know the woman would not take lightly to anyone hurting her sons.

"Go away," Syd said, trying to sound brave.

Kira rolled her eyes. "Sydney, dear, please try to focus here. If I wanted to, I could rip the door from its hinges. Or I could just control your mind to get you to open it. However, I am trying to be civil. Open. The. Door."

"Do you promise you aren't here to bite me as punishment for breaking up with Logan?" she asked inanely.

"Don't be ridiculous, dear," came the response.

Syd thought for a moment. Kira didn't look especially angry this morning. In fact, with her pink Chanel suit she looked downright perky.

Syd threw the deadbolt and slowly opened the door.

Kira wrinkled her nose. "Sydney, we really must discuss the concept of a shower. Is that chocolate on your face?"

"Well, excuse me. I was asleep when you started banging on my door. What time is it anyway?" she asked, using the arm of her T-shirt to swipe next to her mouth.

"There's some on your forehead too, dear. It's seven in the morning," Kira said brightly and brushed past Syd.

"Please, come in," Syd said to the woman's back. When she was ignored, she sighed and closed the door.

She trudged into her living room and flinched at the scene she beheld. In addition to the empty ice cream and candybar wrappers, used tissues littered the floor and the couch. Her green chenille throw lay wadded up in the corner of the couch, and the cushions were in total disarray. A discarded jewel case next to the couch indicated she would find her Air Supply CD in the stereo. She flinched as she remembered belting out "I'm All Out of Love" at one point in the wee hours of the morning.

"My, I see we had ourselves a pity party, hmm?" Kira said as she surveyed the disaster.

Syd's temper flared. "Just yell at me and leave. I am in no mood for this."

Kira picked up a tissue with the tips of her perfectly manicured fingers and dropped it on the coffee table before sitting on the couch. She patted the spot next to her.

"Sit down, young lady. You and I are going to have a little chat," she commanded, her expression serious.

CHAPTER NINETEEN

Syd eyed Kira suspiciously. She sure wasn't acting like a woman bent on destroying the woman who broke her son's heart. However, Sydney was no fool. She knew better than to underestimate a seven-hundred-year-old vampire.

"If you don't mind, I think I'll stand," she said defiantly.

"Sit!"

Syd jumped into action, pushing a clump of tissues off the far end of the couch before sitting. She grabbed a cushion and hugged it to her body like a shield.

"That's better. Now, I can tell from the look of you that you are no happier about the state of affairs than Logan," Kira began. Syd flinched inwardly at the sound of his name and gripped the cushion tighter.

"Where is your gumption? You're cowering on the sofa like a scared rabbit. What happened to the Sydney I know?"

"What do you mean?"

"I hate to see you looking so defeated. What I want to know is why you are running away? Are going to let a little thing like a lover's spat intimidate you?"

"A lover's spat? Is that what he said? The pompous ass!"

Syd said, sitting up straighter.

"That's the spirit! But, Logan didn't say that. Those are my words. In fact, Logan didn't say much to me when I talked to him. He actually hung up on me if you can believe it!" she declared with a huff.

"Oh. Well, what on earth made you call it a lover's spat?"

"Because with you youngsters it usually is," Kira said confidently. Syd really couldn't argue with being called "youngster" seeing the woman had 675 years on her.

"Why don't you tell me what happened," Kira said.

"Can't you just read my mind or something?" Syd asked.

Kira chuckled. "I could, dear, but I think you need to talk."

Syd debated with herself for a moment. On one hand, talking to Logan's mother about Logan didn't seem like a good idea. On the other hand, she didn't have anyone else to talk to, except Jorge. She cringed, imagining Jorge's reaction to the entire story. Probably not a good idea.

She looked at Kira, who seemed genuinely interested in listening to Syd's problems. It had been so long since she had had an older woman to talk to. Actually, not that she thought about it, her own mother had never been a very good listener. She always went into denial mode whenever Syd tried to discuss her feelings. Maybe Kira could help her sort through what had happened.

"Okay." Syd took a deep breath and held it. She had no idea where to begin.

"Just start at the beginning," Kira suggested.

"I guess I need to start at the very beginning then. Three years ago, I was engaged to a man named Cole. My family really supported the match because he was a successful lawyer with a bright future. I thought I wanted it too until he started making demands. He wanted me to give up my master's program and be a housewife. He needed me to help him climb the ladder. He said I wouldn't have time to study in between hosting dinner parties and becoming involved in philanthropic causes. At first I went along with it. Then a few weeks before the wedding, I realized that it would mean giving up my identity to help him pursue his goals. I tried to talk to my parents about my concerns, but they didn't want to hear it. I tried to talk to Cole, but he threw a fit.

"The truth is I didn't love him, at least not enough to sacrifice myself for his success. When I broke off the engagement a week before the wedding, it shocked everyone. I understood Cole's anger, but my parents refused to speak to me at all. Even my friends thought I was nuts. But I knew I had to move on. So I put myself through graduate school and then landed the job at the museum," she explained.

"How awful for you. I don't understand how parents can be so unsupportive," Kira said, patting Syd's clenched hand. "But what does this have to do with Logan?"

Syd open her mouth to speak and then closed it. How could Kira not understand the link between her past and Logan?

"Uh, it has everything to do with Logan," Syd said slowly.

"Nonsense. He is nothing like that Cole person," Kira said with a wave of her hand.

Syd leaned forward. "He told me he wanted me to give up everything so I could become a vampire and be with him."

Kira's brow wrinkled. "Really? That doesn't sound like Logan. I know he can be a bit hardheaded, but he would never ask you to give up your career."

"I am telling you he wants me to give my life up to be with him," Syd said, her voice rising.

"Sydney, are you telling me he actually demanded that you quit your job and leave your life behind?"

"He said if I became a vampire I wouldn't have to work," Syd said and sat back.

Instead of taking her side, as Sydney thought she would, Kira laughed. "He said you wouldn't have to, not that you can't!"

Syd started to respond but stopped herself. Had she been so hell-bent on being angry at Logan that she misunderstood his meaning? Now that she thought about it, she realized maybe he had been trying to make the vampire life sound appealing, not giving her an ultimatum.

"But still. I would have to give it up. Wouldn't I?" she asked.

"Of course not, dear. Do you think we all just sit around on our duffs century after century? Think about it. We all have jobs. We would go crazy if we didn't work. Why would you think Logan, of all people, would want a woman who sits around all day doing nothing? He knows how important your job is to you."

"But . . . but how could I work?"

"You get up, get dressed, and go. If you became one of us, you would take the same supplements that allow us to be out in daylight. But you could easily work at the museum."

"But I thought . . . Oh my God," Syd put her hand to her mouth. How could she have been so stupid? She had jumped to conclusions the minute Logan started talking about forever. He didn't expect her to give up her job to be with him. He just wanted to be with her.

She ruthlessly reminded herself there were other issues. Regrouping her thoughts, she launched into another argument. "Even if he didn't make those demands, there are still major issues we can't get past," Syd said, trying to come up with a list.

"Like what, dear?"

"Well, for starters I don't think I can drink blood," Syd said.

"Oh, please. You know very well Logan is about to release synthetic blood to the market. There's no reason he couldn't alter the taste and color for you. You wouldn't even know it was blood," Kira said.

Syd frowned. "Kira, come on."

Kira shrugged. "Well, okay, you might, but I am sure something can be done. However, I think that issue is minor. After all, you know Logan would do anything to make it easy for you."

Syd was grasping at straws, but as Kira rebutted each of her concerns, she felt more and more frantic

"Okay, the soul mate thing," she said. "Logan didn't tell me about that."

"Sydney, what would you have the boy do? Remember, he has feelings too. What would you have done if he came to you early on and declared he was your soul mate?"

"I would have told him he was crazy. But he could have told me later," Syd countered.

"When?"

"I don't know! Look the whole idea freaks me out, okay?"

"Dear, I know it is a bit overwhelming. But you have to view it from another angle. How many people are lucky enough to find their soul mates? You have to look at it as a gift. Don't waste it because you're scared," Kira said. "You have to take your chances even if you're scared as hell. Take it from me, the gamble is worth it."

"How do you know?" Syd asked.

"Because I was lucky enough find my soul mate. And just like you I was a mortal and Logan's father was a vampire," Kira announced. Syd felt her eyes grow wide with shock.

"Only I was much younger than you and lived during a time when science didn't exist like it does today. I was terrified of Cornelius when he told me he was a vampire. But by then, I was already in love with him. Luckily, he was persistent and finally convinced me. The night he turned me is one of my most cherished memories," she said, dabbing at the corners of her eyes.

"But weren't you scared?" Syd asked, enthralled by the story.

"Of course. But Cornelius had prepared me for what was going to happen. And I knew I would do anything to be with him forever."

"Wow," Syd said, awestruck. She couldn't believe Kira had once been in her shoes.

"We had five hundred years together. I won't say they were all easy. We fought all the time, but then we'd have so much fun making up," she said with a teary giggle.

"I can't believe you were mortal too," Syd said.

"It's true. That is why I feel confident telling you these issues you keep creating can be overcome," Kira said.

"I am not creating issues." Syd felt her righteous indignation rear its head.

"Will you at least admit you love him?"

Syd felt her stomach drop and a cold sweat bead her brow.

"Sydney? Dear, you're awfully pale." Kira's brows knit with concern.

Syd's breath became labored. "Hy—hyper—ventilating," she gasped.

"Put your head down," Kira said, pushing Syd's between her knees.

As she concentrated on getting each labored breath in and out, her heart fluttered like a butterfly on speed. In, out. In, out. Finally, after several repetitions, her heart rate slowed, and her breaths came easier.

"There, there, dear. All better now?"

Syd sat up and immediately regretted it. Dizziness washed over her in waves. She felt Kira get up but didn't care as she swallowed to push down the bile rising in her throat. She wanted to curl up in the fetal position and die. A minute later a cold wash cloth pressed against her neck, making the queasiness recede instantly.

"Thanks," she croaked and held the cloth against her forehead. Kira sat back down and waited patiently for Syd to recover. Finally deciding she wasn't going to hurl, she looked sheepishly at Kira.

"Sorry, I don't know what happened there," she explained lamely.

"I do. For some reason you're terrified to admit you love Logan. I think all of these other excuses are just a smoke screen to hide your insecurity," Kira said.

Syd looked at her. "You sound like a psychologist."

"I've taken a few courses. Don't look so shocked," she said when Syd looked over sharply. "I've had a lot of time on my hands."

Syd just stared at her.

"Forget about my degrees. The fact remains you can't move forward until you face your fear. Now, repeat after me: 'I love Logan.'"

Her heart skipped a beat. "I can't!"

"Yes, you can. Take a deep breath and just say it," Kira

instructed.

Syd took a deep belly breath, and then she blurted, "I love Logan?"

Immediately, her heart rate picked up again, only this time it wasn't so bad. In fact, she felt kind of good.

"That's better. Only this time say it, don't ask it."

Another breath. "I love Logan," she said matter-of-factly. Then she smiled as tension lifted from her shoulders.

Breath. "I love Logan!" she shouted. Her happy laughter followed the announcement, and she grabbed Kira for a hug.

"I can't believe it. I do feel better," Syd said as she let Kria go.

Then she started to think about what had just happened. She'd just admitted, at the top of her lungs no less, to Logan's mother that she loved him. She couldn't take it back now. Collapsing onto the couch, she felt dizzy.

"I need to lie down," she said. She laid her head back on the armrest and closed her eyes.

Kira patted her leg. "It's going to be okay, dear."

"But I love him," Syd whimpered.

"Of course you do," Kira said gaily. "Only I forgot to tell you that being in love can sometimes make you feel like you have the flu."

"I thought that was pregnancy," Syd said.

"That, too. But with love you get to keep having sex," Kira said matter-of-factly. "Speaking of pregnancy . . ."

Syd held her hand up. "Don't even go there!"

"Sorry. I suppose it's a bit premature."

"Definitely. By the way, I forgot to talk to you about the gigantic box of condoms."

"You don't have to thank me. I have a source if you are running low," she said. Syd peeked open one eye to see if the woman was serious. Kira laughed. "Gotcha."

Syd couldn't help but smile. Even if Kira had forced her to admit something she didn't want to face, she was forever grateful for the woman's help.

"So what do I do now?"

"We mustn't be hasty. You only just admitted to loving him. Give yourself a few hours to get used to the idea. Then you can go over to his house and grovel."

"A few hours! Kira, we're talking a major commitment here. And not the fifty-year kind either—the eternity kind. Besides, I can't grovel. I doubt he'd even talk to me after the way I acted last night. When I think about the look on his face when I . . ." She cut herself off as tears threatened to fall.

"Oh dear. Please don't cry, because then I'll cry," Kira sniffed.

"I can't h-help it. I was so m-mean," Syd said, unable to stop her sobs.

"Sydney, you have to understand something about Logan. He should really be telling you this, but I think you need to know. When Logan was younger, around his one-hundredth birthday I think, he thought himself in love with a young woman named Brenna. She was a vain, spoiled young lady. Unfortunately, Logan didn't see that. He was infatuated with her as only the young can be. Anyway, he decided to tell her the truth. She called him a monster and ran as fast and far as she could from him," Kira said.

Jealously churned in Syd's gut.

"Oh, don't worry dear. You're much prettier—and frankly, smarter—than that little hussy. Besides, I know the feelings Logan has for you are real. His foolish obsession with Brenna was nothing more than puppy love.

"But I do fear your actions might bring up some repressed feelings from the experience for Logan."

Syd sat up quickly. "Oh my God. He's never going to listen to me now!"

"Well, I'll admit it won't be easy. But don't lose faith. You have come too far to turn back now. Where's your backbone?"

"But he must hate me now," Syd said, her heart breaking at the thought of his pain.

"I doubt he hates you, but it will definitely take some fast talking on your part to convince him to hear you out. He pretty much withdrew after the Brenna debacle."

"What am I going to do?"

Kira looked at her watch. "It's almost nine. I suggest you get dressed and go to work."

"Crap! It's that late already? I do need to go. But I meant what should I do about Logan?"

"I have a feeling if you go to work the answer will come to you," Kira said with an enigmatic smile. At Syd's curious look, she quickly explained. "I mean perhaps focusing on something else will help you see things more clearly."

"I guess so. Kira, I don't know how to thank you for listening to me. I can't believe I have been such a fool," Syd said.

"We have all made ourselves fools for love at one time or another. Now, don't worry so much. Things will work out. Give yourself some time to think about what we discussed," Kira said.

She enveloped Syd in a hug. The maternal gesture comforted Sydney more than she thought possible.

Kira leaned back with her arms on Syd's shoulders. "I know this is early, but I want you to know I would be very proud to have you as a member of my family."

Syd couldn't control the rush of emotion Kira's words caused. It had been so long since she had felt like she had anyone to lean on, and now this ancient vampire was offering her the one thing she had longed for her whole life—a family to love and support her.

She threw herself back into Kira's arms as tears started to fall again. Soft hands stroked her hair as she cried. After a few moments, the sobs subsided into soft hiccups. Syd looked up, a blush spreading over her cheeks.

"I'm sorry. I have cried more in the last two days than I have in my whole life."

"You can't be strong all the time. Perhaps it's time you learned that sometimes you have to share your burden before it weighs you down. Now, go take a shower. You still have chocolate on your forehead."

Syd let out a watery laugh. After another hug, Kira left.

Leaning against the closed door, Syd took a deep breath. All she wanted to do was collapse back onto the couch and sleep off the exhaustion caused by the emotional burden of the last few days. Instead, she pushed herself away from the door and marched to the bathroom. She had no more time to dwell on her love life.

She had to see if she still had a job.

#

"Hey, Jorge." Syd strolled up to his desk with a concerned frown. "You don't look so good."

"Shhh. Stop shouting." He winced and put a hand to his forehead. Dark sunglasses shielded his eyes and his normally olive skin was pale.

"Are you okay?" she asked.

"No. I don't know what we were drinking last night, but I have never felt this hungover in my life," he groaned.

Confused, Syd stared at him until she remembered Kira's quick thinking last night.

"Oh yeah, uh, you were really tossing back that . . . uh . . . tequila," she said.

"Tequila? Well, that explains it. I didn't get belligerent did I? Tequila tends to make me bitchy."

"You were fine," she said, not wanting him to worry.

"You must have felt like crap this morning too," he said sympathetically.

"Why do you say that?"

He lowered his glasses to get a better look at her. "Well, for starters your eyes are bloodshot, and you have some serious dark circles going on there."

Syd fought her urge to grab her own sunglasses even though she was relieved to have the handy excuse of a hangover to explain the telltale results of her recent crying spells.

"Woo, boy, was I ever hungover. Yep, had to take four aspirin before I even got out of bed."

"I hear ya, sister. Explains why you're late, too. Speaking of which, Stiggler came by about thirty minutes ago looking for you. He seemed agitated. You better call him," Jorge said.

Syd felt her stomach drop. On her way to work, she'd tried to think of a way to handle the painting situation. Stiggler obviously couldn't find out about Logan being a vampire. But she and Logan had never discussed their next steps before The Confrontation, which had left her with no idea what he wanted to do. Her only hope was that Stiggler wanted to see her for a different reason, giving her time to call Kira and figure out how to handle things.

"I'd better go call him and find out what he wants," she said unenthusiastically to Jorge.

He took a gulp of coffee and then dashed all her hopes. "He said something about the Murdoch painting."

"Crap."

On top of losing the love of her life, she was about to lose her job. Deciding to get it over with, she turned to go into her office. Not wanting to waste any time if Stiggler was already on the warpath, she picked up the phone.

"Marvin Stiggler's office, Geraldine speaking."

"Geraldine, thank God."

"Sydney?" the older woman whispered. "How are you?"

"I've been better. I hear Stiggler's looking for me."

"He is. I think you'd better get to the conference room ASAP."

"That bad, huh?"

"You'll see." Syd frowned when she detected a smile in Geraldine's voice. What was she so happy about, anyway? "I'll tell Mr. Stiggler you're on your way."

Syd hung up and took a deep breath. Everything she had worked for came down to this. Stiggler had given her an assignment, and she had failed. She'd known all along that he only wanted her to help the Murdochs so they would give a large donation to the museum.

It didn't make her feel any better that Stiggler would have found a way to get rid of her even if she'd succeeded. Although, now that she thought about it, it seemed odd she didn't feel more devastated about losing her job. But she decided it paled in comparison to what she had already lost. After all, she could find another job, but she could never find another Logan.

She didn't miss the irony that she had accused Logan of wanting her to give up the job she was about to lose anyway. All she could do was march in there, receive her walking papers, and then try to sort through the mess her life had become.

She exited her office and told Jorge where she was going.

"Wait," he said as he stood, followed by a groan. "Geraldine just called and said I needed to get up there too."

"Oh no, Jorge. He's going to can both of us," Syd said, feeling guilty that her failure would impact her friend as well.

"Syd, don't worry about it. If Stiggler lets us go, we'll find a way to recover. Besides, I have been thinking about leaving anyway," he admitted.

Syd gasped. "What? You were going to leave?"

"Nah, so far it was just a thought. I couldn't leave you high and dry. Then you'd have to get an efficient assistant who wouldn't torture you."

Syd smiled and hugged her friend. "Thanks, Jorge. For everything. You're a good friend."

"Now, let's go see what's up. The suspense is killing me." He wrapped an arm around her shoulders, and together they made the trek to the conference room on the other side of the building. Syd felt better knowing she didn't have to face Stiggler alone. No matter what happened, she and Jorge would be fine.

When they neared the conference room, a beaming Geraldine met them. Syd frowned and slowed her pace. She wondered again what made the woman look so happy. Then a thought occurred to her. Had Geraldine not really changed her stripes? Was her upset over Raven's refusal to turn her just a ruse?

"Hi, guys. Mr. Stiggler is waiting for you."

"What's up with the Mona Lisa smile?" Jorge asked.

"Who me? Was I smiling?" she asked. "Don't look so worried, you guys. I think you'll be pleasantly surprised.

"Syd, I just wanted to apologize again. I hope . . . well, I hope we can be friends."

Geraldine's smile seemed too genuine. Syd pushed away her

suspicious thoughts.

"I'd like that," she said with a tentative smile. Who would have thought a woman who had kidnapped her the day before would now be her friend? She shook her head wryly. The surprises just kept coming.

"Okay, you two, scoot. He's about to blow a gasket," Geraldine said, opening the door to the conference room.

Syd took a breath. Time to face the music. She lifted her head and squared her shoulders before confidently strolling into the room. She got about two feet before she stopped abruptly and her jaw dropped open. Jorge ran into her from behind, throwing her forward.

"Oops, sorry, Syd," he said. But she didn't hear him. She was too busy staring. At the far end of the large table an easel stood. Propped on it was the portrait of Royce Logan Murdoch. Stiggler stood next to the easel grinning from ear to ear.

"Wh—what's going on?" she stuttered. How had the panting ended up back at the museum? And what did its presence mean? Her mind raced to figure it out but before she could, Stiggler spoke.

"Sydney, it seems you have been very busy these last couple of days," he began. "Imagine my surprise when I walked into my office this morning and found this painting waiting for me. Next to it was this package." He lifted a large manilla envelope off the table.

"Care to explain yourself?" he asked, his smile taking the edge off his serious tone.

"I . . . uh . . . well—" she began. Luckily, Stiggler seemed so excited that he cut her off.

"In the package was a letter from Logan Murdoch addressed to me. It seems not only were you instrumental in saving the painting from the dangerous group of extremists that stole it, but you also found the letter which proves the authenticity of the Murdoch's claim," he said.

"Well, sir, I don't know what to say."

"You go, girl," Jorge said proudly from his spot beside her. She sent him a lame smile. She had absolutely no idea what was going on.

"Yes, well done. But I am not finished. Mr. Murdoch also included a generous donation to thank the museum for all of its support."

Syd's jaw dropped as she realized what was happening. Despite her cruel rejection, Logan had saved her job. Her mind scrambled to process what that meant.

"Furthermore," Stiggler cut into her thoughts. "He sent a notarized letter passing ownership of the painting to you."

CHAPTER TWENTY

"**W**hat?" Syd shrieked, suddenly feeling faint.

"Yes, Miss Worth. For some reason Mr. Murdoch felt you should be the rightful owner of the painting, not the museum. While I can't say I understand his thinking, I am willing to allow you to sign ownership back to the museum. In return, I would like to offer you a raise and a promotion," he said.

"Promotion?" Syd asked, dumbfounded.

"Yes, your new title will be curatorial director. The only level higher in this museum is director," he chuckled. "Obviously that position is already filled."

Syd's shock turned to suspicion, knowing Stiggler was trying to buy her off. Then it hit her: Logan had not only saved her job, he'd also sacrificed the painting—his last tie to his father—knowing it would give her bargaining power with Stiggler. Normally, she would have sold her soul for the chance to be curatorial director. With the title, she would oversee all of the curators and exhibitions at the museum.

But she knew she couldn't take it. No amount of money or power could make up for working with Marvin Stiggler. Besides, Logan's sacrifice proved that he still loved her. She still had a chance.

Suddenly giddy, she looked at Stiggler.

"Marvin," she began, ignoring his shocked expression at her use of his given name. "You can take that raise and the promotion and shove it."

Eyes bulging, his mouth worked like a catfish out of water. "Excuse me?"

"You heard me. I am tired of dealing with your crap. You can find yourself another curator to push around because this one is walking out the door."

She ignored his outraged noises and walked past him to lift the painting off the easel. Unfortunately, her dramatic exit was hampered by the weight of the piece.

"Hold on Syd. I'll help you," Jorge said as he walked toward her, a brilliant smile on his face.

Then she realized her decision to quit meant Jorge was out of a job too.

"Jorge, I'm sorry," she said when he reached her.

He shrugged. "No sweat, boss. With you gone, there's no reason for me to stay. Now let's get out of here."

"Hold it. If you think I am going to let you walk out of here with that painting, you're crazy," Stiggler growled as he grabbed Syd's arm.

She shrugged off his grasp. "Oh yeah?" She grabbed Logan's letter and waved it in Stiggler's face.

"I have a piece of paper here that says you can't stop me," she said triumphantly.

He paused. "Miss Worth, please, let's be reasonable here. There's no reason for you to leave. I promise I will try to be nicer."

Syd and Jorge snorted at the same time. Then they lifted the painting and marched out of the room. Stiggler tried to follow them, alternating threats with pleas. But Geraldine stopped him at the door.

"Mr. Stiggler, I quit too."

"Please, Miss Stern, can't you see I'm busy?"

"Don't worry. Once the museum board receives the letter I

sent them this morning outlining all of the times you misallocated museum funds for your golfing trips, you'll have all the time in the world."

Stiggler's eyes narrowed. "You wouldn't."

"Watch me," she said, getting in his face. "Now, I suggest you quit your caterwauling and start packing your office."

She turned and ran to catch up with Jorge and Sydney, who held the door of the elevator open for her. As the car began its descent, silence reigned for a few stunned seconds. Then all of a sudden Geraldine giggled. Syd and Jorge soon joined her, and the giggles turned into outright guffaws.

"Did you see the look on his face?" Geraldine said as she wiped the tears of mirth from her cheeks.

"So, now what?" Jorge asked once their laughter had subsided into sporadic chuckles.

As she laughed, Syd looked from one friend to the other, feeling freer than she had in a long time. She finally understood what her life had been missing for the last few years.

Joy.

She was so caught up in trying to prove herself that she had forgotten to live. Her fear of rejection had prevented her from getting close to anyone, which is the reason she'd fought so hard against her attraction to Logan. She had rejected him last night because deep down she was terrified he would eventually turn away from her unless she changed to please him. But Kira was right—Logan wasn't Cole.

No matter what it took, she had to get to Logan and make him understand she wasn't like Brenna.

She needed to tell him she loved him. Even if he turned her away. Even if she had to spend the rest of her life proving her love to him. She just needed a plan to get him to listen to her. And she knew just who to call for help.

The elevator reached the basement and the happy trio exited the building.

"So, what now?" Jorge asked as they walked into late morning sunshine.

"Lunch? I don't know about you guys, but I could sure use a

margarita," Geraldine said.

Jorge groaned. "No alcohol for me, thanks. But I could definitely use some greasy Mexican food. What do you say, Syd?"

She opened the door to her backseat and they carefully loaded the painting in. "No thanks, guys. I need to deal with some stuff," she said gesturing to the painting.

Jorge looked at her with a probing gaze. "Tell Logan we said hi."

Syd sent him a sad smile. "I will." *If he ever speaks to me again.*

"Well, we'll be at Herrera's if you want to meet up with us," Geraldine said. "Come on Jorge, I have a business proposition I want to discuss with you."

The pair turned and walked away, leaving Syd staring after them fondly. She had no idea what Geraldine's idea was, but Syd thought the two of them would probably make a good team at whatever they decided to do.

She got into her car and grabbed her phone from her purse.

"Kira, it's me. I've had enough time to think. It's time for me to make my move."

#

Logan woke up against his will at four in the afternoon. His head pounded, and all he wanted was to throw a pillow over his eyes and go back to sleep. But hunger clawed at his stomach.

After arranging for a courier to deliver the painting to the museum last night, he had gone to his lab. But his work hadn't offered the solace he had hoped to find. His mind kept going over the conversation with Syd, trying to figure out what he could have done differently. But the answers hadn't come. He only hoped signing the painting over to her saved her job and gave her leverage against that creep she worked for. If nothing else, he didn't want her involvement with him to ruin her career—the one thing she cared about most.

He sat up and swung his legs over the side of the bed. Scrubbing his hands over his stubbled cheeks, he tried to wake up. Exhaustion, both mental and physical, weighed down his limbs.

Normally he bounded out of bed, grabbed some blood, and was ready to face the day. But today he could barely manage to drag himself upright, much less bound anywhere.

Even the imminent release of Lifeblood didn't excite him. It seemed Sydney had walked away with not only his heart, but also his motivation. Before she entered his life, he rarely thought about settling down. He always assumed he would but figured he had plenty of time—he was immortal after all.

But with Syd gone, he realized she'd taken away his chance at having the kind of family he grew up in. One where the parents were madly in love and devoted to their children. Sure, he could find someone else, but his chance at the kind of love his parents had walked out the door yesterday.

He forced himself to stand and went into the bathroom. After he had downed a couple of bags of nourishing blood, he showered. Feeling slightly more alive, he threw on a pair of ragged jeans and a T-shirt.

He trudged downstairs and wandered around looking for something to do. He didn't feel any desire to work, and he definitely didn't want to talk to anyone. As if on cue the phone rang. Since he happened to be next to it anyway, he answered it.

"Logan, darling, it's Mother."

He groaned. The last thing he needed was one of his mother's lectures about adversity only making him stronger. Or the dreaded "getting back up on the horse" soliloquy.

"Darling?" she said when he didn't answer.

"Yes, Mother," he said, trying to keep his impatience of out of his tone. Betraying any sign of emotion would only egg her on.

"Logan, I know you are feeling hurt right now, so I am not going to lecture you about the evils of hanging up on your own mother."

Thank God for small favors.

"However," she said, obviously not meaning to let him off the hook completely. "I cannot allow you to waste away in that house of yours alone. You're coming over here."

"Where?" he asked warily.

"To my house. I have decided to make you dinner."

"I'm not really up to company right now. I think I'll just order in."

She tsked. "Absolutely not. You need a home-cooked meal. It is just the thing to mend a broken heart."

"Really. I'm fine," he said through gritted teeth.

"Humph. Fine. I'll just come over there," she said.

Logan panicked. The last thing he wanted was his sanctuary invaded.

"Actually, that won't work either. I . . .uh . . .am going out of town."

"Going out of town? Where on earth are you going?"

Suddenly, Logan had a brain flash. What started out as an excuse to avoid his mother turned into a plan. "I'm heading to Asheville tonight. I need to get away for a few days to get my head straight."

"No!" she exclaimed. "I mean, darling, I know you're hurting, but running away from your problems isn't wise. Give it a couple of days."

"No, I'm going tonight. I think a change of scenery will help me sort through things. Figure out a plan," he said, warming up to the idea.

"Well, darling, if that's what you need, then I suppose I understand. When are you planning on leaving?" she asked.

"I need to pack, so I guess I'll head out in an hour or so."

"Hmmm. Gotta go, love you, darling!" Kira said quickly and hung up.

Logan looked at the phone for a moment, trying to understand his mother's odd behavior. Shaking his head, he hung up the receiver, knowing he'd never figure out women. Luckily, he wouldn't have to deal with any members of the fairer sex in Asheville.

Just me and the mountains, he thought as he ran upstairs to pack.

#

Forty-five minutes later, Logan came back downstairs, suitcase in hand. After packing, he'd called Alaric and given him detailed instructions to move forward with the Lifeblood rollout. He wanted to leave work and everything else behind when he walked out to the door. A few days alone in the mountains with no responsibilities and no worries was just what he needed.

He walked through the house turning off lights and locking up. When he came back to the foyer, he heard the crunch of gravel as a car pulled into his driveway, followed by a screech of brakes. Curious, he went to the door and opened it.

His mouth dropped open in shock when Syd practically fell out of her car and ran toward the door. She seemed so busy trying to stay upright on her ridiculously tall high heels that she didn't see him gawking at her.

Her long auburn hair fell over her chest, which was sheathed in a body-hugging black dress that fell to midthigh. Her strappy heels accentuated the slope of her calves, making her legs look about a mile long. It was the first time he had ever seen her in a short skirt, and the sight made his mouth water.

Wait, he thought. This vision before him was same woman to whom he had handed his heart only to have her throw it back at him. He shook his head to clear it and steeled himself. He had to keep his guard up. The last thing he needed was for Sydney to make a fool of him again.

"What are you doing here?" he demanded.

She gasped and stopped in her tracks as she caught site of him. He crossed his arms and raised an eyebrow when she continued to gape at him without saying a word.

"Well?" he said.

"Y-your mother said you were leaving, so I rushed over," she said, out of breath.

"Ah, my mother," he said, suddenly understanding his mother's hasty retreat from their earlier conversation. He should have suspected something was up when his mother had offered to cook. But that still didn't explain what Sydney was doing here.

"That fails to explain why you're here," he said, hearing the steel in his own voice.

She swallowed and fidgeted with the stair rail. "Can we go inside? I want to talk to you."

"What? You didn't say enough last night? Did you come back to finish the job?" he asked, every word infused with the bitterness he felt.

"Logan, don't," she said brokenly. "I didn't come here to fight. I wanted to explain—"

He cut her off. "Don't bother. You made your feelings, or should I say your lack of feelings, perfectly clear. I think you should go."

He stepped toward the door, his jaw clenched so tight he felt as if his teeth would crack. How dare she come here to torment him further?

"Wait," she pleaded. "I—I brought the painting." She gestured to her car. His eyes widened.

"It's the museum's now. I don't want it," he bit out. The last thing he wanted was a reminder of their time together hanging where he could see if every day.

"No, you don't understand. I quit my job today."

He paused, shocked by her admission. "What? But why?"

Taking a step up, she said, "I realized that in order to keep it I had to give up something I wanted even more."

He hated the hope that flared in his chest at her words. Surely she didn't mean him. He didn't trust himself to speak, so he just stared at her. Daring her to continue.

She saw his reaction and seemed to gather her strength close to her as she took another step. If he hadn't been so angry, he would have admired her courage for facing him like this. Most mortals would have run by now.

"I saw the painting this morning and heard Stiggler talk about how you gave it to me. I even heard him offer me a promotion and a raise. But all I could think about was you. And how your actions had to be a sign that even though I acted like an idiot last night there as still a chance for us."

He snorted. "You thought wrong."

She flinched at his harsh words. "Logan, don't. I know I hurt you. But please let me explain."

He nodded reluctantly, trying to maintain his bored expression. Every minute he was near her it was harder to keep up his façade.

Stepping up next to him on the porch, she grabbed the railing as if needing its support. "A few years ago I was engaged," she began. He felt his eyes widen in response. The rush of jealousy that gripped him was unexpected and unwelcome. He clenched his fists and continued to listen.

"Cole, the man I was going to marry, was very ambitious. He wanted me to give up my own career goals to help him pursue his. Eventually I realized that if he really loved me he would support me instead of demanding I give up something I loved. But more importantly, I realized I didn't love him enough either. When I broke off the engagement, my family was furious. They were more worried about the public embarrassment they faced than in trying to understand my reasons. In the end, they refused to speak to me.

"I tried to move on and put myself through graduate school. But I could never escape their rejection. I felt as if I was somehow flawed that my own parents had turned me away. So I focused all my energy on my job and tried to convince myself it was enough. And it was, until I met you."

Logan's heart softened a fraction as he listened to her story. He could not imagine the pain she must have felt by her family's rejection. He had grown up in a family that supported his dreams, and he knew without a doubt they were there for him.

"What do you mean until you met me?" he asked before he could stop himself.

She stepped closer. The emotion he saw in her eyes made him want to grab her and hold her until she forgot the pain of her past. But he held back, needing to hear her explanation.

"Before you I didn't notice how lonely my life had become. I didn't realize I had built walls to keep everyone out. But then you came along, and from the moment we met, I felt like those walls had been breached. It scared me. I tried to fight my feelings and used my career as an excuse. But in reality I was scared of being vulnerable." She paused, allowing him to digest her words.

Her explanation went a long way to explain the tough façade she tried to maintain. He recalled several times he had wanted to ask her to share her burdens with him.

"Sydney, I understand what you're saying. But I don't know why you're saying it," he said.

She reached out and laid a trembling hand on his arm. "Logan, I—I love you."

A bolt of electricity zinged from his scalp to his toes. The words were so unexpected, yet so vital to his survival. He ruthlessly tamped down the joy that filled his heart. He still didn't dare believe everything would be fine now. He was no longer the naïve boy who thought love could overcome any obstacle.

"Even though I am a monster?" He sneered. Pain filled her eyes, but he had to know if she was ready to accept him for everything he was. If she could love both the man and the vampire.

"You're not a monster," she whispered, placing a soft hand on his cheek. The skin-to-skin contact made him close his eyes for an instant. But her next words had them snapping open again. "Logan, I am not Brenna."

He pulled back as if burned. "Mother had no right to tell you," he growled.

"Don't be angry at her. She was only trying to help me understand you. And I do. I think I am not the only one who withdrew from life to protect myself. I may have fought my love for you because I was scared. But it was not because you are a vampire. If I thought you were a monster, I would not love you as much as I do. And I would not be here begging you to give us another chance."

He really looked at her and realized she was right. She wasn't anything like Brenna. Her bravery for facing him like this and baring her emotions and fears proved that. But he had to be sure she knew what her decision meant.

"You realize that this is forever, don't you? Once you

promise to me mine, I'll never let you go."

"I hope so," she said with a small smile. "Because I am a no-take-backs kind of gal. I expect you to be a one-woman vampire from now on."

A bark of laughter escaped his lips. He grabbed her and pulled her to him, needing to touch her. Unable to believe the impossible had occurred. Just a few hours ago, he'd been sure he had no hope of ever being happy again. Now this amazing woman, his brave Sydney, had just given him the precious gift of her love.

She reached up and rained kisses all over his face, finally settling her soft lips on his own for a scorching kiss. They both poured all of their relief and love into the joining, combining their breath and their hearts. After several long moments, Logan pulled back regretfully. They still had some things to work out.

"Syd, if you need time before you're ready to for me to turn you, we can wait. Being with you, even if you're never ready to become immortal, is what matters."

She smiled. "That's sweet, but if you think I am going to grow old and gray while you stay young and gorgeous, then you're crazy. And I don't want to wait. I am ready to commit myself totally to you. Tonight."

He bit back his smile at her eagerness. "You're sure? Once you're turned there's no going back." He stroked her cheek with one hand, loving the velvety feel of her skin against his own. Thankful he had the privilege to do so.

She sighed and turned her face into the caress. Then she looked him in his eyes and spoke.

"Logan, I know what I am doing. Your mother explained the process to me in detail. While I am nervous about it, I can say without a doubt in my mind I am ready. I want to live with you forever and make babies and fight and make up and face whatever the future brings together."

He lifted her up and twirled her around. "I love you," he shouted as they spun. Syd's happy laughter rained down on him, filling his heart.

Then adjusted her in his arms and strode into the house. He walked purposefully to the library, planting kisses on her precious face the entire way. Once there, he slid her body slowly down his, reveling in every peak and valley of her delectable form.

Gently placing his hands on her face, he drank in the love written clearly on her face, knowing it reflected his own. He pulled her in for a kiss. Gently, he worshipped her mouth, needed to express with his body what he could not put into words. Her soft moans drove him wild as he plunged deeper into her mouth. Her tongue met his, and the kiss turned molten. He backed up to the table and pushed down while continuing to make love to her mouth. Syd ripped her mouth from his and said, "I need you." The heat of her gaze made his cock harden to the point of pain. He needed to be inside her. Now.

He reached under the hem of her short dress. When his hand encountered nothing but skin, he raised his eyebrows in surprise. But Syd's flush had nothing to do with embarrassment and everything to do with the passion she exuded.

"A woman has to be prepared for anything," she purred.

He stroked her heated flesh and smiled. "I see you're prepared in other ways as well."

Her seductive laugh turned him into an animal. He ripped off his clothes and grasped her thighs, pulling her to the edge of the table. His need to be inside her was so strong he was incapable of going slow. He rammed himself home with a groan. The liquid hot feel of her almost made him come right then. Her responding gasp made him look from where they were joined to her face.

"More," she demanded.

He smiled wickedly. "Your wish is my command," he growled and pumped into her.

Faster. Harder.

His action seemed to unleash a beast within Syd as well. She wrapped her feet around his flanks, her heels digging into his flesh, spurring him on. Her moans soon were replaced with outbursts of ecstasy that echoed off the walls. The sight of her reaching for orgasm—the flushed cheeks, the nails dug into the table—caused his fangs to extend. She opened her eyes, and he did not see fear or revulsion there—only love. She reached her arms up for him, and he lay on top of her, his arms supporting his weight.

"Do it now," she whispered as he continued his smooth strokes. He held her eyes for a moment, unable to control the hunger her words caused. "I love you," he said fiercely, holding her gaze.

"I love you," she responded. He lifted his hand and bit into the fleshy part of his palm. She only needed to ingest a small portion of his blood for the virus to pass into her bloodstream. She glanced from him to the trickle of blood running down his hand, and without hesitation she began sucking his flesh. He closed his eyes as he reveled in the erotic sensation.

As she fed from him, his own hunger increased. It had been decades since he had fed from a live mortal, but he'd be damned if he would feed from Sydney. Instead, he gently placed a soft kiss on her neck, just over the pulsing artery.

She grabbed his head and held it to her as she continued to milk his palm. She cut her eyes and met his, silently giving him permission.

"Syd, no," he rasped. But she nodded and pushed his head back down. After a moment's hesitation, the need to bond with her in the most primal way overcame his misgivings. Quickly, to minimize the pain, he jabbed his fangs into her neck. She gasped and tensed, but then she relaxed as he drank. The combination of her sweet blood and the feel of her hot passage on his shaft almost made him come. After so many years drinking bagged blood, the hot, earthy taste of Sydney's essence was like ambrosia to his senses.

Afraid of taking too much from her, he started to pull away, but suddenly he heard her clearly in his head.

Mmmmm. Logan! He paused for a second in shock. It was as if he had a loudspeaker in his head. He tested their mental connection.

You are mine.

Yes, yes, yes . . . Oh my God!

The thought was combined with her scream of pleasure as the combination of his thrusts and the erotic pleasure-pain of his bite overwhelmed her. He withdrew from her neck, entranced by her frenzied response as she thrashed wildly. Soon her movements stilled, and she lay panting with her eyes closed. He smoothed the hair back from her brow and kissed her eyelids.

"Syd?" he whispered.

"Hmmm?"

"Are you okay?"

"I think I blacked out there for a second," she said, lifting the corner of her mouth. "In fact, I was so out of it I was hearing voices."

He chuckled. "Honey, that was me. I think the turning caused our mental connection to open. I could hear your thoughts too."

Both of her eyes popped open. "Can you read my thoughts now?"

I thought you said vampires couldn't read each other's minds.

He smiled. "I guess sharing the blood opened the connection," he said with a shrug. "It's cool, huh?"

Yeah, it is. So am I a vampire now?

He chuckled, "Yes, you're really a vampire."

"Wow, I don't feel any different," she said, looking confused.

"It will take a couple of days for the virus to take effect. By tomorrow night, you'll feel like you were hit by a truck. But then the next day you'll feel healthier than you have in your whole life. It will take you a few weeks beyond that to adjust to the changes though."

"I'm feeling pretty healthy right now," she said with a sly smile. "What should we do?"

"Why don't you read my mind and find out?"

She grabbed his head and stared straight into his eyes. Then she giggled and slapped his shoulder.

"Is that even legal?"

"Darling, we're vampires. Mortal laws can't touch us. So what do you think?"

"Hmmm." She pretended to consider his naughty suggestion. "Okay, but I get to be on top!"

He laughed and pulled her on top of his body. He looked into her green eyes, which were bright with mischief and love. Beyond a doubt, this woman was made for him. He didn't know what power in heaven or on earth was responsible for this miracle he held in his arms, but he would spend the rest of his days paying homage to Sydney in thanks.

She leaned down and kissed him gently. "That was the sweetest thing anyone has ever thought about me. I think you're pretty miraculous, myself."

"Syd, I promise to do everything in my power to make you happy," he vowed. "I—"

She laid a finger on his lips. "Logan, you've already made me happier than I thought possible. Just promise me one thing."

"Anything," he vowed and placed a soft kiss on her lips.

"Promise me you'll never stop loving me."

"Sweetheart, that's not possible," he vowed and kissed her, trying to convince her with his body of what he couldn't put into words. After a few minutes, she pulled away abruptly.

"Wait! I just thought of something. Where did you find that letter you sent Stiggler—the one that proved it was stolen from your family?"

Logan chuckled. "Promise you won't get mad."

She narrowed her eyes suspiciously. "At whom?"

"My mother. When she went to Asheville, she found a letter from our solicitor in Edinburgh confirming he'd look into the theft. Luckily, it described the portrait in detail," he explained.

"But why didn't she show it to me when she got back?" Syd asked, confused.

"Apparently, she felt you and I needed some more time to sort through our problems, so she hid the evidence. She called last night after you left and told me she left it for me in the kitchen before she took Jorge home."

"That . . . that . . ." Syd began, sounding angry. "That

wonderful woman!"

Logan smiled uncertainly. "So you're not mad?"

She chuckled. "I'm mad . . . about you," she said and kissed him to prove her claim. "Now, enough about your mother. Let's see if I can make you black out this time."

-The End-

ABOUT THE AUTHOR

Kate Eden comes from a long line of mouthy broads who love to read, so it's probably no surprise she caught the writing bug early. An avid romance fan since her early teens, Kate loves writing–and reading–stories about plucky heroines, sexy heroes, and the weird and wild journey people take on their way to love. She loves good food, cheap booze, and believes laughter is the cure for just about everything.

Connect with me online:
Twitter: @KateEdenAuthor
Facebook: facebook.com/AuthorKateEden
Web site: www.KateEden.com

If you loved Logan and Sydney's story in **The Hot Scot**, be sure to check out Raven and Callum's story in

REBEL CHILD: Book 2 of the Murdoch Vampires

Raven really doesn't see what all the fuss is about. All she did was kidnap a mortal and try to sabotage one of the most important developments in the history of the vampire race. For some reason, though, her father, who is the leader of the vampire race, is seriously pissed. He gives her an ultimatum: Spend 200 years in exile or submit to a last ditch crash-course in vampire etiquette.

As the poster boy for upstanding, modern vampires, Callum Murdoch stands for everything the rebellious Raven loathes. He's also the brother of the man Raven recently targeted. But this very odd couple is about to find out that opposites don't just attract— they smolder.

See next page for a sneak peek!

CHAPTER ONE

You kidnap one lousy mortal, and everyone freaks out.

That's what I was thinking as my "escorts"—four muscle-bound guards—led me into the office. My boots sunk into the thick Persian rug underfoot. Cocking my hip—both for effect and to take the weight off one of my feet for a blessed second—I thanked the goddess I'd worn my favorite boots.

Here's the thing: Most women can't pull off a red, stiletto-heeled boot.

But I am not most women.

Boots like those required a certain presence—an elusive combination of confidence and a devil-may-care attitude. Oh, and a high tolerance for pain.

The damned things pinched in awful places, and the pointy tips made my toes go numb. But I looked kick-ass, which counted for a lot. The confidence boost was necessary if I was going to get through the coming confrontation.

High Councilman Orpheus Coracino was the most powerful vampire in existence. As the head of the Brethren Sect, it was up to him to decide my punishment.

Oh, yeah, he also happened to be my father.

The room was as imposing as the man who had yet to acknowledge my presence. To mortal eyes it would probably look like the office of any high-powered CEO with the exception of the lit display cases filled with wicked-looking ancient weaponry. Each piece once used by my dear, very old dad in battle.

My father dismissed the goons with a wave of his hand, not bothering to look up from the document he was reading. The guards released my arms and left the room, closing the doors behind them. I almost missed the support of their firm grips. Aching feet, stress, hunger, and the impending sunrise wreaked havoc on my stamina as I struggled to look unaffected. My hands shook anyway.

"What, no hug for the prodigal daughter?" I said into the silence, extending my arms for an embrace I knew would never come.

Orpheus slowly raised his piercing eyes to look at me. He said nothing, just stared at me with the familiar mixture of disappointment and distaste.

I dropped my arms, not quite sure what to say next. It had been ten years since our last meeting. Back then, daddy dearest issued an ultimatum: Clean up my act or else. Well, of course I ignored him. But now I was about to find out what "or else" really meant.

"Gabriella—" he began.

"Stop right there." I held up my index finger with its black lacquered nail. "The name is Raven, you know that."

"Young lady, your name is Gabriella. I named you myself."

His baritone vibrated with authority. It matched his form perfectly. If he'd stood, he would have towered over me. With two black holes for eyes and a jaw so hard and sharp it could cut through metal, the man was a prime example of a civilized predator.

He looked like a highly paid executive in a pinstriped suit instead of an alpha vampire. But the civilized veneer couldn't hide the ruthlessness in his eyes. No wonder he had been the leader of the Brethren Sect for more than one hundred years. Only a fool would dare challenge his authority.

Which made me the fool, I guess.

"You also know I renamed myself a century ago. If you expect a response, you will refer to me as Raven," I shot back. I was probably one of the only vampires in existence with enough bravado to talk back to him. However, egging my father on was sort of a hobby for me.

He ignored the name issue, no doubt considering it not worth his time.

"Would you like to take this opportunity to explain your actions?"

I shrugged. "What's there to explain?"

"You can start with trying to sabotage the most important development in vampire history and finish with kidnapping the mortal woman," he said.

"I am not a member of your precious sect. I don't owe you an explanation."

"You have no excuse for your actions, as usual. Nor do you exhibit one sign of remorse." His voice was maddeningly calm, in complete opposition to my defensive tone.

"Why would I show remorse for standing up for what I believe?" This was an old argument, and I was trying not to let it get my hackles up.

"You could have launched a formal complaint through the proper channels. Instead, you wreaked havoc, as usual."

"Again, what good would a formal complaint have done when I am not in good standing with the council?" I countered.

"Exactly." He steepled his fingers and pressed them lightly to his lips. "Which brings us back to the issue of why you are not in good standing."

Well, shit.

He reached behind the desk, and I heard the sound of a drawer opening and closing. He sat back up, and a large stack of folders thumped on the desktop.

"As you can see, your transgressions have been well documented." He flipped open the top folder and started shuffling through pages. "Here we have the report on the fire alarm you pulled during the council meeting, causing mass panic. Hmmm. And let's not forget the skunk blood incident of 1886." He paused to scowl at me when I snorted with laughter. "Then there's the time you replaced the beds of all the council members with coffins. Shall I go on?" he asked, looking up from the foot-tall pile with fake courtesy.

I bit back a smile. I was damned proud of everything he listed and more. A lot of work and preparation had gone into those feats. Everything he considered a stunt, I considered civil disobedience for a good cause. I hated everything to do with the council's goals to make us more like mortals.

Don't get me wrong. I didn't think everything the council did was bad, but give me a break. Vampires are gods. Mortals are our food. You don't see humans going around eating grass and mooing all the time. And why not? Because mortals understand they are superior to cows.

"Come on," I said. "Nothing you mentioned there was all that bad. No one was hurt. Besides, last time I checked, the council didn't ban freedom of speech or expression. Or is that next on your totalitarian agenda?"

"As the leader of the council, it is my goal to create a democratic life for all of my constituents. I even encourage debate on topics of import. However, your pranks have nothing to do with taking a stand and everything to do with getting attention."

My mouth dropped open. Of all the freakin' nerve! I forgot all about the throbbing in my feet and the hunger pains clenching my stomach as centuries-old resentments bubbled up in me like a volcano.

"You're wrong. You just can't stand the idea that your daughter hasn't toed the line of your administration."

"What I can't stand is the idea that my daughter turned out to be nothing more than a spoiled brat who has not one ounce of self-respect."

"What the hell does that mean?"

"Look at yourself. You're all tarted up like an extra from one of those horrible vampire movies." His eyes raked me with a distasteful glare.

"Excuse me? These clothes are the height of fashion!" No one, but no one, insulted my clothes. The black leather miniskirt and red corset were two of my favorite pieces. He obviously was stuck in the Dark Ages when it came to fashion.

"Where? The Best Little Whorehouse in Transylvania?"

I opened my mouth to rebut, but his words cut so deep I couldn't think of a response. My own father had just called me a whore. Nice.

I took a deep breath to calm the fire in my belly. "My fashion choices have nothing to do with why I am here."

"You're correct." He leaned back in his leather executive chair. "Your behavior is the issue at hand. If I recall, the last time you were in this room I warned you that further disobedience would not be tolerated."

"Disobedience?" I repeated, struggling to keep my voice level. "I am four hundred years old. I will not be treated like an ill-tempered child."

"Then perhaps you should stop acting like one," he said quietly, leaning forward with a clear warning in his cold eyes.

I bit my tongue, hating him for being right. And I was annoyed with myself for taking his bait.

He regarded my silence for a moment. "The council is recommending banishment," he said as if casually commenting on the weather.

My gasp sounded before I could stop myself. He took me completely off guard. My heartbeat kicked up about twenty notches.

"That's insane!" I said.

"Is it?" he asked, raising his eyebrows. "Time and again you have demonstrated your lack of respect for the council. We have threatened, we have cajoled, we have bribed. None of it has worked. You crossed over the line this time."

I stood in sullen silence. My anger and resentment felt like a poison vine in my belly.

"What were you thinking?" he continued. "The Murdoch

family is one of the oldest and most respected among the Brethren." He shook his head with disgust. "I don't have to remind you how important Logan Murdoch's work is. The Lifeblood formula he's creating will make all of our lives better.

"And how is he rewarded? My own daughter tries to cast a spell to gain control of his mind. And if that isn't enough, you kidnapped the mortal woman who may be Logan's soul mate. It's unconscionable."

"Are you more upset by my actions or by how they make you look?" I asked, keeping my voice calm.

"Both." His clipped tone felt like a slap.

"And for that you are ready to throw me to the wolves and let the council use me as an example for all the other naughty vamps? You're going to sacrifice your own daughter?"

"Your actions are a threat to our entire way of life. You bring dangerous attention to all of us with your antics. We, the council, believe you must be rehabilitated by any means necessary."

"So you're going to ship me off to a remote area where you know I will have no source of food? Well, I guess death is the ultimate form of rehabilitation," I said with a bitter laugh.

"Don't be melodramatic. We would provide you with synthetic blood as sustenance. Logan is almost ready to release it to the public, despite your efforts to the contrary. You will be one of the first to use it."

I narrowed my eyes and leaned forward. "A little poetic justice, huh? I tried to stop his efforts to develop Lifeblood, so now I am doomed to depend on it for survival."

I laughed again, the sound hollow. "You know I won't do that. You might as well stake me now."

My words hung in the air for a second. I just knew I had him. He would have no choice but to come up with an alternate punishment.

He laughed instead.

"Don't be ridiculous. Your tantrums don't impress me," he said between chuckles.

If anyone could spontaneously combust, it would be me.

"You're an asshole!" I seethed. "I am sure you would love it if I was dead. Then you wouldn't have that inconvenience of being embarrassed by my every word and action."

"Grow up, Gabriella."

"Raven!" I knew I sounded like a fledgling, but I couldn't help myself. He had me cornered. Like a wild animal I struggled to think of a way, any way, to free myself from this trap of my own making.

"Calm down," he commanded, his voice hard with warning. "I am sure if you look at this rationally you will see it is best for everyone. You get two hundred years to think about what you've done—"

"Two hundred years? Fuck that!"

"Charming language," he admonished. "Yes, two hundred. You must pay for your crimes and have sufficient time to learn your lesson. At least for you, the banishment isn't permanent like it is for some of our more notorious criminals. In fact, it's not really banishment, so much as a period of exile."

Yeah, that made me feel tons better.

"Vampires are banished for murdering other vamps or mortals in cold blood. I kidnapped one measly person and didn't hurt a hair on her head!" I said, trying to make him see reason.

He continued as if I had not spoken. "Now, in addition to exile for the next two hundred years, you must also apologize to the Murdoch family. Since you will be leaving for Norway—"

"Norway? Norway! As in the 'Land of the Midnight Sun?'"

"Yes, that Norway. As I was saying, since you ship out tomorrow, there is no time for you to go back to Raleigh to make a formal apology to the whole Murdoch family. Thus, I have decided an apology to Callum is sufficient until such time as you return from your exile."

"And the hits keep on coming," I grumbled.

Not only was I going to the fucking frozen tundra—where I'd have to deal with two solid months of sunlight a year for two hundred freakin' years—but now I had to apologize to that arrogant asshole, Callum Murdoch, Logan's younger brother.

When the family busted in on my lair to rescue the chick I kidnapped, Callum had volunteered to take me into custody and deliver me home to dear old dad. I couldn't stand the guy. In addition to being the Brethren Golden Boy, Callum ran a company that produced all the products that helped vampires blend into mortal society.

"Do you have any questions?" my father asked.

"Were you born without a heart, or did it dissolve from lack of use?"

He ignored my comment as he pushed the intercom button. As he told Callum to come into the office, I tried to compose myself. Not exactly an easy feat since my entire world had collapsed.

The thought of apologizing to Callum made me want to puke. I never, ever begged anyone for anything, least of all forgiveness. Desperation was a novel and unwelcomed sensation.

The doors opened, and Callum strolled in as confident as you please. Seeing him with the bright light from the reception area framing him in a golden aura was overwhelming. I guess it had something to do with the fact he seemed so . . . capable, while I felt so trapped.

The thought of apologizing to that man made me dizzy and short of breath. I know it probably had more to do with my empty stomach than my pride, but it was there nonetheless.

Finally, I did something I have never done in my four hundred and eleven years on this earth.

I fainted.